MING YELLOW

Captain S. Martin Shelton, USNR (ret.)

Lamplight Press

ACKNOWLEDGEMENT

I thank the estate of John P. Marquand, James Marquand, executor, for permission to make this derivative work of John's novel titled *Ming Yellow*. It was first copyrighted in 1934 and first published in 1935 by Little Brown and Company. John Marquand was the author of the *Mister Moto* series of books and many other popular novels: for example, *H.M. Pulham, Esquire; Point of No Return;* and *The Unspeakable Gentleman*. He was awarded the Pulitzer Prize in 1938 for his novel *The Late George Apley*.

Thanks to the Cole Porter estate for permission to use the lyrics from his song *Love for Sale*.

DEDICATION

I dedicate this book to the indomitable spirit and bravery of the Chinese who valiantly fought the invading Japanese Kwantung Army, suffered under their brutal occupation (the Rape of Nanking, for example), organized guerrilla gangs that harassed the Japanese troops, and rescued the Mitchell B-25 crew from the Doolittle Raid in April 1942. Such conspicuous gallantry is marked from the skirmish at the Marco Polo Bridge, just north of Peiping on 7 July 1937, to the signing of the Instrument of Surrender on board the *USS Missouri* in Tokyo Bay on 2 September 1945.

RECOGNITION

I recognize the following folks who were instrumental in having this book published.

- Danielle H. Acee, Lamplight Press, for her outstanding work in formatting this manuscript and herding it through the publication process.
- Douglas Brown for his sterling cover art.
- Michael Cox for his expertise in creating the China maps.
- Commander Douglas Derrer, USN (ret.) for his eagle-eyed review.
- K. C. Francis for her exceptional follow-through editing.
- Marta Galvan for her superior copy editing of my manuscript.
- Bradley P. Wilson for his excellent content editing of my manuscript.

PROTOCOLS

The *mise en scene* for this novel is China in 1935. Accordingly, I use the Wade-Giles spelling of Chinese names and locations—the standard at the time.

On the whole, the geography is accurate. Please see the map of China on page vii to track the story.

At the time of this story, the capital city of China was Nanking. And, the English name for the city previously called Peking was Peiping. Notwithstanding, I've used Peking in this narrative because it is the more recognized name.

General Wu Pei-fu, 1874–1939, was the fierce and clever warlord of Hubei and Henan Provinces in central China. I've changed his area of rule to the remote Kansu Province to enhance the geographic scope of the narrative and the adventures attendant.

The bandit, Black Viper, is a fictional character. However, I've modeled him after the infamous bandit Sun Mei-yao, who raided the Blue Express railroad train in the early morning of 6 May 1923, near the town Te-chou in Shangtung Province. In an orgy of terror, Feng's bandits raped and murdered dozens of Chinese passengers. In the Occidental's first-class coaches, he killed several British subjects and kidnapped women and men for ransom. Several months later, Nationalist troops and British colonial soldiers brought him to ground and freed the captives.

PROLOGUE

In 1935 China is in chaos: lawlessness prevails. After the revolution that overthrew the Manchu Qing Dynasty in 1912, China has had no effective central government. Its leadership of false emperors, military governors, and ineffective republican presidents changes almost yearly due to coups, assassinations, and resignations. Internal strife rends the country. All manner of corruption rules, and inflation seriously depresses the value of the Chinese dollar.

Warlords control entire provinces, and challenge the weak national government. Bandits roam freely in vast areas of the countryside terrorizing the rural citizens and raiding Christian missions: theft, rape, pillage, and kidnapping are their modus operandi. Pirates raid shipping in the South China Seas. Most officials are corrupt; the judicial system is driven by bribes and favoritism. Mao Tse-tung's Communist party's Eighth Route Army controls Hunan Province and is forcibly expanding into Nationalist and warlord-controlled areas. Japanese patrols of the Kwangtung Army skirmish in northeastern and northwestern China in preparation for their full-scale invasion in July 1937.

What law and order there is in China results mostly from the Occidental powers' numerous treaty ports, widespread legations, and settlements in major cities. They establish international rules of law, constabularies, and juridical systems. Occidental gunboats patrol the Yangtze and Yellow Rivers, and their warships guard the major ports.

Christian missionaries suffuse through eastern and central China in valiant attempts to bring order and succor to people in their missions. All too frequently, however, bandits and warlords raid these missions, raping and murdering the missionaries and the converted Christian Chinese.

MAP: CHINA 1935

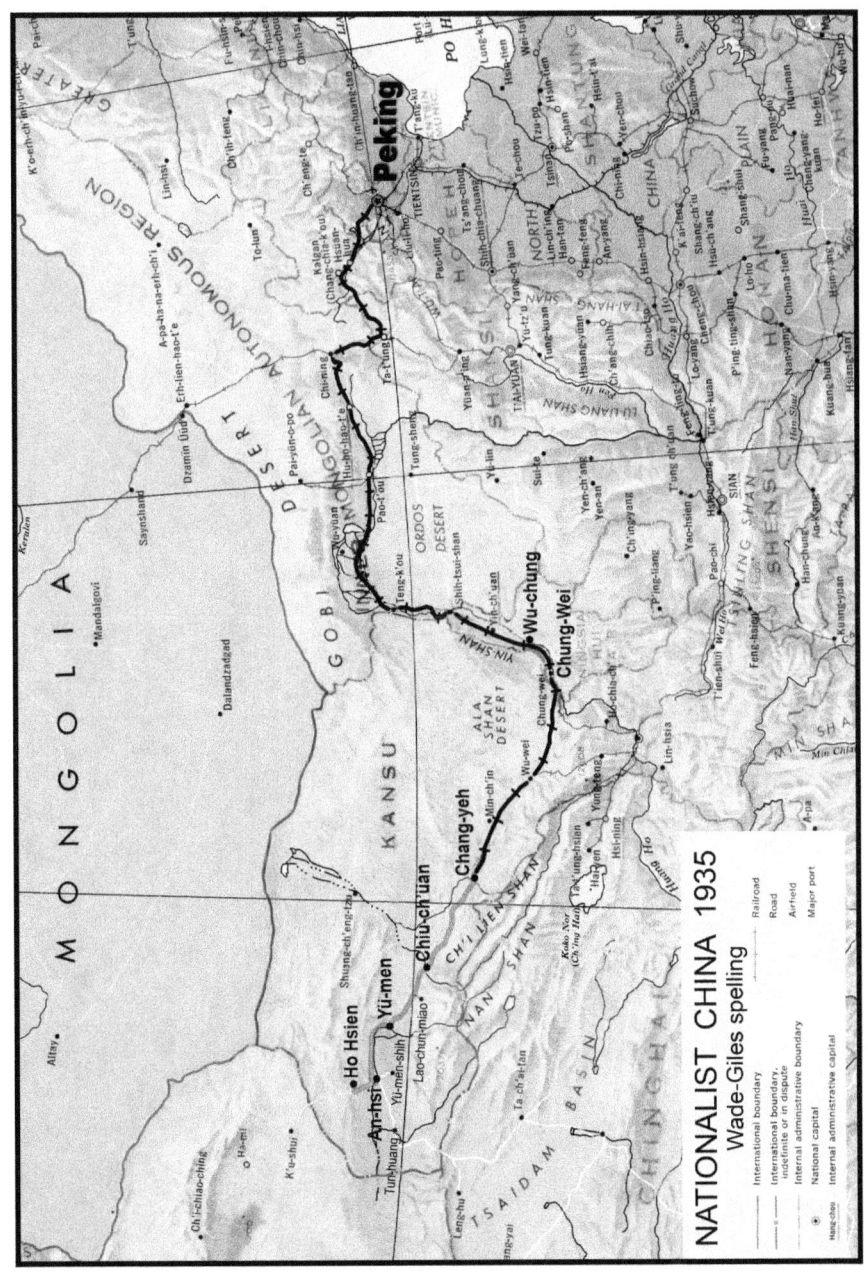

NATIONALIST CHINA 1935
Wade-Giles spelling

CAST OF CHARACTERS

Characters in order of first appearance or mention.

Chapter One

General Wu Pei-fu. Fierce warlord of Kansu Province, Northwestern China. (1874-1939).

Emperor Yung-lo. Third emperor of the Ming Dynasty. (1360 – 1424).

Captain Tze Pie-fu. General Wu's number-two son and executive officer of his Army.

Sergeant Pai Chung-hsi. Warlord soldier on patrol with Captain Tze.

Chapter Two

Matt Drummond. Australian freelance photojournalist based in Peking.

Dah Tung-lu. Barman at the Oriental Hotel, Peking.

Wallace Chung (Yu-feng). Confidence man who hustles business travelers and tourists.

Chin Mao-shu (Black Viper). Leader of an infamous bandit gang.

General Yen Hsishan. Warlord of Sanshi Province. (1883 – 1960).

Randall Kendrick. Multimillionaire businessman from New York.

Ingrid Kendrick. Daughter of Randall Kendrick and CEO of his corporate empire.

Chapter Five

Wuhan Wei-ku. Proprietor of the "Antiks" store and dealer in Oriental antiques.

Chapter Six

Lisan. Matt Drummond's houseboy.

Chapter Seven

Yen Hei-lan. Wuhan niece; seductress.

1

Kansu Province, China. 27 June 1935

Geneneral Wu Pei-fu, powerful warlord of Kansu Province, slaps his horse with his quirt. The steed responds with all its energy forward, and the general leans into the dry desert wind that whips his face. Captain Tze, Wu's second son, rides just behind Wu at the head of two platoons of his well-disciplined mercenaries.

The galloping troop raises a large cloud of dust and sand as they advance toward the Buddhist lamasery at Yü-men, still several kilometers in the distance. The glowing red sky in the west tells Wu that sunset is close. He must enter the lamasery before sunset, when the huge oak doors swing shut. His mission is clear, and today at long last he is determined to fulfill it.

Since he was a boy, Wu had believed that a fabulous treasure was hidden somewhere in his province. No one seemed to know exactly what the treasure was: gold, precious gems, or some exotic talisman that could call evil spirits to do one's bidding. Elders in his village relayed the legend that around the end of the fourteenth century, soldiers of Emperor Yung-lo of the early Ming Dynasty brought this treasure to Kansu Province to secrete it from the invading Mongol barbarians. But there the legend ended. No one knew where Yung-lo's soldiers hid the treasure. Rumors abounded from mountebanks eager for a reward: "It's there!" "No, it's over here!" "Years ago, I saw it in my village." Wu's rigorous investigations dispelled all rumors. Chagrined and frustrated, he dispatched the rumormongers with a swift stroke of his saber. Undeterred, Wu vowed that one day he would find it and become the great Lord of Kansu and all neighboring provinces—perhaps even of all China.

他處。

Kansu Province, China. 20 June 1935 (Several Days Earlier)

Captain Tze leads a mounted patrol many miles to the southeast from his father's isolated base at the Ho Hsien citadel. As they round a large limestone outcrop, Tze's diamond-hard black eyes spot an elderly monk clad in saffron robes walking alone in the desert. *Why would anyone walk alone in this hostile desert, much less a solitary monk?* he wonders. Tze orders his men to halt. "Honorable lama, may I offer you fresh water? Your thirst must be severe in this scorching desert." Tze reaches into his left saddlebag. "Perhaps you would care to share my bread and honey, and dates?"

The monk continues walking without acknowledging him. Tze slips off his steed and grabs the monk's arm. "It is the courtesy of the desert to offer succor to wanderers, and for wanderers to acknowledge the offer with humility and cordiality."

The monk remains silent and with a shake of his head refuses Tze's offer. Tze narrows his eyes, grabs the monk's shoulder, and demands, "What is your destination?"

The monk does not answer, and tries to remove Tze's hand. The monk's silent disrespect sparks Tze's anger and he hits the monk with a vicious slap that knocks him to the ground—a sacrilegious offense. Tze commands, "Lama, where are you going? Answer me."

The monk makes no attempt to rise, or look at Tze, or respond.

Tze looks at the prostrate monk, then briskly issues an order to Sergeant Pai Chung-hsi. "Help this man to his feet and make him stand in front of me." Sergeant Pai grabs the monk and holds him erect. Tze shouts, "Do you have an answer, wanderer?"

The monk stares at the desert and shakes his head several times negatively.

"Sergeant, convince this monk to speak to me and speak truthfully."

After a few minutes of corporeal persuasion, the old monk mumbles through his bleeding mouth, "I am on a pilgrimage to the reliquary at Shung-ch'eng-tzu to make an offering of penance for my evil deeds."

"Pray tell, how does a Buddhist monk commit evil deeds?"

The fellow stares at the ground to avoid eye contact and wipes the blood off his mouth with his sleeve. "My shame is too great."

Tze, now keenly interested, commands, "Tell me, old man. I enjoy tales of misdeeds."

The monk continues to stare at the ground and remains silent.

Sergeant Pai grabs the monk's right arm, twists it hard behind his back, and applies continuous pressure.

The monk emits a scream at the increasing pain. "Yes! Enough."

Tze nods to the sergeant, who releases the monk.

The monk rubs his damaged arm. "My shame is onerous and I am embarrassed to speak." He pauses to gather his courage. "For several weeks past I have had carnal knowledge with a visiting nun at our lamasery."

Tze and Sergeant Pai roar in raucous laughter. Calmed, Tze says, "Indeed, you are a rake and your transgressions must be forgiven."

Sensing the possibility of profit, Tze slaps the battered monk. "What manner of penance? "

"A token—a small porcelain," he answers feebly.

That is curious, a small porcelain is no penance for evil deeds. Tze reflexively adjusts his cap. *His penance should be a purse of gold or box of precious gems.* Puzzled, he demands, "Show me this small porcelain that has enough value for your superiors to forgive your transgressions, old man."

The monk withdraws a small package from deep in his robe. His words are weak, "This is my humble penance."

Tze grabs the package. It is tied with a strong string, sealed with wax, covered in paper, and wrapped in straw. With some difficulty, he cuts away the coverings and discovers that the monk's penance is a small yellow saucer. Tze sees that the porcelain has marginal value and certainly not enough for his seniors to forgive the monk's sins—no matter how onerous or minor. Tze is about to toss the saucer into the desert when a reflection from the yellow porcelain flashes into his right eye. Stunned by the radiance of the yellow light, he lifts the yellow porcelain close to his face and stares at it. The saucer's brilliance fixes his eyes on the yellow and it mesmerizes him. Deep inside the saucer, he sees a cache of other yellow porcelains—urns, bowls, tureens, dinnerware, pitchers, and a large jar at least four feet tall. They seem to move in random patterns, transfixing him.

Sergeant Pai sees that Captain Tze is immobile and has an unblinking stare. Pai is startled and confounded to see his commander in a trance. He grabs Tze by the shoulders, shakes him, and shouts, "Captain Tze. Captain Tze. It is Sergeant Pai. Wake up! Wake up! Wake up, Captain Tze."

The sharpness of Pai's tone shakes Tze from his stupor. He grabs Pai, "Sergeant, a devil must have stolen my mind. I was spellbound—unable to move, speak, or think. I saw in that saucer a peculiar mirage of yellow porcelains moving about in some strange space." Tze pauses and rubs his eyes. "Sergeant, I am in your debt for driving that demon away from me. As a reward, you will have first pick of the women we capture."

He draws a silver cigarette case from the inner pocket of his jacket, strikes a match, lights the tobacco, and inhales deeply. The nicotine invigorates Tze. He exhales slowly, letting the smoke drift lazily upward. He turns the saucer over to inspect the inscription. Though the ideographs are faint and in an ancient script, he can read "Ming" and "Emperor Yung-lo." He wonders if this entrancing yellow saucer is a part of the legendary Ming treasure.

Tze grabs the shoulders of the monk and shakes him vigorously. "Tell me, old man, where did you get this yellow saucer?"

The monk shakes his head negatively and remains mute. His black eyes are arrogantly defiant.

"Sergeant Pai, convince this wanderer that it is to his advantage to answer my question."

Some minutes later, Tze commands, "Enough, sergeant. Bring him to me." The sergeant holds the bloodied, barely-conscious monk upright in front of Captain Tze. "You are a brave man and uselessly stubborn." Tze draws his saber and sticks it under the monk's chin. "If you want to conclude your journey and have your evil deeds forgiven, it would be prudent for you to answer my question. Where did you get this yellow saucer?"

His body racked with pain and his mind clouded with fear that the captain will murder him before he can gain absolution, the monk murmurs, "At the lamasery in Yü-men."

Tze bellows, "You do not speak truthfully, old man." That lamasery is many miles away to the southwest—on the edge of the camel trail to Anhis. Tze presses his saber into the monk's throat just enough to draw blood. "Where did you get this yellow saucer? The truth, old man." Tze flicks his saber sending a spasm of pain into the monk's neck.

Barely able to speak, the monk utters through the blood in his mouth, "I speak honestly. This yellow saucer comes from the lamasery at Yü-men."

Convinced that the monk is being truthful, Tze shouts into the old monk's battered face, "Are there other yellow porcelains at this lamasery?" Tze twists his saber to open the cut until the monk's blood stains the front of his robe.

On Tze's command, the sergeant pins the monk's arms tight behind his back. The monk cannot move. "I do not know. Only the abbot knows." He vainly tries to squirm to ease the pain in his arms and back. However, in Sergeant Pai's steel grip, he is immobile. Hoping to ease his pain he says, "I have heard rumors among the older monks that there is a cache of yellow porcelains hidden there."

"How many? What kind?" Tze demands.

"I do not know. Many, I assume." The monk pleads, "Release me."

"Yes. Later."

His curiosity now heightened, Tze asks in a smoother voice, "How do you have this yellow saucer?"

"I took it." The monk lowers his eyes. "Carelessly, several nights ago, the abbot left the saucer on a stool in his room. I went to see him to plead for a token for my penance. I saw it unattended and, on irrational impulse, I took it. Then I gathered a few items and began this journey."

Tze leans forward and stares at the monk with unbridled attention. "In addition to your 'onerous sins,' you are a liar and a thief."

"It is true, Captain. But I have no reason to speak a falsehood now. I must continue my pilgrimage. Return the yellow saucer to me and let me proceed."

Tze barks, "I believe you, monk." He jams his saber fully into the monk's throat. "I absolve you of your evil deeds."

Tze retrieves his saber and points at the body. "Unfortunately, it appears the monk has died of a heart attack." He smiles faintly toward Sergeant Pai. "Let the carrion animals finish him."

他處。

The citadel at Ho Hsien resembles a medieval walled city. During the eleventh century, Ho Hsien was an important and wealthy hub on the Silk Road; its wells were full of crystal-clear water from the Ai-pi mountain range. Merchants of all types traded and transshipped commodities to the West and East: silk, jewels, slaves, and many other goods. Perhaps more importantly, merchants and intellectuals at Ho Hsien exchanged technologies, as well as religious and philosophical thought. Around 1025, Buddhist monks established a lamasery. This trade in goods and reason brought immense wealth, culture, and scholarship to the town. Over the years, the wells dried, the Silk Road waned, and Ho Hsien began a slow decline. Around 1915, a few years after the collapse of the Qing Dynasty,

General Wu Pei-fu established his base there. Over time, he built his army and consolidated his position as warlord of Kansu province.

Tonight, Tze stands stiffly at attention and addresses General Wu. "Honorable father, I have discovered information about the nature and location of the legendary Ming treasure of Kansu Province."

Wu leans back in his chair, inhales a deep draw from his cigar, and looks at his number-two son with quizzical eyes. Wu is a tall, heavyset man with deep-brown eyes, a high forehead, and a "Fu Manchu" mustache. "And this is your report from a fourteen-day patrol? Another treasure rumor, is it?"

"I believe my report is true."

"What else? Did you see any Nationalist soldiers?"

"No, sir."

"Japanese patrols?"

"No sign of them."

With a rising voice, Wu quizzes, "What activity is on the railroad at Chang-yeh?"

"Because of the importance of my report, I rushed to see you. I did not get to Chang-yeh."

"What are the peasants grouching about?"

With his eyes downcast, Tze responds, "I do not know. We did not linger in any villages."

Wu rises and jabs his index finger at his son. "Nothing else, Tze?"

"General, please give my report your attention."

"Go to your whore. You are wasting my time."

"General, I beg you, listen to me." Tze's voice is a trifle forced. "I am convinced that my information is accurate, and I have evidence to support my claim."

"A rumor is not evidence. Do you have gold bars?" Wu draws his saber and slams the flat edge on his desk. "My saber is for rumormongers."

Before Wu can continue, Tze leans over the desk and pushes the yellow saucer in front of him. "Here is my evidence: a saucer from the cache of Ming yellow porcelains."

"What Ming yellow porcelains?" Wu grabs the saucer, puts on his reading glasses, and gives it a cursory inspection. "I see no value in this yellow trinket. Why do you bother me with such nonsense? Go away. Your concubine awaits." He thrusts the saucer at Tze. "Get rid of this junk. Yellow porcelains are in every bazaar and sell for only a few coppers. They are a drag on the market."

Tze takes a deep breath and with wide eyes says, "Before you dismiss my report, may I suggest that you look at the inscription on the bottom?"

Wu looks at the saucer, then at Tze, then flips the saucer over and brings it close to his glasses so that his eyes can focus sharply on it. He stares at the inscription for a full minute. "What have you given me, Tze? I see ancient Chinese ideographs that I cannot read." He puts the saucer on his desk and leans back in the chair. "To what end, my son? I am not schooled in the subtleties of ancient porcelains or their value. Is this yet another trinket for the tourists? This junk cannot be a part of the treasure of Kansu." With emphasis, Wu continues, "We are looking for gold and precious gems, and true Fei T'sui pale-green jade. Not tourist porcelains."

Frustrated at his father's intransigence, Tze's initial reaction is to pound the desk but, on second thought, he realizes that only evidence logically presented will convince his father. In a firm voice he says, "I have read most of the inscription, and I am convinced that this saucer is from the Ming Emperor Yung-lo's reign in the early fifteenth century. It is a Ming yellow porcelain. That makes it very rare and much sought by Occidental collectors, who will bid a fortune for such a piece. If the Department of Antiquity in Peking knew about this Ming yellow saucer, then they would confiscate it with all the power of the state." He pauses for a beat. "My esteemed father, please hold the saucer to the light and gaze into the deep yellow."

"As you say, my son." Wu picks up the saucer, places it in the light from a flickering oil lamp, adjusts his glasses, and fixes his eyes on the yellow glaze. He narrows his eyes and rubs his weather-beaten face. His mouth remains firmly shut.

Tze wonders if his father sees the yellow cache.

Several minutes later, Wu places the saucer on his desk. He studies his second son as he speculates to himself: *Has my son found a clue to the fabled Kansu treasure? Can it be true? Is it mere porcelain?* He strokes his chin. *If it is, how do I turn this treasure into gold or perhaps a hard currency, British pounds sterling?*

Tze notices a slight smile creep across Wu's once skeptical face.

After several seconds, Wu rises and grabs his son in a strong hug. He exclaims, "My son, congratulations. You indeed have uncovered the secret of the Kansu treasure. I saw the apparition in the bottomless yellow." He returns to his chair. "In this entire world, I would never have thought that porcelains were the Kansu treasure. Sit, my son Tze! Join me in a fine Napoleon brandy." He pours the dark-amber liquid into two snifters, hands one to Tze, and swigs his in one gulp.

Wu commands, "Give me a full report of your discovery. Where are these Ming yellow porcelains? How many are there? What kind? How are they guarded? I need all the fine details."

An hour or so later, Tze concludes his report. "Indeed, there are perhaps several dozen Ming yellow pieces in the lamasery at Yü-men. I would say that monk's statements are authentic enough that we should investigate with force. Of course, the monk needed persuasion to tell all. Sergeant Pai seemed to enjoy his task. Unfortunately, the monk had a heart attack and died shortly afterward."

General Wu stares at the ceiling and has another brandy. Eventually he shouts, "Yes!" and surges to his full height. "Now the fabulous Kansu treasure will be mine—as will be our neighbors, Nigsia and Shensi Provinces, and those beyond."

Tze cautions, "General Wu, before we launch our attack on the lamasery, we must have detailed intelligence on the disposition of Nationalist troops in the area. It is risky to stray so far from our base now that General Chiang Kai-shek is waging a fierce campaign against the Northern warlords."

"Captain Tze, do you think me a fool? I will have patrols in the area within a few days."

彼時，

The sun dips below the horizon as several monks work the leverage mechanism to close the nearly impenetrable doors of the lamasery at Yü-men. The huge oak slabs begin to grind shut for the night. It's too late.

General Wu and Captain Tze charge through the opening. They split: Wu slashes to the right, cutting down two monks with his saber. Tze sprays bullets into two more with his semi-automatic pistol. Wu's troops flood into the courtyard and butcher monks at random.

After the chaos subsides and the last screams fade, Wu charges his Sergeant Major with securing the lamasery. Soldiers scatter throughout the lamasery grounds and several three-man patrols immediately head back through the open gate to scout the nearby area for Nationalist troops.

Wu, Tze, and the two platoon leaders rush inside the main building. The lamasery sprawls helter-skelter in a dark maze of small rooms and narrow halls. Wu keeps his party together as they search for the treasure. He soon realizes that his goal of a quick strike and equally quick withdrawal is not possible.

As they wander in the maze, they interrogate the remaining monks, demanding to know the treasure's location. The survivors either do not know or refuse to answer. Wu dispatches them with his saber. He lets his frustration show in his blade work as critical time passes and their futile search in the warren continues. Earlier, one of his scouts had reported that a battalion of Nationalist cavalry was about twenty-five miles south and headed in this direction. Wu silently curses. Rounding a sharp corner, they spot the abbot standing in front of a huge oak door secured with a heavy chain and a massive lock. His robe is splashed in blood and he holds his right hand over his left shoulder—obviously wounded.

Wu waves his saber, "Stand aside, abbot, and I might spare you."

The abbot stands firm and challenges Wu, "You are committing a sacrilege and the phantoms guarding this door will plague you for all time."

"Nonsense, abbot. I know no phantoms—only men with blood."

"You are a fool. Go away. The Ming Emperor Yung-lo has infused this chamber with heinous spirits to protect these porcelains and has charged this lamasery with safeguarding them for his royal court when he returns."

Wu points his saber at the abbot's heart. "Move aside, spinner of yarns. Open that lock and show us the booty behind this door."

Realizing the futility of resistance, the abbot, with his eyes downcast, shuffles away from the door. He mumbles, "Save yourself, one who desecrates."

Wu slaps the abbot on one side of his face with the flat of his saber, sending the fellow spinning to the floor.

Captain Tze raises his pistol and blasts the lock off with three well-placed shots. The chains fall away. Wu grabs the handles and swings the door open. He parts a thick, silk curtain and plays his flashlight over the room. Carefully placed on shelves and stands is the cache of Ming yellow porcelains. He smiles broadly and beckons his son. "Captain Tze, enter and behold the riches of a Ming Emperor."

Tze holds back. "General, we'll admire and inventory these porcelains later. It is late. We must pack these porcelains, load them in our wagons, and leave. Now. The Nationalist cavalry must be closing in."

"Indeed, Tze. Your counsel is sound." Wu orders the platoon leaders to fetch soldiers and packing materials from the wagons. When the work party arrives, he shouts, "If any of you dolts damages even one of these porcelains, I will crucify you and have the buzzards pick out your eyes."

The wounded abbot stumbles into the chamber and falls to his knees before Wu. "Commander, end this malevolence. Honor the commands of the Ming Emperor to keep these yellow porcelains in sanctuary for his return."

Wu, annoyed by the abbot's interruption of his reverie, draws his saber and is poised to impale the intruding abbot. Suddenly, a foot soldier rushes headlong into the chamber, anxious to see the yellows, and bumps against Wu, causing him to stumble. As his arms swing to catch his balance, Wu's saber rips a terrible gash across the abbot's face. He staggers out of the room and falls to the floor, motionless.

The General recovers his balance, turns, and plunges his saber into the offending soldier. The man's dying eyes plead for help as he crumples to the floor with blood pumping out of his body. "You bumbling fool." Wu kicks him. "My anger saved you from a prolonged flogging and slow, painful death by crucifixion."

Under Captain Tze's supervision, the work party wraps the yellows in pounds of straw and tarpaulin. Stout ropes secure the bundles. He inspects each pack. Finally, he reports their readiness to his father. Satisfied, Tze orders the yellows loaded onto the wagons and secured firmly.

On completion, General Wu orders his troops to move out. Swiftly, the raiding party gallops clear of the gate and disappears into the night.

2

Oriental Hotel, Peking. 5 July 1935

Matt Drummond enters the Cygnet Blanc Lounge in the Oriental Hotel at the cocktail hour, spots two empty stools at the bar, and settles in. He places his camera bag on the bar, and his Australian Jacaru hat on the seat next to him. Drummond is in his early thirties, tall with blue-green eyes, and square-jawed. His mien reflects his rugged upbringing in the Australian outback.

The barman, Dah Tung-lu, fluent in the banter of Occidentals, smiles and ignores the trail of dried mud clots from the Occidental's worn leather boots. He says in Mandarin, "Welcome home, Mister Drummond. I am pleased to see that you are in good health."

Drummond responds, "Yes, thanks. And you, in excellent health also?"

"Indeed, Mister Drummond."

Drummond switches to English. "I'll have a bourbon straight." He puts both elbows on the bar and leans forward. "Double the bourbon. I'm exhausted." His khaki trousers and short-sleeved bush jacket are wrinkled and soiled. He pulls halfheartedly at the loose-hanging tan scarf around his neck.

Dah, preparing Drummond's drink, smirks. *When will Mister Drummond ever learn to speak the Queen's English?*

Placing the whiskey on the bar in front of Drummond, Dah eyes his customer's matted hair and three-day beard and asks, "Your trip to Shansi Province was productive?"

Drummond swigs the whiskey and comments, "Yes. Very much so. I'll be busy in my darkroom for several days processing the negatives and making prints."

Drummond covers China as a freelance photojournalist for several international news media. He'd quietly left Australia after the *Herald Sun* newspaper in Melbourne broke the scandal regarding his indiscretions with a socialite woman married to the leader of the political party in opposition. Currently, he has no girlfriend, but he's known to cavort with Occidental women of the international community. His social life consists mostly of palling around with other expatriates in the Foreign Concessions. He is the reigning dart champion in the Bloody Mary Pub.

Drummond tosses down his drink and orders another.

It's a quiet night at the Cygnet Blanc Lounge. A Eurasian chanteuse in a bright-green strapless gown and matching elbow-length gloves sways in front of a five-musician combo, singing American show tunes in a throaty voice. On the microscopic dance floor, a few well-dressed couples sway to the music. The lounge is decorated in art-deco style—chrome trim, etched glass, and leather chairs. On the cream wall are autographed photographs of Clark Gable, Shirley Temple, Fred Astaire, Jean Harlow, and other motion-picture stars.

Wallace Chung climbs onto the bar stool next to Drummond. "Welcome home, Matt. I see that you seem to be in good health. Have an interesting trip? Any news? Take lots of photographs?"

"Hi, Wallace. Very interesting adventure, and I shot several dozen rolls of film. What are you up to? Perhaps I ought to say, 'Who are you hustling now?'"

"No one, my dear fellow. There are no tourists and the few busi-nessmen I've encountered are miserly." He orders a gin and bitters. "It's a lean summer in this Depression year." Wallace sits straight in his chair and turns his Stanford class ring on his finger. He is about the same age as Drummond, but attired in an impeccably tailored white suit, pale-blue tie, and white shoes. He is cultured and handsome, yet he projects an ambiguous and affected mien. "Then I take it that you've not heard the news about the bandit Black Viper's rape and pillage of the small village of Chung-wei in Shansi Province."

"Nothing. Fill me in."

Wallace nods. "The news is just trickling in. That merciless barbarian and his gang of brigands kidnapped all the nubile women, massacred all the remaining inhabitants, looted what valuables there were, and burned all the structures."

Surprised at this news, Drummond reflects for a few moments. "Unfortunate. Just a couple of weeks ago I traveled through that village. I just missed the carnage." He takes a swig from his bourbon. "That blackguard bandit has a charmed existence. The Nationalist patrols are always two or three days behind him. I wonder if General Wu and he have a concord not to interfere with each other."

Chung sips his gin. "Past is past. Bring me up to date on your adventure in Shansi Province. Obviously, your luck held. You are here and apparently unharmed."

"I'll tell you about it shortly. Now, I need to unwind with this bourbon." He finishes the drink, puts the empty glass on the bar, and nods slightly to the bartender, indicating it's time for another bourbon.

He takes his time with this whiskey.

Wallace Chung needlessly adjusts the handsome Windsor knot at his throat, settling in with his own drink to wait for Drummond to continue. He watches the Australian from the sides of his eyes.

Refreshed, Drummond sips a bit longer before he continues. "Indeed, yes. Unharmed. But just barely." He shakes his head remembering. "Probably the most 'interesting' trip I've taken to the interior. Dodged a few bullets." Before he can continue, the combo segues into a rousing arrangement of Cole Porter's *Begin the Beguine.* He raises his two palms toward Wallace indicating 'time out.' He swings his barstool around to watch the singer. A few minutes later, the combo begins another tune in a softer tone. He continues. "A cobra damn near struck me. A Japanese patrol from the Kwangtung Army took me prisoner for a few days. And General Yen Hsishan, the warlord of Sanshi Province, almost impaled me on his saber. Nonetheless, I got a great story and sensational photographs of Yen's raid on General Chang Tso-lin's headquarters. As soon as I process the photographs, I'll file this story about the chaos in Sanshi Province by wirephoto to New York and London."

Wallace gives a perfunctory nod and comments, "Best of luck, old chap!"

Drummond sips his whiskey and notices that, as usual, Wallace has barely wet his lips with his gin drink. "How is it, Wallace, that I never see you take a proper swig?"

Wallace looks at Drummond with a cocked eyebrow and questioning eyes. "Because one must keep one's wits about oneself in case an opportunity should arise."

"Smart, very smart, Wallace. You'll never miss a 'mark' being sober." Their conversation fades and they turn to listen to the combo and watch the dancers.

They are content to enjoy the music. After a time, a ruckus breaks out at the registration desk. Randall Kendrick, a well-dressed Occidental, pounds the desk and loudly shouts, "I have your cablegram confirming my request for the Imperial Suite, and I demand it. I don't give a damn if the King of England is in there. I want it now."

Flustered by the fuss and the fear of offending this important guest, the manager responds, "Yes, Mister Kendrick. We'll move the party in there to another suite. Please give us a few minutes to complete this transfer." He continues, "Meanwhile, please relax in our lobby's comfortable lounge, and enjoy our complimentary champagne."

"Champagne be damned," Kendrick growls. "Send scotch whiskey— single malt."

Drummond, wondering what this confusion is about, looks to Wallace for an update. "Who is that blowhard causing such a flapdoodle?"

"Blowhard? Perhaps. Nonetheless, that fellow is Mister Randall Kendrick from New York, the American businessman, adventurer, and collector of Oriental antiques—also one of the richest men in the United States of America."

Taken aback for the moment, Drummond focuses his eyes on the loud newcomer and comments, "Mister Randall Kendrick! The man in person? I've heard he has more money than God." Matt continues his stare and sees that the gray-streaked, brown-headed Kendrick cuts an imposing presence with his tall and erect stance, and his commanding voice. After a few beats, he says, "What do you reckon Kendrick is worth?"

Wallace smiles. "I can't imagine how much wealth Kendrick has. He probably doesn't even know."

Drummond continues to evaluate the scene. With calm irony, he continues, "Since the world is engulfed in this worldwide depression, I suppose that he donates most of his wealth to the unemployed standing in the bread lines."

Alarmed at this suggestion, Wallace blusters, "No. No. I understand that he is not a charitable person."

His curiosity piqued, Drummond asks, "What's a tycoon that rich doing in this chaos of a country?"

Wallace, in an excited voice, leans close and whispers into Matt's ear. "He's here on a quest of some sort—to collect antiquities, I suspect." Smiling broadly, he continues, "An opportunity for me to earn some serious profit, if I am not mistaken."

"Take it easy, Wallace. Best to leave Kendrick alone. He is out of your class."

With a voice too intense, Wallace says, "I've heard that Kendrick uses his vast wealth to satisfy a compulsion to add to his impressive collection of Oriental art. Nothing will stop him from acquiring a treasure once his mind has vectored on it." Wallace's hand shakes slightly as he grabs his gin cocktail and drinks deep. "I was born to profit from this man. Yes." He raises his glass. "I will find a way to earn a handsome fee for my singular services."

Drummond laughs mockingly. "Do you really believe that nouveau riche tycoon will pay any attention to you?"

"Yes. I intend to introduce myself to Mister Kendrick and offer my services as an interpreter, or perhaps as a guide with unique knowledge of China and some of its most intricate secrets."

Matt looks at Wallace with incredulity. "Secrets? Swell! Best of luck. Keep me posted on your progress. The drinks are on me if you succeed."

Wallace slips off the bar stool. "Excuse me, Matt." He moves to the registration desk where Kendrick is signing the register.

"Sir."

The tycoon does not look up.

"Mister Kendrick. Sir, please allow me to—"

Kendrick snaps, "A bellboy, good. Boy, tell the Bell Captain to get my luggage to the Imperial Suite *pronto*. Bring ice for the refrigerator, put fresh flowers in all the vases, and get four bottles of single-malt scotch."

"No, sir. I'm not—"

"Give me a room service menu. I'll order dinner from my suite."

With that order, Kendrick turns and enters the elevator, leaving the humiliated Wallace standing with business card in hand, mumbling, "My card …"

Defeated, Wallace returns to the bar.

Drummond pats his slumped shoulder sympathetically and suggests, "Finish your drink, Wallace. There'll be other opportunities."

A miffed Wallace does not respond. He orders another gin and bitters. As soon as Dah sets the cocktail on the bar, Wallace grabs it and takes a large gulp in one swift move. He scribbles on his business card, gets up quickly, and returns to the lobby. He finds the head bellman. "Here is a one pound note, British pound sterling. It is yours should you put my card in Mister Kendrick's hand and tell him that the fellow who sent him the cablegram regarding the porcelains is in the lobby and is anxious to see him. Do you understand?"

The bell captain nods, and scurries off.

In a few minutes, the messenger boy strolls the lobby announcing, "Paging Mister Chung." A few steps later he repeats, "Paging for Mister Chung."

Wallace calls out, "Here, boy." Wallace picks up the note in the boy's silver tray, reads it, and smiles broadly. "I've cracked the wall, as it were. Seems I have an appointment with Mister Kendrick." He toasts once more with his gin and bitters. "'Hoo roo,' mate."

Drummond sips his bourbon whiskey and wonders about Wallace's credulity. *It's only a matter of time before that con artist is going to get into serious trouble with the authorities. Or worse.* The Australian is about to speak to the bartender when he hears a husky female voice behind him.

"Please remove your hat, or whatever that thing is, from this stool." She taps him on the shoulder. "This is the only stool left at the bar, and I need a place to park and get a drink."

"Of course," Drummond responds. He turns and sees a rather striking, well-dressed Occidental female with long, flaming-red hair and with a sparkle of youth in her intense, green eyes. He picks up his hat and places it over his camera bag. "My apologies." With his right hand palm up, he indicates the vacant bar stool. "Please, madam."

She cracks a crooked, mischievous smile, climbing onto the barstool. "It's *mademoiselle, amigo.*" Her skirt crawls up her long, sensuous legs. She gets the bartender's attention. "Rye whiskey. Straight. Damn, I need a quick refresher." When her drink arrives, she tosses it down in one gulp.

Starting to relax, she gives Drummond a soul-appraising perusal, and she likes what she sees. This time she orders a double rye whiskey. "Straight," she tells the barman. On delivery, she takes a healthy swallow, leans back on the stool, with a high-wattage smile offers her right hand to Drummond, and says, "Hi."

Drummond, taken aback by this attractive woman's forthrightness, takes a long look at her, and reflects, *a first-class sheila*. He reckons that she is in her early thirties and takes in her sensual mouth that smiles easily. He finally cracks a thin smile, shakes her hand, and manages to say, "Good day, *mademoiselle*."

Not offering the customary response, she continues rapidly, "What's your racket? Legit? Hustle the tourists? Level with me. What are you doing in Peking? I don't imagine you're a tourist or a missionary."

"No. Not at all." Trying to recover some advantage, he asks, "How about you? Tourist?"

"Not hardly," she responds tartly, with a laugh that's too long and too loud. "I'm here on business with my father. Looking at the scene. Taking in the environment. Having a time." She pinches Matt's hat between two fingers, lifts it off his camera bag, and twirls it about. "Pray tell, what is this abomination?"

"That, my lady, is my hat. It's a 'fair dinkum' Diggers headpiece from 'down under'—ideal for traveling about this country."

No longer interested in his hat, she opens his camera bag and withdraws his Leica. Impressed with this expensive camera, she says, "I see you're a photographer. Any good?" She takes a quick look through the viewfinder and returns the camera. She continues, "Finally, I'm hearing someone speak English, sort of. That Aussie accent of yours is heavy." She lifts a hand. "Bartender," she says, pointing to the empty glasses, "Fill 'em up."

"Come on, Aussie, let's toast to 'down under' and Yankee camaraderie."

The bartender places two more drinks on the bar in front of them. She picks hers up, and looks Matt in the eye.

"Cheers, ol' chum. My name's Ingrid."

"Cheers, then."

"My pleasure, ol' chap." A sly grin crosses Ingrid's mouth.

Their eyes lock.

She takes a healthy swig, and states, "This round is on me. The next one is yours, if you're game." She offers him her hand once more and swigs again. "Just who are you, mate?"

Drummond takes her hand and looks into her intense, green eyes. "My pleasure. I'm Matt Drummond of Peking, China—the center of the universe. And, yes, I'm a photojournalist of some talent, or so I'm told. I also work as a stringer for several international news services: The Composite Press Newsreels, Acme Pictures Today, World-Wide Press Service, and some other news services." He reluctantly releases her hand. Then her name rings a bell. "In fact, if you're *the* Ingrid Kendrick, executive editor of World-Wide Press Service, you frequently publish my photo-articles. Moreover, I'm pleased to report your checks are prompt and always clear. In fact, you published my photo-article on warlordism in northwest China last year in your magazine *Copy*."

Ingrid, taken aback by her *faux pas*, blushes at not recognizing Drummond's name, but quickly smiles again and says, "Of course! That photo-article won the Carl Mollenhoff Award for Investigative Reporting." She hoists her drink to Drummond. "May I offer a too-long-delayed congratulations?"

"Yes, indeed. Congratulations accepted. Thank you, editor Ingrid."

To recover from her embarrassment, Ingrid watches the dancers for a few seconds. "My apologies for not recognizing your name. Your Australian accent should have been my first clue." She sips her rye whiskey. "Indeed, your stories and photographs always are first class. We are delighted to publish your work on our wire-service and in our publications."

The combo begins to play Cole Porter's *Night and Day* with a slow, Latin beat. Ingrid takes Matt's arm, slips off the barstool, and says, "Let's dance. This is my favorite song."

"Ingrid, I'm not presentable. I have a three-day-old beard, my clothes are filthy, and I'm exhausted. Not to mention a little tipsy."

"Don't be a fuddy-duddy. Dance with me." It is clear from Ingrid's manner that she is accustomed to having her way.

He bows and responds mockingly, "Yes, my lady. As you command."

They glide smoothly to the rhythm of the music. The combo segues into Cole Porter's *Love for Sale*. After a brief musical introduction, the chanteuse moans the lyrics, "Love that's fresh and still unspoiled, love that's only slightly soiled. Love for sale ..."

Ingrid moves closer to Matt and, with a faint, wistful smile, says softly, "Once more, please." She flutters her eyelashes at him. As they gently sway to the erotic music, she puts her cheek on his shoulder. Matt draws her a little closer and senses a simmering passion in her.

As the music fades, they return to the bar, each of their pulses beating a little faster.

Ingrid says, with a cryptic miniature smile, "Come up to my suite." After a pause for Matt to savor the erotic implications, she says, "I want you to meet Dad. Have dinner with us. We're working on an enterprise that ought to pique your interest as a photojournalist. If it develops, as we suspect it might, you'll have a fantastic story of great historical import. Obviously, World-Wide Press Service will cover your expenses and will pay handsomely for your photographs and story. In return, you will let us publish the story exclusively."

Preparing to leave, Drummond picks up his camera bag, puts on his hat, and says, "You've stirred my curiosity. Tell me more."

She replies in a cool, sober, businesslike voice, "Can't. Not until you make a firm commitment."

Puzzled at the sudden transformation of Ingrid's demeanor, Drummond says, "Fair enough. I'm going to my flat to get this grime off, change into clean clothes, and in general to make myself presentable."

"Deal. It's suite 412. We'll expect you about seven. Please don't dress for dinner. We're not that formal." She tosses down the last of her whiskey and in a mocking English accent says, "Cheers. Here's to good times. 'Toodle-doo' and all that, ol' chap."

3

Oriental Hotel, Peking. 5 July 1935

Randall Kendrick sits in a leather-covered club chair in a dark corner of the lobby lounge sipping a double scotch whiskey. He scans the lobby looking for the Chinaman. He empties his glass, then pounds it on the small enameled table next to him to attract the attention of someone who will bring him another drink. His pique is evident—he does not wait for anyone. Kendrick is a large, tall man with a harsh face surrounded by straight brown hair and white-tinged sideburns. His sharp blue eyes immediately lock onto an exotic Oriental woman, dressed in a skin-tight cheongsam split to mid-thigh, walking toward the elevators. He muses, *I didn't realize the hotel offered that sort of service.*

Wallace Chung enters the lobby, spots Kendrick, and veers toward him. In a rush, he sidesteps a waiter to reach the tycoon. "Mister Kendrick—"

Kendrick glances at Chung. "At last, a waiter. Bring me a double scotch—bartender knows my brand."

Unprepared for Kendrick's bluster, Chung manages, "Mister Kendrick, I am not an employee of the hotel. I am the—"

Kendrick has quickly appraised Chung with a questioning eye and, without waiting for more information, he spouts, "I'm not interested in what you're selling. Go away. Or I'll have you tossed out."

This time Chung refuses to be cowed. Gathering his resolve, he affirms, "You have my card, sir, and we have an appointment for six o' clock this evening." Chung glances at his watch. "My apologies for being a few minutes late."

Kendrick's growl abates somewhat as he states, "You sound American. What's your pitch? No bullshit. Get to your point without embellishments."

A waiter brings Kendrick's scotch. "Excuse me for interrupting. I saw your empty glass and assumed you wanted a refill." He places the drink on the table.

"Don't ever interrupt me again, you yellow Chink. I'll have your job."

"My sincere apologies, Mister Kendrick."

As the waiter turns to leave, Kendrick snaps, "Charge it to my suite."

Waiting patiently, Chung asks, "May I sit in this other chair?"

"Sit, and get started." Kendrick makes a point of looking at his watch, "I've another appointment shortly. You've got five minutes."

With his most sincere mien, Chung takes his seat, composes himself, and says, "I am Wallace Chung. It was I who sent you the cablegram about the porcelains—the Ming yellow porcelains."

Kendrick puts down his drink and leans forward slightly. "So, how do you know about these porcelains? I want all the details, and tell me, what's your interest? Your take?"

Chung smiles internally. He's got his hook in Kendrick. He speaks in a soft, conspiratorial tone. "I have special knowledge about these Ming yellow porcelains because the owner is an acquaintance of mine, and I can facilitate your acquisition of them." Chung spreads his hands and smiles. "That is your intent, is it not?"

Kendrick leans back in his chair, swigs his scotch, and assesses Chung's mettle. He lets the silence hang for a time before he responds. "Yes. If these porcelains are genuine Ming yellows." He raises his right hand with the palm forward to keep Chung from responding. "If you pull any chicanery, I'll kill you."

Stung, Chung speaks forthrightly. "No chicanery, Mister Kendrick, I assure you. My credentials are impeccable. I offer a straightforward deal without any knavery." Chung places his left hand on the chair's arm, his Stanford ring prominent. "Mister Kendrick, I am aware of your keen interest in collecting Oriental antiquities. Specifically, you have a long-time compulsion to own a cache of authentic Ming yellows. Is it not so?" Chung feels the hook beginning to set, but he resists pulling the line taut just yet.

Kendrick, still cautious, responds, "Yes. Chung, what's your game?"

"I am privileged to know where there are twenty authentic, magnificent yellows, all in perfect condition, available for you to purchase. And quite reasonably priced, I might add."

Kendrick gapes at Wallace and wonders, *Can it be true? Does this fellow have such singular intelligence? Or, is he just another flimflam artist?* "Really! How do you know about these yellows? What's your cut?"

"Please, Mister Kendrick. I am here to look after your interests." Chung smiles. "I ask only to earn a modest finder's fee for facilitating your quest for these yellow porcelains. But I can be of even greater assistance to you. I have contacts throughout China, and I speak several dialects." He bows his head once before finishing. "I offer myself as your personal translator and guide."

Kendrick's interest is piqued keenly. "Does anyone else know about these yellows?" Kendrick presses. "How about Gaspar Wickham in New York? If you lie to me, Chinaman, I'll personally wring your neck."

Chung does not let his smile falter. "I assure you wholeheartedly that I am the owner's sole agent. And that I have told only you about these yellows, which are in a private collection some distance from Peking."

"Are you sure? Are you damn sure?"

"Mister Kendrick, I am an honest businessman with excellent references, one of whom happens to live near this hotel. Please contact Mister Matt Drummond. He is a stringer for your World-Wide Press Service. He will vouch for my integrity."

Kendrick taps his fingers on the table as he continues to take the measure of this Chinese fellow. *Damn, I'm usually quick to size up a peddler. But this Chink is difficult to figure.* "You want a drink?"

Chung responds respectfully. "No, thank you, Mister Kendrick. I seldom drink alcohol."

Not to press the issue with Chung, Kendrick shrugs. "No matter." He fidgets in his chair as questions and doubts slash through his mind. "All right, Chung. Where exactly are these Ming yellow porcelains?"

"Please, Mister Kendrick, unfortunately, I am not empowered at the moment to share the whereabouts of these yellows. At least not until we reach an agreement about my fee for services. But, I can tell you that I have personally seen one of these yellows, and it truly is exquisite. And, I should add that an expert has verified that the calligraphy is authentic." Sensing he's set the hook, Chung waits silently.

Kendrick, in deep thought, lifts his glass to his lips before he realizes it's empty and sets it down. "Come to my suite this evening at eight thirty—number 412. I'll see what you have in mind."

Wallace smiles broadly, confident he has landed his mark. *I have got him.* "Yes, sir, I'll be there. And I shall bring a yellow sample to substantiate my authenticity."

4

Kendrick's Suite, Oriental Hotel, Peking. 5 July 1935

The knock on the door sends a warm shiver through Ingrid. She reasons that the visitor is Matt. She twirls to flare the skirt of her coral-colored dress and shakes her head vigorously, sending her long, red hair swirling; it falls into place as if it were a frame. Ingrid's pace quickens as she approaches the door.

Drummond flashes a large smile, "Good evening, *mademoiselle* Ingrid." He wears a tan sport jacket and white linen trousers. A subdued red tie in a neat Windsor knot complements his crisp white shirt.

Ingrid opens the door wide, and stands aside. In a soft voice she says, "Please come in." She eyes Matt approvingly. "My, my, you are a new man." She kisses him on the cheek. "Welcome." She smiles with her wide, tempting mouth. "I want you to meet my father." Her short-sleeved dress is ankle-length and fits tight at the waist, highlighting her winsome figure. She wears a pair of discreet pearl earrings—small, but of high quality.

The Kendrick suite is large and sumptuously decorated in subdued colors. The furniture is of the ubiquitous art-deco style. Vases of fresh roses fill the air with delicate perfume. Original paintings by contemporary artists hang on the walls.

Matt and Ingrid approach Kendrick. "Matt, this is my father, Randall Kendrick. Dad, this is my new friend, Matt Drummond."

"My pleasure, sir," says Matt as he extends his right hand to Kendrick.

Kendrick does not accept Matt's offer. Nonetheless, with his sharp eyes he sees instantly why his daughter is impressed—a promising fellow. "Sit down, young man. Have a drink with me." He points to a tan leather armchair. "Call me Kendrick, that's my moniker with my inner circle." He continues to size up the Australian. "So, you're the fellow that Ingrid has been babbling about. I hear we publish your photo-stories. I'm impressed." He manages a faint smile that matches his friendly tone, yet his eyes seem to pierce into Matt's soul.

"Thank you." Matt settles comfortably into the chair.

Ingrid asks, "Bourbon?"

Matt's eyes bathe Ingrid with delight. He responds softly, "Yes. Thanks." Somewhat intimidated by Kendrick, he decides quickly that his best strategy is to observe the unfolding scene and speak only when necessary.

Kendrick watches the interplay between the Aussie and his daughter. Satisfied for now he avers, "Ingrid is the love of my life. Bears a striking resemblance to my departed wife, Hilda. Ingrid is my aide-de-camp. Armed with her MBA from Columbia, she is the Chief Operating Officer of my industrial holdings and financial business, and my best pal."

This evening, Kendrick wears a dark-blue double-breasted sport coat and plain white trousers with a knife-sharp crease. "I understand that you're here to find out about the deal that inveigled me to Peking and to decide if you want to get involved. Do I have this correct?"

"Yes, sir, that's correct."

Ingrid pours two stiff bourbon drinks and an equally stiff scotch in tall, thin crystal glasses. "Ice or soda, anyone?"

Matt responds, "Soda, please."

"Straight," Kendrick grunts. He looks Matt straight in the eyes. "What's your take?"

Matt sips his bourbon, then says, "Please, sir, I'd want to know what sort of enterprise you're planning and if it's worth my time. What's involved? That sort of thing."

Kendrick, still not fully confident about Drummond, points his index finger towards him, and with a straight face says, "I've not made any deal—not enough reliable information. And I'm not sure I trust that Chinaman, Wally Chung or something or other. He's spieled lots of mumbo jumbo about a rare treasure ensconced somewhere in the interior. I'll get detailed information from him this evening. He's coming here later to spell out the particulars."

Matt Drummond takes a long drink of his whisky. His mind whirls in incredulity. *Can it be that the hustler Wallace Chung has finagled his shenanigans cleverly enough to snare Kendrick's attention? Randall Kendrick, the sharpest of all the hucksters? If so, I'll owe Wallace a stiff drink.* "If I may, I'd urge caution, Mister Kendrick. In this chaos within China, scams abound in all manner of tomfoolery."

In a too loud voice, Kendrick retorts, "I am the one who hornswoggles the flimflam artists."

Matt responds, "So I've heard."

Ingrid, off to one side, nods to her father and mouths, "Matt's okay," giving a thumbs-up sign.

Assured by his daughter's confidence and his assessment, he says, "Here's the deal, Drummond. It's fine with me if you tag along. In which case, the terms Ingrid offered earlier apply. No matter how you decide, I need your word that everything you hear and see here tonight is strictly confidential and will remain so until either Ingrid or I relieve you of your promise. Do I have your word?"

Matt evaluates what he has learned so far. Satisfied, he says, "You have my word."

A faint smile flickers across Kendrick's face. "Understand, my avocation is the acquisition of rare, and usually expensive, Oriental artifacts. And, I have the resources to pay for them. Yesterday, for instance, we were in Shanghai to inspect a Tang Dynasty, Fei T'sui jade figurine collection called 'The Songs of the Emperor.'" He opens a small teak box on the table, picks up one of the miniature pieces, looks at it carefully, and shows it to Drummond. "The delicate carving on this jade highlights intricate details not seen on most figurines of this period. It's a beautiful collection that I'm proud to own." He returns it to the box.

Ingrid interrupts, "A refill, Dad?"

"Of course." Kendrick takes a long swallow of his newly poured drink. "Drummond, let's get down to business. At eight thirty that Chinaman will be here with a sample of an authentic Ming yellow porcelain—so he claims. Supposedly, it's part of that rare treasure he's peddling."

Matt gasps at Kendrick's announcement and chokes on his whiskey. After wiping his mouth and regaining his composure a few moments later, he manages to speak. "Wallace Chung! Ming yellows? Is that what Chung is hawking this evening?" Matt shakes his head in amazement at Wallace's brazen pluck in such a preposterous scam. He thought Wallace had more finesse in his schemes. "Mister Kendrick, I would urge caution. These exceptionally rare and priceless yellows are impossible to find on the legitimate market because the Department of Antiquities has banned their trade and export. The Chinese authorities regard Ming yellow porcelains as national treasures. Any deal Chung is offering is sub rosa and fraught with danger and legal traps."

"That's not new information, Drummond. I understand these inconveniences. Chung suggested you as a reference. What say you?"

Drummond squirms slightly. "I've known Wallace Chung for several years. Occasionally, he gives me tips on news events and I give him tips on visiting dignitaries. Understand that Wallace Chung is a slick hustler. He provides various services—legal and not so—to the well-to-do tourists and business travelers. So far, he's avoided any serious legal trouble, and he's always been square with me. Can't speak for others. In summary, I would not trust him with my bank account."

"I understand." Kendrick smiles inwardly. "I've dealt with hustlers, flimflam artists, swindlers, and blatherskites all my life. On the whole, I'm way ahead, and those jokers are much the poorer. A few are now the unwilling guests at various state and federal facilities for many years to come."

Ingrid doesn't share her father's sanguine view and interrupts. "Dad, caution. I'm getting uncomfortable with this Ming yellow business. Let's reconsider."

"Not yet, daughter. Let's see what the Chinaman brings and what he has to say."

Matt glances at Ingrid, and then back to Kendrick. "I support Ingrid's caution. Keep the onus on Chung to prove his claims."

Kendrick thunders, "Drummond, do not take me for a fool."

Ingrid puts a soft hand on her father's arm. "Dad, there's no need to be bearish with our guest."

"Yes, daughter. You are correct. I apologize, Mister Drummond, for raising my voice."

"No matter. Please continue."

"Very well. Chung avers that the yellow porcelain he's bringing is genuine and its history is written in blood." He swigs deeply and cracks a thin smile. "What's critical is Chung's avowal that the yellow he's bringing is from a cache that consists of twenty of these porcelains somewhere deep in western China."

Matt leans back in his chair and considers. *A cache of twenty Ming yellow porcelains? On the illicit market now? Amazing if true. How did Chung get involved? What chicanery is he conjuring?* Seriously concerned, he asks, "Did Chung offer any specifics about the yellows' location? Or who has them?"

Kendrick frowns. "Excellent questions, Drummond. No. He was evasive—just teasing me. I'll demand and get more information from him. Meanwhile, let's eat. I've ordered porterhouse steak dinners, rare, with all the trimmings."

5

Kendrick's Suite, Oriental Hotel, Peking. 5 July 1935

At eight thirty sharp, there is a soft rap on the door. Ingrid opens it and says, "Good evening. You must be Mister Wallace Chung. Please come in."

Chung gives a short bow. "I am he. Thank you." He wears a white doubled-breasted suit with a white silk shirt, a cream-white tie, and white shoes. He carries a white panama hat in one hand and a small teak box in the other.

Ingrid escorts Chung to her father. "Mister Chung, you've met my father."

Chung bows and says, "Good evening, Mister Kendrick." He quickly surveys the suite.

Ingrid gestures toward Matt and asks, "Mister Chung, you know Mister Drummond?"

"Yes, I know Matt Drummond. He and I are old friends." He bows to Matt and sits on the divan without an invitation. He looks at Kendrick with a slight frown. "Mister Kendrick, may we speak in private? As a journalist, Mister Drummond should not be privy to the information I have. It would be to his advantage to publish a story about our negotiations."

"Whatever you have to say, say it in front of all of us," Kendrick snaps. "Mister Drummond and I have made an arrangement. He's considering accompanying us to the interior if we go."

Dismayed, Wallace glances at Drummond. He has fraternized with him on a professional basis from time to time; he just doesn't want Matt snooping around this deal that's taken several months to plan. But, it's also plain that he has no choice. He speaks directly to the Australian. "What I have to say must be kept in strict confidence. Or else the deal to get the yellows will collapse."

Matt retorts, "If you have a problem with my trust, discuss it with Mister Kendrick. Now, I'm on his team."

To ease the tension, Ingrid asks, "Mister Chung, would you care for some tea?"

Chung smiles, grateful for the distraction, and says softly, "That would be most kind."

Ingrid brings a tea service from the suite's kitchen and pours the tea into a thin, white, porcelain cup decorated with a black dragon. She places the cup in a matching saucer and hands it to him.

"Thank you, Mistress Kendrick." Chung takes a sip.

Kendrick, anxious to find out what Chung has for sale, rises, goes to the divan, stands in front of him, and says, "Enough of this nonsense. Let's get down to business. Show me this yellow porcelain sample, bibelot, or whatever you've got."

"As you wish, Mister Kendrick." Placing his cup carefully in its saucer, Chung reaches for the box, opens it with showmanship, and withdraws a yellow saucer. He holds it in his right hand for a few seconds for effect. He smiles as six eyes focus intently on the saucer. The bright light from the standing lamp hits the yellow saucer and its color sprays throughout the room.

The room is singularly quiet.

Finally, Kendrick says, "That's a beauty. What is it?"

Chung, with deliberate articulation, says, "It is a genuine Ming yellow saucer from the collection we've discussed." He hands it to Kendrick. "Please."

Kendrick brings the saucer to the light and looks deeply into the yellow glaze. His eyes narrow as he examines the saucer. After a time, he exclaims, "Well, I'll be damned! This is indeed a beauty." He hands it to Ingrid. "What do you make of it?"

"I know nothing about antique porcelains. But I must say this saucer is gorgeous. The yellow is so wondrously deep." She passes it to Drummond. "Matt, do you have an opinion?"

Chung interrupts. "Matt, use my ten-power loupe."

"Thanks." Drummond inspects the saucer at length, turning it over to view the calligraphy on its base. After several moments, he hands the saucer to Kendrick. "The calligraphy is faint, but I can read one of the characters. It is 'Yung-lo.' Several others, I suspect, are 'Inner Court.' I cannot read the rest." He returns the loupe to Chung. "We need to check, but I believe Yung-lo was a Ming Dynasty Emperor who ruled around 1400."

Chung interjects, "You are quite correct, Mister Drummond. Yung-lo was the third Emperor of the Ming Dynasty and he ruled for about twenty years in the early fifteenth century."

Ingrid smiles and addresses Matt, "You have more talents than are apparent."

"Yes, *mademoiselle*." He turns to Kendrick. "I do not have the expertise to authenticate this yellow saucer. If it is a forgery, it is exceptionally well done. The yellow is so mystically deep that it's mesmerizing. Clearly, the craftsman was a profound master of high-temperature-fired porcelain."

Kendrick demands of Chung, "How do we know this yellow saucer is genuine and that your story about the cache of twenty more is true? Fess up, Chung. Any deal we might make hangs in the balance. If you try to hoodwink me, I'll personally send you to your ancestors—head first. Are we clear?"

"I understand your concern quite well, Mister Kendrick. I have learned from an unimpeachable source that the entire yellow cache is authentic."

"What unimpeachable source? Where did you get this yellow?"

"I am reticent to reveal confidential information about my business. I am sure you understand."

"I don't understand one damn bit," growls Kendrick.

Faced with Kendrick's ultimatum, Chung decides to leak enough information to keep Kendrick interested. "Very well. Several days ago, an emissary from the rightful owner brought this saucer to me. For reasons I do not understand, this emissary has firsthand knowledge of the saucer's provenance. He confirmed that there are twenty more such yellows in his employer's care. His instructions were to show this saucer to potential buyers as a sign of my good faith. If necessary, I may sell it—a prerequisite for a potential buyer to purchase the entire cache of yellows." He glances about the room and sees that his audience is paying rapt attention to his story. "We completed the exchange, and that is the last I saw of him." He pauses to sip his tea and to gather his thoughts. "An independent expert has confirmed this yellow saucer's authenticity."

Kendrick doesn't bother hiding his frustration, and in an accusing voice says, "What expert?"

Chung freezes with his cup halfway to his lips.

"Chung, you've babbled a lot. But, without telling us any of the particulars. I need to know specific names, places, and other details." His anger rising, he yanks Chung out of his chair by his lapels and pulls him until their faces almost touch. The cup falls to the carpet and the tea stains Chung's jacket and trousers. "Where did you get this saucer and from whom?" He shoves Chung back into his chair. "If you can't answer forthrightly, we will have no more dealings. Am I clear?"

"Dad! Stop it. Be civilized. Mister Chung is simply protecting his interests by being reticent." She goes to Chung and hands him a large cloth napkin. "Let me refill your cup."

Kendrick grabs his drink and finishes it. He does the same with the near-empty scotch bottle and says, "My apologies, Chung. My temper too often overwhelms my propriety."

Still smarting from Kendrick's untoward behavior, Chung mops the front of his suit as best he can. "Please let me reiterate that I cannot reveal any details until we complete a deal. However, I can assure you that your interests will be well served by engaging me to guide you to the yellows."

Kendrick, accepting defeat, returns to his chair. While making up his mind, he's torn between his desire and his caution. He stares at the yellow saucer. It feels like cool cream in his hand. He turns it over again and again to stare at the faint marking. "Who's your expert authority, Chung?"

"I can tell you that Mister Wuhan Wei-ku authenticated this yellow as genuine. He is the premier expert regarding Ming porcelains."

Kendrick looks to Matt Drummond.

"Wu is the recognized expert."

Chung allows himself the tiniest of smiles. He has seduced Kendrick.

Kendrick takes a healthy swallow of his refilled whiskey glass and glares at Chung. He looks to Ingrid and then brings his gaze back to Chung. He clenches his right hand into a fist, points a threatening finger at Chung, and growls, "What's your price for this yellow?"

Chung, not intimidated, flashes his thin, professional smile. *Now I'm reeling him in.* "I am authorized to offer this Ming yellow saucer for only five thousand British pounds sterling."

A stunned silence permeates the suite. Then, almost in unison, incredulous gasps erupt from Ingrid and Matt. Kendrick stares at Chung with narrow eyes.

For a few seconds Ingrid sits silently, coldly rigid with a stony face. Then she leaps out of her chair, puts her hands on her hips, and cries, "Dad, this is ludicrous! You can't spend twenty-five thousand dollars on a saucer. That's insanity!"

Ingrid addresses Chung sharply, "Mister Chung, you cannot be serious." Tempering her voice, she turns to Kendrick. "Dad, this is nonsense. Return the saucer right now to Mister Chung, tell him goodbye, and let's go home." She tosses her hands up to cover her face as soft tears flood her cheeks. She mumbles through her frustration, "I'm sick of China and all these dealings of yours. I want to get back to my office and my job. I want to see the Yankees play the Dodgers in Ebbets Field in a World Series game. I want to eat a hotdog covered with mustard and dripping with relish. I want to sleep in my own bed." She takes Kendrick's free hand in both of hers. "It's time we quit this collecting compulsion of yours and return to our business in New York."

Kendrick remains stoic, caressing the saucer. He does not look at Ingrid.

With her adrenaline abating, she returns to her chair, wipes her tears with a handkerchief, and finishes her drink in two deep swallows. Then she covers her face with her hands and rocks her head back and forth, hoping to clear her anger and frustration.

Kendrick continues to fondle the saucer.

Chung is somewhat taken aback by Ingrid's outburst. "Mistress Kendrick, I assure you that I am quite serious. What I ask for this spectacular Ming yellow saucer is far below market value. And please recall that the buyer of this saucer will have the opportunity to purchase the remainder of a truly fabulous and historically significant collection of twenty more Ming yellow porcelains."

Before Ingrid can respond, Kendrick snarls in his last-and-best-counteroffer voice, "Three thousand pounds sterling. Either accept my offer or get out."

Wallace Chung sits quietly while he calculates his strategy and the odds that Kendrick's offer is in fact firm. He sips some tea, then carefully places the cup on its saucer. His mind whirls. *If Kendrick purchases the entire cache I will get an exceptionally large finder's fee, and I can earn serious money as Kendrick's guide and interpreter in the interior.* Chung realizes that he has no other potential buyers, and it is to his benefit to accept Kendrick's offer. He nods to Kendrick and says, "I accept."

Suddenly the tension in the suite evaporates. Ingrid slumps in her chair, her energy spent. Matt gulps down his bourbon, and makes mental notes.

Kendrick whips out his checkbook. He quickly writes a check and signs it with his bold signature. He hands it to Chung and says, "I presume you will take a check. It's drawn on the China National Bank and Trust Company. It will clear on your presentation."

"Of course. Thank you, Mister Kendrick. You drive a hard bargain. I am confident that there will be no problem with your check. The bank's senior teller is an old friend." Chung retrieves the saucer and carefully returns it to the box. He hands the box to Kendrick with a flourish. "You have made an exceptional purchase."

Kendrick, satisfied that he has made a propitious bargain, places the box on the table and turns to his daughter. "Please refresh our drinks, and make them potent. I need a boost."

"Dad, you're an idiot! Our country is in a deep depression. We could have used those funds to expand our business, buy machine tools, create jobs, and boost the economy." Ingrid refills the glasses and grumbles, "Fifteen thousand dollars for a yellow saucer."

"Don't worry about it. We have plenty more in accounts and investments all over the world—we'll expand when the market demands it." He tosses down a large gulp of whiskey and says to Chung, "What's the deal with the remainder of this yellow collection? What type are they? Who has them? And where are they? I need straight answers, Chung. And tell me how you profit from any deal we might make."

Chung calmly sips his tea. Then he sits forward on the divan and replies, "Your questions are relevant. Unfortunately, I do not have answers to all of them. As I understand, the owner is in need of funds to purchase various items of equipment to meet unexpected demands on his services. Accordingly, the yellows are for sale at a very reasonable price. The owner's representative has insisted that I act as his sole agent. That is why only I am authorized to negotiate the sale and to guide the potential buyer to the yellow porcelains." He pauses for effect and to gather his thoughts. "Here is my proposition: On my word of honor, I will tell you all that I know, truthfully. You may accept the deal or not. If you decline, I would expect you to keep the information confidential as I try to find another buyer. Do you accept?"

Kendrick grumbles, "So far, yes. What're the logistics, and what's your take?"

Chung responds, "As your guide and to protect my own interest, as it were, I will accompany you to the yellows' location. I will make all travel arrangements and pay all upfront expenses. My finder's fee is twenty-five percent of the purchase price of the yellows. Naturally, you will reimburse all my expenses with an added twenty-percent handling fee."

Kendrick blusters, "A twenty-five percent finder's fee is outrageous. The usual finder's fee is twenty percent and the handling fee for expenses usually is fifteen percent. Why do you merit such thievery?"

Chung ignores his insult and responds patiently. "My fee is higher than in customary transactions because of my specialized knowledge, unique charge as the sole agent, and for the extensive travel to the yellows." Wallace knows that he has keenly whetted Kendrick's appetite for the porcelains. "Sir, it would be a tragedy for these magnificent yellows to be in the hands of another collector. Or displayed in a glass case in some provincial museum. I must insist that my fee is twenty-five percent."

"Damn you, Chung." Kendrick takes another swallow and grumbles. "You are a blackguard. I repeat, if you pull any monkey business on me, I'll wring your Chinaman's neck."

"Is that an affirmative answer, Mister Kendrick?"

Kendrick nods his head. "Yes." His eyes narrow and lips tighten. "Now, answer my questions regarding the details of this yellow collection. No more games, Chung. Out with it!"

Chung, in an uncharacteristic response, says, "Mister Kendrick, we must be courteous and trusting if we are to conclude an auspicious arrangement."

Kendrick grunts, "Yes. Yes. Yes. God's sakes, man, to the point."

"Very well, Mister Kendrick, here is what I do know. I am led to believe that this cache of Ming yellow porcelains is in the citadel Ho Hsien, in Kansu Province."

Matt, who has been silent, interrupts Chung's spiel. "Kansu Province! That's insane. You can't go there." He rises and talks directly to Kendrick. "Ho Hsien is well over sixteen hundred miles to the northwest, and over a hundred miles from the end of the railroad line at Chung-weh." He takes a deep breath. "Ho Hsien is a fading Silk Road city in the Ala Shan Desert— one of the hottest, driest, largest deserts in Asia. Warlords, bandits, and renegade soldiers control most of the area between Peking and Kansu Province. There are Japanese patrols from the Kwangtung Army in the area. Finally, there's minimal Nationalist government presence anywhere near there. This scheme is foolhardy at best." Spent, Matt retreats to his chair and checks the whiskey remaining in his glass.

Ingrid hears Matt's rant, and it confirms her foreboding. She rises and glares at Chung. Her mouth is tight, eyes narrow, and her hands in tight fists. She turns her stare on her father. "Dad, Chung is spinning fairy tales. You can't fall for his twaddle. Let's go home."

Chung hurries to reassure Kendrick. "Mister Drummond exaggerates the hazards. The local warlord keeps the area reasonably secure. However, I will make arrangements that will ensure a strong measure of safety. I have a strong connection in Kansu Province."

Kendrick, with his eyes wide, calculates the odds of Chung's surety.

"Insanity," mumbles Drummond as he empties his glass. In a stronger voice, he looks first to Ingrid then to Kendrick. "This is bloody madness. The odds are that you'll be swindled, kidnapped, or worse."

Kendrick points his open hand at Drummond, "Calm down. I hear your objections. You have a point. I'm considering them."

Ingrid nearly hisses. "Mister Chung, the mission you've outlined is fraught with grave danger and unknowns. By what measure can we be assured of your integrity?"

With faux hurt in his voice, Wallace Chung responds, "Mistress Kendrick, it is unfortunate that you and Drummond question my sincerity. Please understand that I would not be so witless as to fabricate any of these details and jeopardize my fees. Clearly it is to my advantage that your party remains safe, that the transaction for the yellows goes smoothly, and that you return to Peking pleased with your adventure into 'the wilds of the Celestial Kingdom.'" He sips his tea. "I remain hopeful there will be other profitable deals in the future."

Kendrick, his eyes steely, still can't let one question go. He demands, "Before we proceed further, Chung, tell me straightforwardly, who has these yellows? What's his name? If I don't get an honest answer right now, our deal is *kaput*. And I promise that you will never see another cent from me."

Chung, playing his captive audience on a fine string, responds in a conspiratorial voice, "The Ming yellow porcelains are in the safe hands of General Wu Pei-fu, in his citadel at Ho Hsien."

Instantly, Matt sees the entire scheme. "General Wu! You folks are batty even to consider this scheme. Wu is the vicious warlord of Kansu Province. He's a total animal. Hear me! Four days ago, I heard a rumor via the journalist grapevine that last month General Wu sacked the Buddhist lamasery at Yü-men! The surviving monks and acolytes scattered and hid in the nearby hills. You're best advised to stay away from this notorious warlord and the bandits that roam in the area."

Kendrick and Ingrid are stunned at Matt's outburst and graphic message.

Needing to seize the initiative, Wallace Chung tries to reassure his audience. "Again, Mister Drummond overstates the conditions in Kansu Province. I must say that General Wu is in complete control of this entire area. He governs with a firm but fair hand. I know him personally and I will vouch for his integrity regarding the sale of these Ming yellow porcelains. May I continue?"

Kendrick nods. Ingrid falls back in her chair and mutters, "Damn."

Matt remains silent and wonders, *Should I get out now and leave these loonies to their fate?* Matt speaks emphatically. "Kendrick, don't be seduced by Chung's balderdash. Again, I tell you that General Wu is a megalomaniac without any scruples. He is notorious for kidnapping, rape, murder, pillage, and God knows what all."

Before Drummond can continue, Chung interrupts. "Mister Kendrick, I can assure your safety. I have family who have lived peacefully in Kansu Province for hundreds of years."

Kendrick looks at Ingrid to assess her reaction.

She sinks deeper in her chair, hands palms up. Protest is useless.

Satisfied, he snaps, "Continue, Chung."

Wallace inches forward in his chair. "You have asked about the details of the yellow porcelain collection. I understand that all of them date from the Emperor Yung-lo's reign. Those types of porcelains are the most magnificent of the Ming yellows, are they not?" He pauses for effect. "I've not seen the other yellows; however, I have a complete inventory." He withdraws foolscap from his inner coat pocket, opens and scans it. "A matching cup for your saucer, several plates, an assortment of jars, urns, plates, other cups, and vases. Each piece's dimensions are listed in centimeters and weight in grams or kilograms, as appropriate." Wallace Chung pauses and, for dramatic effect, flashes an intriguing glance at each person in the room. Then, with intense eyes, he focuses on Kendrick and says, "The major piece in the collection is a vase some four feet tall!" Chung pauses for his audience to absorb the import of this revelation.

Gasps and reactions reverberate throughout the room. Matt exclaims, "Four feet! That's incredible. Wallace, I wonder if you believe we're *drongo*."

Chung responds, "Not at all, Matt. I have the greatest respect for your keen perception." Chung hands the list to Kendrick.

Kendrick puts on his reading glasses, studies the inventory, and snaps, "How valid is this information?"

Chung responds with unctuous sincerity, "I am confident that the inventory is true. The emissary is close to General Wu, and he is a boyhood chum of mine whom I trust implicitly."

Ingrid laments, "Dad, don't. The risk is too great. You should not make such a critical decision based on apocryphal information from a man whom we do not know and whose sincerity we cannot verify."

Kendrick does not move for several seconds. His face is devoid of expression. He closes his eyes as he slowly and carefully weighs Ingrid's concerns against the potential rewards and the intoxicating thrill of another intriguing adventure. He rises from his chair, wanders to a window, and gazes down at the activities in Tiananmen Square. He drinks his whiskey with small, deliberate sips, and scratches where it does not itch.

After several minutes, Kendrick returns to his chair, sits on its edge, and stares at Wallace for several seconds. "All right. You've got a deal, Chung. Let's get those yellow porcelains."

Ingrid, resigned, says in a cool, collected voice, "Dad, this is a huge mistake. But if you're determined to go, I'll do what I can to support you. But—this is the last time." She adds with a forced smile, "I mean it."

Drummond remains silent as he observes the drama unfolding before him. He wonders, *Is Kendrick wacko? What's the real story behind Chung's narrative? Is it a lark? Or is it the story of the century?* He looks at Kendrick with questioning eyes, then turns to focus on Ingrid, and smiles inwardly. *She is enchanting.* He twirls his glass and takes a deep swig. With finality he avers, "Kendrick, I'm in."

Chung glares at Drummond before he rises and goes to Kendrick to shake his hand to conclude the deal. "You have made the correct decision, Mister Kendrick."

Kendrick does not rise, nor does he accept Chung's extended hand. "My word is my bond. You know that. However, I'm going to have this saucer authenticated. If it's a forgery, our deal is off. And I'll come after you with all the forces I can muster."

"Very well. Ho Hsien is about sixteen hundred miles northwest of Peking. It would be prudent for us to travel by train to rails-end at Chang-yeh, about fifteen hundred miles away and several miles into Kansu Province. For your comfort and privacy, I would suggest that you authorize me to charter an executive railroad club car. I will also need to arrange transportation for us to travel the remaining one hundred miles or so to Ho Hsien. I expect that it will take me a few days to complete these plans." He bows and picks up his hat. "I will begin making arrangements tomorrow."

"Do it," murmurs Kendrick. In a more positive tone, he tells Ingrid, "Please show Chung to the door. We have concluded our business."

There is a restful quiet in the suite after Chung leaves. In a minute or two, Ingrid picks up the glasses and the tea tray and returns them to the kitchen.

Kendrick finally speaks, "Another whiskey, please." After Ingrid returns with his drink, he gulps it down. He points his index finger at Matt and says, "Frankly, I'm delighted that you are with us, Matt Drummond."

"Absolutely! This caper has potential for scoop of the year. If we survive."

Satisfied, Kendrick lets his excitement creep into his voice. He exuberantly tells Matt, "What the hell. The night is early. And you two young people ought to be out having fun, not moping around with me." He shoos them toward the door. "Skedaddle, the both of you. Matt, show my Ingrid a good time!"

6

Matt Drummond's Apartment, Peking. 6 July 1935

K endrick pounds loudly on Matt's front door. Under his left arm is
.the teak box containing the yellow saucer. Today he wears a light-
weight seersucker suit, blue silk shirt, dark-blue tie, and white shoes.

Matt's fashionable apartment is in the International Settlement. It's
nicely decorated with a mix of European and Chinese furniture and accessories. Matt's houseboy, Lisan, is busy arranging books and photographic equipment, and tidying Matt's desk, piled with all manner of notes from his trip.

Lisan opens the door, and stares at the tall, well-dressed Occidental
a moment before he says, "Good morning, sir."

"This is Matt Drummond's apartment."

Lisan waits.

"Right?"

"That is correct, sir. May I help you?"

Kendrick, without invitation, enters the foyer, barrels past the as-
tounded Lisan, and goes into the living room. "Good! Tell Drummond that
Randall Kendrick is here and wants to see him."

Lisan composes himself and asks courteously, "Is Mister Drummond
expecting you?"

With impatience, Kendrick snaps, "No. But get him. I have business to discuss."

Lisan recovers, somewhat taken aback by Kendrick's boorish behavior, and presses on. "Sir, I cannot tell Mister Drummond that you want to see him. I do not know the purpose of your visit."

"Chinaboy, tell him Kendrick is here on important business. Chop! Chop!"

Lisan, not outwardly fazed by the racist pidgin English, responds, "Mister Drummond cannot see you. He is asleep. He worked until early this morning. Very sorry, I cannot help you."

Kendrick's impatience begins to soar, and his voice rises in volume and tone. "Get him, boy. It does not matter what he is doing."

Aroused by the ruckus, the half-awake Matt shakes Ingrid, who lies next to him. "My God! It's Kendrick. Ingrid, get up. Your father is here."

With sleepy eyes, she asks, "Why? What time is it?" She uses both hands to rub her forehead. "Damn, my head is about to explode. I reckon we indulged far too much in the fruit of the vine."

"Ingrid, Kendrick is here to see me. Get up, gather your clothes, and hide in the bathroom."

Drummond's words finally penetrate her fogged brain and, realizing her embarrassing predicament, Ingrid rolls out of bed and spouts, "Damn! You might know he'd show up."

Matt tosses back his hair, slips into his robe, and shuffles into the living room. He glances at Kendrick and grunts, "Hello, Kendrick." He checks his watch. "It's sort of early for a visit."

Kendrick says, "It's never too early for business."

"Okay, Kendrick. Find a place to sit, and I'll have Lisan bring coffee." Drummond speaks in Mandarin to Lisan. "It's okay, Lisan. Don't let this Occidental barbarian perturb you. I'm going to work with this fellow." His ire aroused, Matt says in a too loud voice, "Kendrick, you will be civil in my home. Lisan has been my houseboy for many years. He is my responsibility."

Kendrick realizes that his waspishness has almost quashed the deal with Matt. "You're right, Drummond. My sincere apologies to you and Lisan. Impatience and passion are my cross. When I start a project, I'm singularly focused on the task at hand. May I start over?"

Matt, his ire subsiding, nods in agreement. "How may I be of service this early morning in the heavenly kingdom?"

Kendrick looks past Matt and in a robust voice speaks loud enough to be heard in the bedroom. "Ingrid, come in here, I need your help."

Matt turns scarlet. He can't stop himself from looking at the bedroom door.

Ingrid's soft voice drifts out from the bedroom. "In a couple of minutes, Dad. I've got to get presentable."

Drummond watches as Kendrick sits on the sofa, seemingly unfazed. "Matt, I need your help. On reflection, the deal I made with Wallace Chung last evening makes me uncomfortable. Perhaps it was too hasty. I'm in a strange land. I don't know much about its customs, and sure as heck don't know the language. And you are right. That trip to Ho Hsien is going to be a 'piss-cutter.'"

Lisan enters softly and asks Drummond, "Shall I prepare coffee?"

Kendrick ignores the intrusion and continues. "Frankly, I need a sidekick to steer me away from making tactical blunders. I need a white man I can trust, one who knows his way around the chaos of this country—someone to keep Ingrid and me out of trouble. You game?"

Drummond fidgets a bit and says, "I don't understand. I've already made the commitment to go with you and to document your activities and then to publish my work in your media. What more do you want?"

"I want lots more. I want your commitment to me personally—my contract assistant—an Occidental to protect my interests and offer relevant advice. You have a working knowledge of Mandarin, know the mores of this country, and you have a reputation as a man of integrity. You're familiar with the subtleties and etiquette of bargaining with Orientals, and apparently have some knowledge about porcelains."

Stunned at Kendrick's proposal, Drummond does not respond at first. Too many conflicting thoughts whirl in his mind. A few seconds later, he responds, "I don't know." After another short pause, he says, "What's your offer—the deal?"

Lisan brings a silver service and pours two coffees into beautiful blue porcelain cups set on matching saucers. He makes a short bow toward Drummond, "Shall I pour a cup for the missy?"

Almost on cue, Ingrid, with her hair combed back, and dressed in a man's tan dressing gown, enters and says, "Please pour, Lisan." She winks at Kendrick, and unabashedly says. "Good morning, Dad. What's up?"

"I'm trying to hire Drummond as my *aide-de-camp* on our upcoming trip."

Ingrid smiles broadly, "That's a great idea. I don't relish the thought of traveling almost sixteen hundred miles west into this untamed area without a competent and trustworthy paladin." She goes to Matt and kisses him on the cheek. "Do it, Matt."

Drummond pulls away. "I'm a photojournalist, not a bodyguard or a major-domo."

Kendrick beams, "I see no conflict. You'll get your story. We'll publish it. And Ingrid and I will have a measure of mental and physical security. Accept, and your salary will be one thousand British pounds sterling per week plus all expenses, and I'll prepare an exclusive contract to publish all your work for five years with right of first refusal."

Drummond does not respond. He goes to the window and stares at his well-tended garden. A few moments later, Ingrid moves next to him and stands in silence. He becomes keenly aware of her aura and her faint scent. He turns to Kendrick. "It's a deal on two conditions: I'll not be your servant, and you won't interfere with my photojournalist work. I'll photograph and write about anything that I choose."

Kendrick grabs Drummond's right hand and shakes it vigorously. "Deal. You're on the payroll now."

Drummond beckons Lisan. "Spike our coffee with brandy."

Kendrick plops on Matt's chaise lounge. "Tell us about your skill level in identifying these porcelains."

Ingrid interrupts, "You fellows talk. I'm going to get dressed."

Drummond nods toward Ingrid, swigs his spiked coffee, and addresses Kendrick. "To set the record straight, I have minimal expertise. But, I'm reasonably sure that I would recognize a gross counterfeit. A few years ago, I did a photographic essay on Ming porcelains. The curator of the Peking Hall of Antiquities let me inspect several Ming pieces. Most were the blue. A couple pinks. There was one magnificent yellow jar, perhaps twenty centimeters tall, with exquisitely detailed paintings. I have photographs of all the pieces from several angles. Additionally, I took tight close-ups of the calligraphy on the porcelains' bases. Those markings would be near impossible to duplicate with authenticity."

Hearing this, Kendrick is even more convinced he's made the right choice in hiring Drummond. "Excellent! Do you have prints of those marks? We'll need them."

"Yes. They are in my photographic files."

"Excellent. Make a couple of duplicate prints and bring them with you." He withdraws Wallace Chung's inventory of the twenty yellows and hands it to Drummond. "Amazing! Twenty Ming yellows! For sale. Any idea what they could be worth?"

Matt scans the list. "Can't tell. In this 'off-record' deal you're working on, the primary factor determining the price is the owner's desperation to sell. We, on the other hand, need to consider several factors: authenticity of the calligraphy, condition, size, depth of color. Details of the designs." Drummond leans forward in his chair. "I must warn you, Kendrick. There's no active market in these yellows. One, perhaps two, trade in several years—illegally, I'll add. Understand, these Ming yellows are part of China's national treasure. Even if you get them, you'll have a difficult time getting them past Chinese customs and shipping them out of the country."

Kendrick responds, "That's not your problem. I'll take care of it when the time comes." He boasts, "I own a shipping line that works in these seas and have enough money to buy this country."

Matt looks at Kendrick. He's not pleased with himself for agreeing to work with this vulgar fellow in a shady deal. *But, there is Ingrid! And, there is that fabulous salary—more than I'd earn in several years. Perhaps enough to let me get out of here and back to Queensland.*

"Do you know this Wuhan fellow who is supposed to be an expert on Ming porcelains?"

"Yes, I know him. Over the last few years, he and I have made a few minor deals."

"Let's go to his place and have him authenticate the yellow saucer I bought last evening. Before I get into this miasma any deeper, I want to be convinced that I'm 'playing with a full deck.'"

"Excellent suggestion. But you should know that Wuhan's reputation is somewhat shady. Nonetheless, he was of great help to me in interpreting the calligraphy on those Ming porcelains I photographed in the museum. To return the favor, I gave him a complete set of prints for his reference."

Kendrick looks at Drummond with increased respect.

In a soft, warning voice, Drummond says, "Rumor has it that it was Wuhan who negotiated the last Ming yellow sale—*sub rosa*, of course."

Smiling broadly, Kendrick stands and announces, "My kind of Chinaman. Let's go. Now!"

7

Tsingtao Street, a Few Blocks South of Tiananmen Square, Peking.
6 July 1935

K endrick and Matt bump along the cobblestone streets riding in a rick-shaw pulled by a tall and powerful fellow. Kendrick is amazed by the sights and sounds of this Oriental city teeming with beggars, peddlers, pe-destrians, and helter-skelter traffic—a cacophony of sounds and innumer-able rickshaws recklessly crisscrossing every which way. The panting man pulling their rickshaw maneuvers it deftly through the traffic and maze of narrow streets. Finally, they stop in front of a nondescript shop in a dark, narrow alley. The sign over the door reads "Antiks."

"This is it, Kendrick. Since I know the proprietor of this shop, Wuhan Wu-ku, I'll make the introductions and handle the initial inqui-ries. Please, Kendrick, do nothing and say nothing. Just watch and listen. Wuhan has knowledge of English. However, as a courtesy, I'll speak in Mandarin at first."

Kendrick, somewhat miffed by such a stern request from a subordi-nate, pouts. "Nonsense, I'll talk whenever I want."

Matt's hand freezes mid-air just as he is about to open the door. With clenched fists, he commands, "No, you won't. Not as long as I have the responsibility of negotiating and deciding when I deem it best for you to keep your trap shut. Your bluster and vile treatment of these people will quash my efforts to facilitate our trip and purchase the yellows. Understand?"

Retorting with a vengeance, Kendrick commands, "No. I do not understand. I'm in charge."

"Very well." Matt turns and walks down the alley. "Get yourself a lackey. I'm through with you."

Stung by the Australian's rejection of him and his authority, Kendrick simmers with bitter exasperation. As he sees Matt walking away, his better judgment kicks in. He realizes that his quick temper and narcissism are about to destroy his quest for the yellows and are driving away one of the best men he's ever met. Drummond's on-target comments ring true. He shouts, "Drummond, you are right. Accept my apologies. I'll defer to your suggestions."

Matt returns to the Antiks door. "Absolutely? No more finagling?"

"Absolutely. You have my word."

They shake hands to conclude the deal. Kendrick comments, "You're a man of many talents, Drummond—a jack of all trades." He nods toward the door, "Let's get with it."

As the pair enter the shop, a small bell attached to the door tinkles softly. Seemingly out of nowhere, a strikingly beautiful female with an exquisite body clad in a skin-tight crimson cheongsam greets them. An embroidered golden-dragon design winds around her body. Its open mouth hovers over her left breast. She bows deeply, and Matt returns the bow.

Kendrick gapes in awe at this Oriental enchantress. Matt ignores his employer's rudeness and speaks. "Good afternoon, Mistress Yen. I am pleased to visit with you again. All goes well, I assume?"

Yen Hei-lan speaks in her low, raspy voice. "Welcome, Mister Drummond, to my uncle's poor shop." She looks at Kendrick and recognizes him from his photographs. "We are honored to have you and your associate grace our humble place." Her faintly rouged lips form a thin smile.

"You have come possibly to do some small business? Perhaps we can be of service." Her inference speaks perhaps of a relationship with Matt more intimate than merely professional.

The Antiks shop is jammed with bric-a-brac, posters, old books, and tourist souvenirs. There is barely enough room for one person to move about. The light from a single bulb hanging from the ceiling casts a chiaroscuro ambiance. However, the shop's ramshackle appearance belies its wealth of rare Oriental treasures.

Matt smiles professionally. "Your day is pleasant?" He meets her jet-black eyes. "It is we who are honored to be here. Is it possible that we may speak with your uncle? My colleague has expressed some interest in rare porcelains."

With a smile that now breathes of wicked sin, Yen speaks in near-perfect English. "Please. I will see after my uncle." She moves to the rear of the shop.

Kendrick locks his eyes on her *derrière* as she swings in erotic syncopation. She parts a beaded curtain, glances back at her visitors, and disappears into another room.

Matt notices Kendrick's reaction to the striking Yen Hei-lan. With a stern voice he cautions, "Forget it, Kendrick. She has a dangerous reputation."

Shortly, the proprietor, Wuhan Wei-ku, emerges from behind the beaded curtain. He is of indeterminate age and short of stature. He wears a spectacular green dressing gown, and a black skullcap that covers his short black hair. His deep black eyes dominate his lean, expressionless face. With his alert manner, he projects no-nonsense business.

Kendrick tries to appraise Wuhan from his American perspective—without much success. Wuhan is more discreet and accurate in his evaluation of Kendrick.

Drummond opens the conversation in Mandarin. "This humble one has deigned to bring an associate so that he may be permitted to see fine porcelains, perhaps a thing or two from the Ming Dynasty. If that would please you."

Wuhan responds, "Your friend does this simple one honor. He comes, I suspect, from the Excellent Country."

Matt turns to Kendrick. "Wuhan has spotted you for an American."

"Tell him I'm pleased to meet him."

Drummond complies.

Wuhan returns a perfunctory bow.

Drummond says, "We would ask a favor of you, also—to look at the calligraphy on a yellow saucer."

Yen Hei-lan appears and speaks to Matt, "Please invite your friend to join us for tea and cakes in our reception room. Today we have a special oolong tea imported especially for us from Ceylon." She makes a point of working the hip-high slit in her cheongsam to expose fully her long, sensuous leg.

Drummond wonders if her coquetry is meant for him or Kendrick. No matter, he knows that it's prudent to ignore after-hours activities with her. "It is our pleasure to join you and your uncle."

Yen leads the pair into a softly lit lounge behind the jumbled shop. It is furnished with thick silk carpets, soft leather chairs, and a large teak and ebony coffee table. An *étagère* holds a collection of exquisite Sung celadons, and a magnificent brush painting of a karst mountain landscape hangs on the paneled wall.

Kendrick, not much impressed with the setting and the verbal parley, tugs at the hem of his jacket in frustration at these time-consuming customs. "Ask Wuhan, when will we see the porcelains? We can't take all day."

"Kendrick, be quiet and learn," Drummond whispers. "This is the customary way to do business. Your boorishness is close to nixing any deal we might make. Be patient. I know that's not your style, but follow my lead—your word, recall."

Yen, pretending not to understand the exchange, indicates the pair should sit in two large, soft, leather-covered teak chairs. She has a faint, knowing smile as she prepares the tea service.

Wuhan slides into a high-backed chair covered with bright pink silk.

Matt Drummond makes small talk with Wuhan in Mandarin as Yen brings tea and scones. She pours. Matt addresses Wuhan, "I have told my associate that your knowledge of Ming porcelains is extensive. That, perhaps, you might know of a yellow or two that were sold a few years ago."

Wuhan continues in English. "Yes, Mister Drummond, I was privileged to be the intermediary in that sale of yellows. A magnificent tea set. Thirteen cups, saucers, and the teapot. The finest yellows I have ever seen." Wuhan sips his tea and his blank affect continues. "Thanks to your photographs of the calligraphy on the museum's Ming porcelains, I am able to authenticate many more of these rare pieces. Unfortunately, there are many fakes. One has to be most careful."

Kendrick is unable to control himself and exclaims in a loud voice, "Wuhan facilitated that deal for those yellows that Caspar Wickham got." His temper begins to abate. "I've seen that collection in the Museum of Oriental Art in Philadelphia. Damnation."

Wuhan's black eyes narrow, as he is taken aback by Kendrick's inopportune outburst.

Drummond jabs his elbow hard in Kendrick's ribs. "You fool. Shut up! Else we're finished." He glares at Kendrick. "I'm running this show. Do you understand without equivocation?"

Wuhan speaks in a soft voice. "My most humble apologies for causing such distress to your associate."

Kendrick's face flushes red with embarrassment. He's broken his deal with Matt and understands the seriousness of the play he is in. He uses all his mental strength to remain silent. His clenched fist comes open slowly. He nods "very well" to Drummond. "My apologies to Mister Wuhan."

Drummond smiles weakly at Wuhan. "Please excuse my associate. He is uninformed about your customs."

Wuhan nods. "So it seems."

The tension in the room slowly eases as the participants sip tea and munch on the sweet scones.

Drummond asks Kendrick to hand him the yellow saucer. "Mister Wuhan, may I ask you to look at this yellow and tell us what you see?"

"Indeed." Wuhan takes the yellow, withdraws a powerful loupe from an inner pocket, and inspects the saucer. "I authenticated this saucer several days ago for that rascal Wallace Chung."

Matt is not surprised. "I suspected as much. Thank you. My associate purchased this saucer from Chung last evening and we needed to confirm its authenticity."

"Indeed."

As the silence becomes burdensome, Wuhan suggests, "Perhaps the honored gentleman would care to see a Ming blue currently in my possession."

Drummond responds, "You are most kind."

Wuhan makes a silent signal to Yen. Shortly she appears with a bright blue, silk-covered box fastened with an ivory clasp. She sets it before Wuhan. He slowly turns the box towards Kendrick and opens it carefully. He removes a sparkling Ming blue plate, about twenty centimeters wide, and sets it with great care on the polished rosewood tabletop.

Kendrick stares at the plate with eager eyes. He's never seen such a deep blue, and he is enthralled with the plate's beauty. With ultimate restraint, he refrains from reaching to touch the plate.

Wuhan sees Kendrick's keen interest. He says, "I offer my apologies for showing such a poor specimen of a Ming porcelain." After a beat, Wuhan says, "If your associate would care to examine this blue, please ask him to bring it close to his eyes."

Kendrick, unable to resist, takes the delicate blue in his huge, rough hands. A smile slowly forms. He scrutinizes the blue porcelain with a sharp eye—turning it every which way. He looks at the calligraphy on the base, unsure of its authenticity. Almost convinced, he hands the blue to Matt. "This plate is a beauty. Tell me, Drummond, about the markings. What do you make of them?"

Wuhan hands Matt the loupe.

Matt carefully examines the plate's calligraphy. "It looks authentic."

Kendrick, with his eyes aglow, says, "This is a fantastic piece. A prize for any collection."

Drummond looks to Wuhan. "You have compared these markings against my photographs?"

"Indeed, I have. And I see coherence."

Kendrick whispers to Drummond, "I'll buy it. Find the price."

Matt addresses Wuhan. "My associate is delighted with this blue plate. We wonder if you would consider parting with this spectacular porcelain."

Wuhan responds, "With great sorrow, I would see this Ming plate leave my shop with your associate."

"What fee would entice you to part with this blue plate?"

Wuhan pretends to contemplate. At length he responds, "I would reluctantly part with this blue plate for the simple sum of fifteen thousand U.S. dollars in gold certificates—one-thousand-dollar dominations, please."

"Tell Mister Wuhan that I agree. It's a deal!" Kendrick cracks a large smile. He is delighted, pleased that he's scored a coup over his arch rival, Caspar Wickham. "Tell Wuhan to wrap it up. I'll take it now."

Matt silently fidgets. There's business undone. Kendrick realizes what's missing. He pulls a pad out of his coat pocket, writes, and hands it to Wuhan. "Here's my promissory note. I'll have the gold certificates ready for you by tomorrow afternoon at the China National Bank and Trust Company, Limited."

Wuhan looks to Drummond, who nods affirmatively. Satisfied, he addresses Kendrick. "Your payment option is satisfactory. My niece is preparing the blue for you. My thanks for honoring my shop with your presence."

Soon, Yen appears and hands the package to Kendrick. She escorts the pair to the front door and smiles invitingly at Matt. "Good day, Matt Drummond. We look with favor on your next visit." She smiles coquettishly. "Perhaps we will have some treasures for you."

Drummond cracks a crooked smile, "And to you, fair lady."

Matt hails a passing rickshaw. The pair get aboard and Drummond tells the man, "The Oriental Hotel."

Kendrick says, "You did a bang-up job back there, Drummond. I'm much obliged. This blue is marvelous."

"Thanks. Wuhan is an excellent contact. He probably knows more about Ming porcelains than anyone in China."

"Listen, Drummond, do you suppose that fellow, Wuhan, knows about that cache of yellows Wallace is hawking?"

"I don't know. But, understand that Wuhan is shrewd. If he has any inkling, he'll keep it to himself. Wuhan looks to finesse profit in many ways." Matt reflects for a few seconds. "It's nigh impossible to read Wuhan. I'd never play poker with him."

Kendrick congratulates himself for purchasing the marvelous blue porcelain at such a bargain price, and he's satisfied that probably only his party know about the yellows for sale at Ho Hsien. "We've done well this afternoon. Got anything else on your schedule? No? Let's go to my suite for liquid refreshments—100-proof kind. I want to review the day and to figure what kind of hand I hold with that Wallace fellow."

Matt, tired of Kendrick, nods, and looks at the passing scene.

Matt Drummond's Apartment, Peking. 6 July 1935

Matt enters his apartment. His mind is whirling with conflicting images. He's having second thoughts about his commitment to Kendrick. He's perplexed about his feelings toward Ingrid, and tempted beyond reason by the generous salary he'll earn. And he's convinced that the trip to Ho Hsien is a fool's errand.

Lisan senses his master's distress. As he takes Matt's hat and jacket he asks, "Is everything satisfactory, Mister Drummond?"

"No. Maybe. I don't know. I've got to relax. I've got to think. Things are happening too fast. I've got to sort it out."

"Shall I make tea?"

"Sure." Matt manages a sad smile for Lisan. "A fine idea. I'll be in the study."

Matt sits at his desk, pushes aside his typewriter, opens the bottom drawer, and removes a dozen or so competition darts. In rapid succession, he slings the darts at the target board on the opposite wall. To his dismay, most are scattered on the wall. A few actually hit the board, but not near the bull's-eye. He stares at his scattershot pattern. *Not good, Matt. You're slipping.* He leans back in his chair and breathes deeply. He recalls his games in the championship tournament in the Bloody Mary Pub last month. His near-perfect score propelled him to the rank of Champion of the International Settlement.

Lisan raps lightly. "I have prepared a special tea to ease your distress." He pours the tea into a deep-blue cup, set in a matching saucer.

"Thanks, Lisan." Drummond sips the tea. "Don't prepare dinner for me. I've got to sort this yellow porcelain business into coherence." He sips the tea and lets his mind wander. *It's going to be a long night. Ingrid. Porcelains. Ingrid. Kendrick. Warlords. Ingrid. Wallace. Ingrid. Fees. Ingrid.*

प

Matt Drummond's Apartment, Peking. 7 July 1935

त is several minutes after midnight. Matt is asleep at his desk when the telephone rings in the living room. Within a few rings, Lisan answers. "Mister Matt Drummond's residence. How may I be of service?" After a brief pause, he says, "A moment, please. I shall get Mister Drummond."

Lisan enters the study. He gently shakes Matt's shoulder. "For you. The telephone."

With sleep gently fading, Matt mutters, "Who is it, Lisan?" He glances at his watch. "What the hell do they want at this time of the morning?" He asks rhetorically.

Lisan hands the telephone to Matt. He answers with muffled excitement, "It is Colonel Peng T'su-si. Peng of the Nationalist Intelligence Service."

The name of the Nationalist's chief intelligence officer jerks Matt fully awake. *To what purpose would Colonel Peng call me?*

"Drummond here. Yes, I am … I see … into Kansu province? You're sure? I need to make notes. Yes, continue. I've got it. Many thanks, Colonel Peng. I'll make sure to include your name."

Lisan looks at Matt, too discreet to ask what Colonel Peng had to say, but he's eager to know. "Shall I make tea?"

Matt, on keen alert, says, "Of course. Big news, Lisan. I've got to file a hot, breaking story. Colonel Peng says that his agents have spotted Japanese troops from the Kwangtung Army in Kansu Province. To what end are the Japanese in Kansu? We could be in a major war soon."

Lisan whispers a benediction when he returns with the tea. "Please drink my tea to have a sharp mind and an intelligent pen."

Oblivious, Matt scribbles a few notes as he gulps the tea. Then he grabs his hat and jacket, and dashes out the door—unaware of the worried look on Lisan's face.

10

Matt Drummond's Apartment, Peking. 8 July 1935

I t's about ten o'clock in the morning. Lisan quietly enters Drummond's bedroom. He places a tea service on the bedside table.

Matt begins to stir from his deep sleep. It was only a few hours ago that he filed his story about the Japanese Army in Kansu Province, along with stock photographs he took on his last assignment.

"Good morning, Mister Drummond. I have hot tea for you." He pours a cup. "I have also the morning paper." He unfolds the English-language newspaper *The Peking Times.* "Congratulations. Your story about the Japanese Army is the lead story on the front page, and you have the byline."

Matt props himself up on his pillow and takes a long sip of tea. A faint smile of satisfaction creeps across his face as he scans his story. "They got it right and did not slash-edit it." He slaps the paper into his lap. "Lisan, I'll be ready for breakfast shortly. I'm famished."

Matt, dressed in a light-blue seersucker suit, white shirt, and light-tan tie, enters the dining room, where Lisan has laid out breakfast. Matt picks up the *London Times* Hong Kong edition and scans a few pages.

The ever-present Lisan asks, "More tea, Mister Drummond?"

"Damn! My story about General Yen's raid on his rival is on the back page of the Rotogravure section." He tosses it aside. "That's just lovely! I can read about the revolution in Spain and the Italian invasion of Abyssinia, Stalin purging his old Bolshevik comrades, and Hitler occupying the Rhineland. No wonder editors relegate my stories to the back pages. In the scheme of world events, I reckon that's where they belong." He stares at Lisan, "Does no one care about the monumental events developing in the Far East? We'll be in a ghastly war in just a few years."

"Let me pour more tea for you."

There is a gentle rap on the front door. Lisan goes to answer. He returns shortly. "Sir, Mister Chung is here to visit with you."

Wallace bursts into the dining room extremely excited. "Forgive me for disturbing you at this early hour. I have come upon some secret information that will be of immense value for you."

Matt returns the teacup to the saucer and looks at Wallace Chung with questioning eyes. With a touch of sarcasm he says, "That's interesting. What's in it for you, Chung?"

With faux hurt, Chung responds, "You wound me, Matt. I always give you the best tips. What information I have is of grave importance, and I ask nothing in return but your continued good will. Are we not associates who exchange tidbits of information from time to time?"

Matt's interest has been slightly piqued. "All right. What have you got that's so confidential and so valuable?"

Wallace moves close to Matt and whispers in a conspiratorial voice, "I have it from an impeccable source in the National Government that General Chiang Kai-shek is preparing a sizeable military expedition into the northwestern provinces to quell the chaos. General Chiang's immediate goal is Kansu province. In the last few days, if one were watching, one could hear and see the preparations being taken in and about the Lungtow arsenal."

Matt has completely forgotten about his breakfast; now his mind is attuned to Chung's news. "What else?"

Now, Wallace knows he has Matt's attention. "Should you have inter-est, my source guarantees that he will arrange for you an exclusive inter-view with General Chiang. Photographs, of course. You will have unfet-tered access to all the mobilization activities."

Matt does not bother to hide his skepticism and asks, "Tell me, Wallace, how'd you manage such a coup? Every reporter in China would crawl on nails for such an interview."

Wallace speaks with assurance. "I have many contacts inside the Nationalist government that I must keep confidential. Unfortunately, there is only a small time opening for the interview with General Chiang. My source says that you must leave for his headquarters in Nanking tonight. That is where General Chiang is planning the campaign. Your interview with the General will be tomorrow morning. I believe the Express train leaves at eight o'clock this evening."

Matt is not totally convinced that Wallace has a *bona fide* scoop. However, he does not have a choice. He can't skip this once-in-a-lifetime opportunity. No matter that he knows he can't fully trust the man standing before him. As he evaluates Wallace's spiel, he realizes that such a mili-tary campaign makes Kendrick's trip to Ho Hsien untenable. Matt, with urgency, demands, "You've told Kendrick, of course. General Chiang's campaign will end his wild-goose chase to Ho Hsien. I reckon even that bull Kendrick won't venture into a war zone."

Wallace says, "Mister Kendrick and I talked on the telephone this morning. Notwithstanding the developments in the northwest, he is bent on going after the yellows. He must have had a fruitful rest to make such a propitious decision. Now, of course, my role has become all the more important."

Alarmed, Matt manages, "Good Lord! He's going? What about Ingrid—Ingrid Kendrick?"

"She'll remain in Peking, of course."

"I wonder if Kendrick can keep her here in Peking. She has a mind of her own and is determined to look after her father." He drains his cup while evaluating his commitment to Kendrick. He stares into the leaves at the bottom and decides to renege on his deal with Kendrick. Matt has conscientious misgivings. *That's not my style but it's ludicrous to consider accompanying Kendrick to Kansu Province in the middle of a war. He'll not come back.*

Lisan refills Matt's teacup and purposely ignores Wallace Chung.

Matt considers how incredible Kendrick's trip is. "And you're going? That's stupid, Wallace. Your greed will be your undoing. Stay here. That'll keep Kendrick in Peking."

"I've made too many arrangements and commitments to key personnel. And my expenses are exorbitant. I am going. I must recoup."

Realizing that it's useless to try and dissuade Chung from going, Matt tries another tack. He demands, "Wallace, I'm charging you to keep Kendrick safe. That's your responsibility. Don't fail me."

Wallace deliberately ignores Matt's prescription. "My contact will meet you tomorrow morning at the train station in Nanking and take you to General Chiang. I'm delighted that you are going to have such an important story. It is a real scoop for you."

11

World-Wide Press Service Office, Peking. Noon, 8 July 1935

Matt is researching the background of General Chiang, and the state and composition of his army. He screens stock footage on the Moviola.

Kendrick enters and spots Matt. "There you are, Drummond. Lisan thought you'd be here. Let's talk. We've got to firm up our travel plans."

With incredulity, Matt exclaims, "What! What travel plans? I'm not going with you to Kansu. I don't mean to be rude, but I have a critical interview scheduled in Nanking. I'm taking the evening train."

Kendrick is stunned by his new *protégé's* betrayal but quickly recovers and angrily responds, "Listen, Drummond, you made a deal with me and I expect you to honor it. Cancel your trip to Nanking. We're going to Ho Hsien."

"Pardon me?"

With a smoldering anger, Kendrick demands, "You heard me." Kendrick roars, "Cancel your trip to Nanking. You're going with Ingrid and me to Kansu Province. No more nonsense, Drummond."

With equal fire, Matt counters, "All the area around Kansu will be a war zone in a few days. And I will not be bullied. I've got the scoop of the year waiting for me in Nanking." He pauses, forcing himself to calm down. "It's foolish. No, it's stupid for you to go to Ho Hsien—especially now that Wallace has told you of the upcoming Nationalist Army's expedition to pacify Kansu and to engage Japanese patrols in the area. It will be a war zone. I will not be involved in the slaughter of you and your daughter."

Kendrick, taken aback by Drummond's renege, demands, "What the hell are you babbling about? What expedition? What war zone?" He doesn't wait for Drummond to answer. "I do not have any idea what you're talking about. Know this, Drummond: I've not talked with Wallace Chung this morning and I know nothing about an upcoming war in Kansu. Here's the bottom line. Ingrid and I are going to Ho Hsien. She is determined to come with me to look after my financial interest. We're leaving shortly. There's lots to arrange and you're going to help me."

"What? You haven't talked with Wallace Chung today?" In an instant, Matt realizes he's been duped. Wallace's tip was so much folderol to get him out of the way—to keep him from going to Ho Hsien. "Wallace, that sonofabitch. That wanker! He lied to me."

Kendrick chuckles at the hurt look on Matt's face. "I don't know what's between you two. And I don't care. Ingrid and I need you. I'll double your fee, and if we conclude the deal with the yellows successfully, I'll deposit 50,000 United States dollars in your bank account."

Matt's anger and chagrin begin to evaporate. *If I go, I'll maintain my honor by keeping my pledge to Kendrick. I'll be with Ingrid, and earning a fee larger than I could ever have imagined.*

Kendrick lowers his voice and approaches Matt. "I made my first stake when I struck the mother lode in the gold rush of '98. Look cross-eyed at a prospector and you'd likely be shot. I was a wily schemer. I survived. Got my poke. And got out with a fortune. With that stake, I built my industrial empire." He grins. "And now Ingrid keeps it running smoothly."

"Kendrick, that's not relevant now. Kansu has become significantly more dangerous now than I detailed in your suite. I know from an unimpeachable source in the National Government's Intelligence Agency that

Japanese patrols are roaming unabated in Kansu Province. I've seen first-hand how these people work, and they are neither polite nor forgiving— believe me when I tell you they shoot first and ask questions later."

"Perhaps true. Nevertheless, Ingrid and I are going." He points his large and rough index finger at Matt. "You going to sit on your ass as the world goes by? There are other kinds of gold for you on this trip. This trip across China to get those yellows could be one of the best stories you'll ever write and photograph. Do it right, and I'll push for the Pulitzer." He rests his hands on Drummond's shoulders. "And, Matt, I'm not stupid. I see the electricity between Ingrid and you. You going to desert the best woman you'll ever know?"

Kendrick's exhortation melts Matt's reservations. "You win. I'm in."

"That's a firm commitment, Drummond? Shake."

Matt grins wide. "It's moronic, but yes, it's a yes."

"Great. Our train leaves at one tomorrow afternoon."

12

*Yin-Shan Mountains, Ala Shan Desert, Inner Mongolian
Autonomous Region. Noon, 9 July 1935*

A convoy of four supply trucks of the Japanese Kwangtung Army snakes along a narrow mountain road. The convoy slows as it winds through a narrow, steep canyon.

Suddenly, a fusillade of rifle fire smashes into the lead truck. The windshield explodes and the driver and his shotgun passenger, instantly slump dead. The truck careens and crashes into the hillside, rolls over, and effectively blocks the road. Ambush!

The remaining trucks screech to a halt. Soldiers pile out of the backs of the trucks and aimlessly return fire toward the bushwhackers hidden on both sides of the canyon. The firefight continues for a few minutes. Soon, most of the Japanese are killed, and the rest are seriously wounded.

Black Viper directs members of his bandit gang to blindfold the wounded soldiers and forces those that are able to kneel. With cold precision, he walks down the row of kneeling soldiers and carefully places his pistol at the back of each of their heads and pulls the trigger. His gang members bayonet the more seriously wounded.

Black Viper climbs in the back of one of the captured trucks. Shortly, he emerges with a crooked grin, a rifle in each hand, and a bandolier around his chest. They have captured the mother lode of arms: modern rifles, pistols, machine guns, and ammunition. Other cases contain sake, dried fish, and rice. The gang loots the trucks and then burns them. The gang absconds on secret mountain trails, their horses and pack mules loaded with loot.

13

Matt Drummond's Apartment, Peking. 9 July 1935

Lisan carefully packs Matt's freshly washed and pressed clothes into his employer's leather suitcase. He places each item in the best manner to prevent wrinkles and ensures that his employer's essential toiletries are stowed in the leather ditty bag.

Matt works at his desk to inspect, clean, and check the operations of his Leica 35mm camera, auxiliary lenses, and accessories. He places each item in its proper slot in his camera case and stows forty rolls of Agfapan 100 film in an auxiliary case. He rings the small brass bell on the desk to attract Lisan's attention. "The train leaves this afternoon at one o'clock. How close to completing the packing are you?"

"Yes, Mister Drummond. I have completed the packing task for you. All is in order for your trip. With your permission, I will tend to my things for the long journey. I've arranged transportation for us to the railroad station."

"Well done. My cameras are ready. The usual precautions, Lisan."

"As always, Mister Drummond."

"Lisan, I'm going to the World-Wide Press Service Office to make arrangements for the stories I'll file. Have our luggage on the doorstep and have that taxicab standing by when I return."

"Yes, Mister Drummond." Lisan escorts Matt to the door, opens it, and says, "I shall have everything ready on your return."

Matt nods in understanding as he exits.

Lisan closes the door gently, moves to a window, slightly parts the print curtains, and watches Matt climb into a rickshaw and disappear down the street. He slips into the study, picks up the telephone, and checks to hear the sometimes-unreliable dial tone. Satisfied that all is correct, Lisan dials a memorized number. After the first ring, someone picks up the receiver and remains silent. Lisan says in a whisper, "Comrade, the Kendrick party leaves this afternoon at one o'clock for Ho Hsien to get the Ming yellows." Lisan gets no response and, in a second, he hears the receiver set down, the line shut, and the dial tone return.

Peking Railroad Station. 9 July 1935

Chung's chartered Executive Club Coach is opulent. The décor is the modern art-deco style—rich colors and bold, symmetric, rectilinear designs set off by swirling curves and chrome. The walls are decorated with excellent reproductions of famous prints by great art-deco artists: Tamara de Lempicka's *The Musician* and *Tamara in the Green Bugatti,* Georg Barbier's *Le Feu,* and Jean-Gabriel Domergue's *La Garçonne.* A twenty-inch-high copy of the Chrysler building hangs over the bar—the landmark where Kendrick has his offices. The Occidentals will be travelling in grand style.

There are four sleeping compartments in the front of the coach, a communal bath on each side of the aisle, a kitchen-bar combination, and a lounge area with six large leather chairs and side tables. Outside the rear door is a railed platform with steps that are just a foot short of the railroad's concrete walkway.

Standing on the platform beside the baggage car, the stationmaster stares at his railroad pocket watch. The second hand ticks click-by-click to 1250 hours. He puts the watch in his vest pocket, blows his sharp-toned whistle ten times, and vigorously waves his red and white flag back and forth over his head. The whistle's shrill tone echoes throughout the station. The fireman shovels coal into the locomotive's blazing furnace, and the engineer bleeds steam that hisses loudly and engulfs the nearby area in a white cloud.

Lau, the steward assigned to the Kendrick party, places a steel stool at the foot of the iron steps that lead to the coach's rear platform. As Kendrick, Ingrid, and Wallace approach, the steward tips his hat, bows, and says in broken English and a raspy voice, "Good this afternoon. My name is Lau Jian-kang. I am assigned to this club car for our long trip to Changyeh. I will be your porter, cook, and bartender." Lau is tall and has a thick, solid body that he carries erectly. He has large, soft, black eyes that exude honesty and keen perception. With a large smile and a glint of pearl-white teeth, he continues, "Our larder is well stocked with your favorite victuals, and our bar inventory is varied and ample." He checks his watch and, with his right hand extended, indicates that the party ought to board. Once in the lounge area, Lau bows once more and continues. "Please ask and I am pleased to do my best for you."

Ingrid, delighted with their sumptuous accommodations, slides into one of the chairs, and looks at the steward. "Thank you, Lau. We are pleased that you will be taking care of us. We are looking forward to a pleasant trip in your capable hands."

Lau bows deeply. "Thank you, missy. It will be so."

Even Kendrick is impressed by the car's luxury, and he is especially pleased with the art-deco ambiance. "Yes, indeed, this club coach will do very well."

Wallace Chung smiles and says, "Thank you, Mister Kendrick. I did research into your pleasures and had this coach decorated accordingly. Please notice how close these excellent lithographs are to the originals of these famous art-deco artists." He indicates the art on the walls with his left hand extended in a wide sweeping turn. "Without expert knowledge, one could easily be duped into thinking that they are originals."

Ingrid is somewhat concerned. She asks, "Mister Chung, what is the cost for this railroad palace?" Despite her concerns, she can't help running her fingers along the creamy-smooth arm of her chair.

"Do not be concerned, Mistress Kendrick. The rental cost for the coach is minimal and will be itemized on my invoice, which I shall prepare for you in the next few days." *Minimal indeed compared to the fortune I'll make on this adventure.*

"Don't double-talk me, Wallace Chung. When I ask a question, I expect a direct and honest answer." Now, she clenches the leather. "How much is this coach costing my father?"

Quickly realizing he's misread the situation, he changes his tenor and responds, "Yes, Mistress Kendrick. I will invoice your father one hundred thousand Chinese dollars per diem or, preferably, 250 British pounds sterling per diem, plus, of course, my handling fee."

"Very well. That is not unreasonable." Not completely satisfied, she charges Chung, "Be sure to include the receipt from the railroad line."

"Yes, Mistress Kendrick." Chung fumes. *I abhor doing business with females, especially pushy females. But this Kendrick woman is smart and tough. I'll be cautious with her; else she'll disrupt my whole scheme.* He forces himself not to grit his teeth in the smug face of this overbearing, spoiled girl. "Of course, Mistress Kendrick. I will compile an itemized invoice for all expenses related to this coach." He smiles with frosted courtesy. "Naturally, this will include my fees and expenses, most notably my sizeable deposit." Realizing that it would be a serious tactical error to make Ingrid Kendrick his enemy, he continues in his most professional voice, "Shall I pay Lau's gratuity, or will you?"

Offended by Chung's not-so-subtle, pettish response, she snaps, "I will."

Chung nods. "Very well."

Lau leads a cadre of luggage-toting porters into the coach. Ingrid indicates the compartments in which they are to stow Kendrick's and her bags. Chung's one valise remains on the floor near the bar. "Mister Chung, please take care of your luggage," directs Ingrid.

Chung does not move at first. Out of the corner of his eye, he catches Lau looking away and Kendrick staring at him. Kendrick cocks his head and stares. Chung is miffed that this haughty white female has set the ground rules. All too clearly, he understands. *The Occidentals regard me as just another Chinaman hired hand.* Keeping his mind on the handsome payday ahead, he complies. "Yes, indeed." He moves his valise to the far compartment on the right side of the coach.

The Kendricks follow their luggage into their own compartments. After the trio have unpacked and refreshed, Kendrick returns to the lounge, followed shortly by Ingrid, who settles into what has already become her favorite chair. Chung enters last and sits at the bar. On cue, Lau brings the trio iced tea. "This is a special green tea that was much favored by the emperors of this Celestial Empire. It will refresh you deeply."

"Thank you, Lau, for your thoughtful consideration," says Ingrid.

"It is my pleasure, Miss," Lau replies. He takes the measure of his charges and knows that Mistress Kendrick is 'number one.'

Matt and Lisan arrive at the coach's forward door. Matt enters while Lisan remains in the foyer. Matt has his ever-present Leica hanging from his neck. He surveys the scene and quickly sees that Wallace Chung is painfully surprised at his arrival. "Good day, all." Matt jams his fists onto his hips and with his best smile, beams. "You can rest easy now. The Aussie is here."

Wallace, brooding, mumbles a sarcastic curse under his breath. *I don't understand. Drummond is supposed to be in Nanking on a fool's errand and to have skipped this trip.*

Matt takes a moment to relish Wallace's obvious chagrin. "G'day, mate. I decided to forgo your tip regarding that interview with General Chiang in Nanking. Thought the trip to Ho Hsien would be more interesting."

Kendrick jumps up and shakes Matt's hand vigorously. "Welcome aboard, Drummond. Delighted you've made it. I've been wondering when you would show up." He motions to Lau. "Innkeeper, your special tea for Mister Matt Drummond."

Ingrid suppresses a smile and considers once again just what her feelings are for this genial Australian. With his forthright 'down under' manners, he's nothing like the affected northeastern dandies she's used to in her circle of gallants and friends. *Am I falling in love or is it just animal passion?* She can no longer contain her smile and it spreads across her face. *Either way, I'll be on a great adventure with a great guy. Who knows? Maybe I'll find the answer to my question.*

Matt places his suitcase on the floor next to the bar. "My apologies, Mister Kendrick, if I've caused you alarm. I had lots to take care of at the last minute." He sips his tea deeply. "Is there room in this coach for me, or should I look for other digs?"

Wallace stares at Matt with a face that is taut and drained. *Drummond now knows that I've tried to trick him and he'll be especially watchful. Somehow, I'll have to divert him to other interests.* He keeps it cordial even though he tastes bitter venom. "It would be best, Matt, old chap, if you camped in the coach ahead. It doesn't make sense for all of us to squeeze into this coach. We would be too crowded with a fourth person."

Sick of Chung's machinations, with a quick riposte, Matt snaps, "I wasn't speaking to you, Wallace, ol' chap." He practically spits the words. "And, if you're so concerned about crowding, maybe you should move out!"

Kendrick, amused at the verbal sparring between the two, says, "You sure showed up ornery, Drummond. Do I have to treat you two as little boys? I've chartered this entire coach. Drummond, you're staying in here with us. Take compartment D—across from Chung. Get settled in and then let's discuss the adventure we're headed for."

"Very well. Lisan is waiting for me in the coach's foyer. I'm going to see that he gets settled in the second-class coach, and I will return shortly."

Kendrick snaps, "All the other coolies are in the third-class car. That's where Lisan belongs."

Suppressing his anger at Kendrick's slur, Drummond retorts, "Lisan is my loyal servant and is my responsibility. He'll travel in the second-class coach, and you'll pay for it."

Matt's tone is not one Kendrick's used to hearing from anyone. But he knows he needs the Australian. "Okay. Whatever it takes to keep you content and on our team. I simply figured he'd want to be with his own kind." Considering the matter closed, Kendrick figures that he's settled the issue to all's liking and turns to the bar, completely unaware of his insensitivity.

Standing on the station platform, the stationmaster stares at his pocket watch. The second hand on his watch snaps to the 12. Exactly at 1300 hours, he vigorously waves the red and white flag over his head and continuously blows a series of sharp, short blasts on his whistle. Last minute passengers scramble aboard, porters slam coach doors shut, and the locomotive's sonorous bell clangs incessantly. The engineer releases the brakes. Billowing white steam surrounds the train and temporarily enshrouds the stationmaster in a ghost-like mist. Within the cacophonous din of screeching, clanging, and clamor, the locomotive's six drive wheels spin, spitting sparks as they try to gain purchase to pull the seven heavy coaches. Ever so slowly, the train inches forward.

14

Gobi Desert, Inner Mongolian Autonomous Region. 10 July 1935

The train slowly winds through rolling hills on the southern edge of the Gobi Desert. It has been twenty-seven hours since the train left the Peking Station and the quiet in the club car is overwhelming. The travelers are hot, bored, irritable, and just about talked out. Ingrid works on a financial report. Matt idly scribbles information in his note pad about the background and environment of his story and writes captions for the photographs he's snapped. Wallace nurses a beer at the bar and reviews again and again his scheme. Kendrick is fidgety with inaction and is bored. He slumps in his lounge chair and stares unseeingly at the passing scene. His only escape is to review sullenly the inventory of the Ming yellows once again. He tries and fails to conjure mental images of how they'll look in his private museum of Oriental art. He slaps the arm of his chair and orders in a too-loud voice, "Lau, a large scotch with ice." The echo of his bark permeates the lounge like rolling thunder, stirring its quiet ambiance.

Ingrid stows her report. "Fine idea, Dad. Lau, rye bourbon for me."

Matt clears his mind and says, "Same for me, Lau."

From the other side of the bar, Lau moves to Wallace. "What may I serve you, Mister Chung?"

Wallace, mindful of his place, orders, "Tonic water with a lime, please."

Kendrick, revived by the scotch, commands, "Chung, come over here and sit in that chair across from me. Tell me about yourself. Is Chung truly your family name?"

"Yes, Mister Kendrick." With shoulders erect, he walks purposefully to the chair and sits upright. He avoids eye contact with Ingrid and Matt. "My Christian name, Wallace, is only for the convenience of your Occidental language. My surname indeed is Chung. Please know that there are just a few surnames in my country—one hundred, perhaps a few more."

Matt interrupts. "And where are you from? In all the years I've known you, you've not talked about your background. Is it a secret?"

Ingrid looks out the window and snickers quietly.

Kendrick doesn't find Matt's comment appropriate. "Don't interrupt him, Drummond. I'm interested in his story."

Matt, properly chastised, swings his chair so that it faces Ingrid and whispers, "The pooh-bah has spoken."

Wallace continues. "Thank you, Mister Kendrick. My given name is Yu-feng. It means jade peak. My father gave me this name only after a Confucian scholar sanctioned it." Now that he has a clear field to talk uninterrupted, he continues. "I was raised in the country in Shansi Province on a large farm. Fortunately, my father was a man of means and sent me to the United States for my formal education; first, at St. Mary's Catholic High School in Pasadena, California, and then I attended Stanford University in Palo Alto. I earned my Bachelor of Science degree in Business Administration with the goal of helping my father run his business." He sips his tonic water and continues to talk directly to Kendrick, emotionlessly relating the tale of his father's death during a bandit raid, and the local warlord's confiscation of his land.

Ingrid is concerned that the contretemps between Matt and Wallace will engender a hostile ambiance in the expedition, perhaps even put the expedition in jeopardy. She whispers to Matt, "What's between you two?

Why don't you like Wallace Chung? So far, he's been forthright with me, after some prodding, and his travel arrangements are excellent."

Matt stares into the brown liquid in his glass, deciding how much he should say. With a look of incredulity, "I don't like him because he's a damn liar, among other things." Matt continues with odium-filled eyes, speaking with clear-cut clarity of sober facts. "He's a bamboozle artist— 'untrustworthy' says it best."

Ingrid looks at Matt with wonder in her eyes, brow furrowed, and lips tight. "A misunderstanding perhaps, Matt?"

"Absolutely not. Wallace tried to hoodwink me with some fanciful interview with General Chiang Kai-shek as he prepares for his campaign against the warlords in these northwestern provinces—a critically impor-tant interview any journalist would jump at. Understand that Chiang is in Nanking—a day's journey south of Peking. If I had taken that evening train to Nanking as Wallace suggested, I would have missed this trip. For reasons yet unclear, it's obvious that he does not want me here." With steady eyes, he looks at Ingrid. "I fear he's far worse than a liar. I don't trust him one damn bit."

She smiles, dismissing Matt's wariness. "Chung is a little too slick and pompous for my taste, but he's probably harmless."

"Harmless is not the appropriate term for a fellow like Wallace. Not in this part of the world."

Almost on cue, Wallace approaches. "Tomorrow morning our train will stop at Wu-chung for service. You'll have time to explore this old town on the Silk Road."

15

Yin-Shan Mountains, Ala Shan Desert, Inner Mongolian Autonomous Region. 10 July 1935

A column of Japanese soldiers rides at the gallop along a narrow moun-.tain trail. Leading the column is Major Komio Terauchi. Beneath his handsome veneer is a ruthless disciple of Bushido, the way of the samurai. Suddenly, he raises his right hand, signaling the column to halt. They have arrived at the site of the Black Viper's ambush.

Major Terauchi views the carnage with manifest shock and rising anger. Dead Japanese soldiers are scattered throughout the area. His trucks are looted and burned. The stench of decaying bodies suffuses throughout the canyon. He spots six executed soldiers lying in a ditch—blindfolded and with their hands tied behind their backs. One bullet hole is in the back of each of their skulls.

Terauchi vows to find the murderers and take wrathful vengeance.

He is distracted by a loud groan. Sergeant Matuso drags a severely wounded bandit, and drops the fellow at Terauchi's boots. The man has bullet wounds in the shoulder and upper thigh. He's covered in blood.

Major Terauchi orders the sergeant, "Make him stand before me."

The sergeant directs two privates to do as Colonel Terauchi ordered.

The privates grab the wounded bandit under his armpits and prop him upright. The bandit screams in pain. Terauchi examines him critically, taking his time before he speaks. Shortly, he asks, "Who is responsible for this slaughter?"

The fellow pleads, "Please, sir, I do not know. I stumbled onto the fighting and was wounded in the crossfire. I am a humble farmer going to the market in Wu-chung."

Major Terauchi, standing tall, fingers the man's half-full bandolier. "Fool! Your lie is transparent. There is a bandolier across your shoulder. Farmers do not have such military gear. You are a common criminal, a bandit, abandoned by your comrades and left to die. Now answer me, who is responsible for this massacre?"

The bandit drops his eyes and does not respond.

Terauchi nods to one of the privates, who slams his rifle into the bandit's wounded shoulder. The bandit screams in searing pain and shakes back and forth in a failed attempt to ease his suffering.

Terauchi orders, "Keep this bandit standing." He draws his samurai sword. "It appears that Japanese bullets are still in your wounds. Perhaps I can help you by digging them out." He places the tip of his sword exactly on the wound site in the bandit's shoulder and pushes it slightly. The bandit screams in excruciating pain, and his knees buckle. The two soldiers continue to hold him erect and facing Major Terauchi. The bandit realize that his only survival option is to cooperate. *Did not my compatriots abandon me—severely wounded and lying in the ditch?* With renewed energy, the bandit shouts, "The Black Viper! The Black Viper and his gang did this. He is running guns for General Wu. I saw him execute your soldiers."

The Major looks over the carnage of his supply train once more. "It is as I suspected." He slaps the bandit, snapping the wounded man's head onto his neck and almost knocking him free of the soldiers' grip. The privates manage to hold the bandit erect. "How is the Black Viper moving my guns and supplies to that corrupt warlord Wu? And where is your bandit leader?" Terauchi pushes his sword in slightly.

The bandit howls. He gasps for breath and grimaces with tortuous pain. In a stumbling voice, he says, "Your guns and equipment are on pack mules, moving on hidden trails through the mountains. I heard the Viper say that he has business in Chung-wei. He goes by train. Please, sir, that is all I know."

Major Terauchi orders, "Let the fool go."

The two soldiers let the bandit fall to the ground and he moans.

"If I knew more, sir."

Terauchi looks at the fallen bandit. "I cannot just leave you here as wounded as you are and suffering such intense pain. Let me assist you with that wound in your thigh. You are losing much blood." The Major plunges his sword into the bandit's stomach, and kicks him hard. The hapless bandit rolls into the ditch and expires.

Armed with this intelligence, Terauchi and his column mount and gallop toward the railroad tracks that lead to Chung-wei.

16

Railroad Station, Wu-chung, Ningsai Hui Autonomous Region.
11 July 1935

With screeching brakes, the lumbering train chugs to a halting stop at the railroad station in Wu-chung, a small railroad town deep in the Ordos Desert. Locals mill about as railroad workers swarm over the train. Brakemen tap the wheels with metal rods, checking to see if they are sound. Second men squirt oil in change boxes. The fireman directs the colliers loading coal into the tender car. The engineer supervises the replenishment of water in the locomotive. Stewards bring supplies. Coolies haul freight out of and into the baggage car. Passengers from the third-class compartment tumble off with all manner of bags, boxes, and animals. A large group of pilgrims with their baggage board the third-class coaches.

Ingrid looks out the window of her compartment at the unfolding scene. She spots Matt on the platform snapping photographs of the frenetic activity with his Leica. Wallace is on the station steps haranguing the conductor about something. Kendrick is in the lounge feasting on a sumptuous breakfast.

Ingrid, dressed, enters the lounge area. Lau greets Ingrid with a huge mug of steaming black coffee. She takes it from him and says,

"Thanks." She hoists the mug toward Kendrick. "Good morning, Dad. How will we ever survive this long, hot, boring trip? I need a Fifth Avenue spa for 'the works'—hair, body, and soul." She yearns for private time with Matt, but this cramped coach has afforded no opportunity. *He seems more dedicated to documenting this trip with his camera than to being with me. The first chance I get, I'm going to crucify him—afterwards, of course.*

Wallace enters and sits by Kendrick. To no one in particular, he announces, "The conductor has agreed to increase the speed of this train. We were delayed several hours chugging slowly in those hills. He tells me that he'll try to make up some of the lost time."

Ingrid responds, "Thank you, Mister Chung. I am anxious to get to our destination. This club car is luxurious but it's becoming stifling."

Wallace continues, "The conductor is seeing to preparations for the next leg of our journey. All in all, I might say that our trip has gone rather smoothly so far. Would you not say so, Mister Kendrick?"

Kendrick looks up, but chooses to ignore Chung's question, and finishes his breakfast. "More coffee, Lau."

Matt enters and goes to Ingrid. "Good morning, young lady." He sits next to her and begins to change film in his Leica. "I shot an entire roll of thirty-six exposures this morning. Pictures of the activities in and about this train will make good background stuff." On impulse, he changes to a slightly longer focal-length lens and snaps close-up photographs of Ingrid, Kendrick, and Wallace. Ingrid raises her hands and protests "too much." Kendrick doesn't seem to care. Wallace turns away, goes to the bar, and asks for a glass of orange juice.

Shortly, the conductor climbs onto the rear platform and knocks on the door. Wallace opens it, exits, and stands with the conductor on the platform. The passengers inside hear tidbits of Mandarin spoken too loudly and see Wallace grimacing.

After several minutes, the conductor leaves and Wallace returns to the club car with a solemn face. "The conductor says the train will be delayed until late afternoon. Maybe as late as four o'clock. One of the wheels on the baggage car is out of round and needs to be replaced."

The silence that permeates the club car is deafening. After a few seconds, Ingrid exclaims, "Damn! I'm bored. I can't sit in this car for eight hours." She rises. "I'm going to look the town over and stretch my legs. Come with me, Dad."

"Can't. Want to mull over things. Matt, you go with her."

Matt comments, "I shouldn't. I've got to catch up on my caption writing and continue developing the background for this story. Ingrid, don't go." He taps his pencil on the bar. "Especially don't go alone. Your venture into town will not be a stroll down Fifth Avenue. The people here haven't had much contact with Occidentals, let alone an unescorted Occidental woman."

"She needs you, Drummond," Kendrick barks. "Go into town with my daughter," he adds in his patented command voice. "You've plenty of time to write your story."

Ingrid queries Wallace, "What is your opinion, Mister Chung? Should we go?"

He answers unequivocally, "Though Wu-chung is remote, it is a peaceful place. There are several ancient shrines to visit. I should not worry. If you take the main road to the end of town, there is a shrine with a large statue of the reclining Buddha—some several centuries old. The scene, with hundreds of flickering joss sticks, is mesmerizing and their aroma is mystical. In the Buddhist religion, lighting a joss stick is a form of prayer to honor the ancestors and ask for their protection." Wallace goes to the rear door, opens it, and looks at the activity in the town. "I am confident that you will have no problems in Wu-chung. I shall remain near the train and will send a messenger to fetch you when our departure is imminent."

Ingrid moves to the coach door, opens it, and looks at Matt with a 'come hither' glance.

Several hours later, Ingrid and Matt have completed their tour of the Buddhist shrine, lit several joss sticks, purchased from a nearby vendor, and strolled some of the back streets. Matt has snapped photos of the local scene at almost every turn. The pair are alone, strolling hand in hand, enjoying being alone together in this strange town, and having a delightful time. Occasionally, Ingrid clowns around with outlandish poses—that Matt duly captures with his camera. When they enter the town's market, the villagers stop their chattering and bargaining to stare at the Occidental couple. Most have never seen white people. Business prevails, nonetheless, and soon all activity returns to normal.

Matt remarks, "I reckon we look like exhibits in a zoo."

Ingrid, with a devilish quip, asks, "And what would you be? The orangutan?" She leans to him and kisses him on the cheek. "I'll be the seductive serpent." Another kiss follows, longer, and closer to his mouth. "More follows," she teases.

Before Matt can make a snappy riposte, he spots Lisan approaching.

Lisan, with appropriate deference, bows and says, "Good afternoon, Mistress Kendrick, Mister Drummond. Mister Wallace Chung has sent me to find you. Our train will be leaving shortly. I am instructed to ask you if you would be so kind as to return to the train with me."

17

Ch'i Lien Plain, Kansu Province. 12 July 1935

The dawn is bright, clear, and warm. A fresh breeze from the north promises a cool afternoon. The train accelerates on the flat plain, having spent the night crawling its way through the Ch'i Lien Mountains. The next stop is the desert outpost Wu-wei, about forty miles ahead, where the frenetic activity of servicing the train will be repeated.

The sunlight peeking through the window's opaque curtains in Ingrid's compartment rouses her from a light sleep. She yawns, stretches with her hand high over her head, and then draws back the curtain to view the morning scene. She spots a man on horseback keeping pace with the train. After a few seconds, other riders appear—galloping hard toward the engine. She rubs her eyes to make sure that they are not an illusion. The horseman just outside her window sees her and grins. Quickly, she snaps the curtains shut. The rider veers close and taps his saber several times on the window of her compartment. She gasps in fright. Alarmed, she wonders, *Who are these riders and what do they want of us in this God-forsaken desert?* Her curiosity rises. She peeks out the window again and sees that the horsemen wear uniforms of some sort. She throws on her robe, rushes down the aisle, and raps hard on each door. She shouts. "Get up! Everyone get up. There are cavalrymen attacking our train."

The male club-car passengers, now awakened by the hubbub, scramble out of their rooms in various states of undress and dishevelment. They race to the lounge area, and see the mounted soldiers keeping pace with the train. Lau has coffee brewing.

Kendrick turns away from the window and complains, "Damn it. This means that we'll be delayed further." The train starts to slow. "Why can't these Chinamen just keep this damn train moving? Who the hell are those fellows on horseback? We're already hours behind schedule."

By now, the mounted soldiers have surrounded the train, captured the train's engine, and are holding the engineer and fireman at gunpoint.

Matt offers, "I reckon we'll find out shortly."

Wallace peeks out of a curtained window and exclaims, "Whoever they are, these soldiers have commandeered the train. Though I cannot imagine why." On reflection, he trembles, fearing the worst. One soldier gallops close by the window. Wallace gets a good look and begins breathing hard. He slumps onto the couch. The blood drains from his face, and he feels his head grow light. He shouts, "They are Japanese!" He grabs the arm of his chair and mumbles, "My honorable ancestors, protect me."

Lau remains unfazed by the ruckus. "May I serve freshly brewed and steaming hot coffee? My biscuits are freshly baked and delicious, I must say."

Matt looks out another window and spots the Rising Sun patches on the soldiers' khaki uniforms. "This is trouble. Big trouble." He goes to the bar and gets coffee. With the calmest voice he can muster, he addresses the group. "It's a Japanese patrol from the Kwantung Army, and it looks like they mean business. We're slowing down. That can only mean they've taken control of the locomotive, the engineer, and his train."

Ingrid cries out, "My God! What's going to happen to us? We are not at war with Japan."

Kendrick comments, "Ingrid is correct. We've no business with those fellows. Let's see what they're up to and let's get moving again."

At that moment, the train jerks to a halting stop, forcing Ingrid and Wallace to stumble toward the back door. They grab railings to stop their progress and bump into each other. Wallace offers a subdued, "Please excuse me."

Matt continues, "These soldiers are from Manchukuo—Japan's puppet state that was formerly the Chinese province of Manchuria. They're not supposed to be this far west, much less this deep into China proper. I reckon that these soldiers are part of the group that Major Peng's agents spotted. I can't imagine what they want."

Almost on cue, Major Terauchi enters the coach and several of his soldiers follow. He surveys the scene. After a few words to his men in Japanese, Terauchi makes a short bow and addresses the Occidentals in near-perfect English. "Good morning. I am Major Komio Terauchi of my Emperor's Imperial Kwantung Army. At your service. Your passports and travel documents, please."

Kendrick rises from his chair and in his blustering voice spouts, "Now see here, Major, or whatever you are—"

Matt quickly interrupts, "Kendrick, sit down and be quiet. I will handle this. The Major is just doing his duty. Some routine procedure, I reckon."

Kendrick does not like taking orders from his subordinates, but he recalls his deal with Matt. "Okay." He returns to his chair and growls under his breath, "Last time I looked, we were in China. What's this Jap gang doing here, anyway?"

Ingrid exclaims, "Dad. It doesn't matter. Let's cooperate with the Major and help him conclude his business. The sooner we cooperate, the sooner we'll be on our way."

Insulted by and thoroughly annoyed with these pompous Occidentals, Major Terauchi rudely barks at them, "Do not delay. Give me your passports and travel documents. Tell me why you are on this train. What is your destination?"

Beads of sweat appear on Wallace's forehead and he shakes as he fumbles for his papers.

Finally realizing that the Major is serious, Kendrick thinks about pressing his rights as an American citizen, but something in the Japanese major's flat eyes makes him back down. He says, "Fine. Fine. Okay." As Kendrick shoves his hand inside his jacket pocket to retrieve the documents, he freezes when a soldier sticks a bayonet in his face.

Ingrid cries, "Dad, be careful!"

Kendrick slowly raises both hands, the passport packet in his left hand. "Here. Take it." With his best poker face, he smiles at the soldier with the bayonet. "No need for all that, son. Take it easy and get that pig-sticker out of my face."

The soldier lowers his bayonet when the major nods.

Sergeant Matuso retrieves the passports and hands them to Major Terauchi. As the major reviews the documents, a scream permeates the coach. It's coming from the area between the coach and the next car.

The Occidentals tense in wonderment and fear. Through the coach windows, they see soldiers dragging the kicking and screaming Lisan off the train. Drummond's servant grabs the coach's handrail. A soldier slams the butt of his rifle on Lisan's hand.

Lisan screams and shouts, "Mister Drummond, please! Please help me!"

Other soldiers pull five more Chinese passengers off the train.

Matt and the travelers hear Lisan's screaming plea. He rushes to the coach's door to rescue his houseboy. He hollers, "Lisan!"

On a hand signal from Major Terauchi, a private soldier blocks him with a bayonet pointed at his midsection. Matt turns and blurts to Terauchi, "Major, I am a British subject from the Commonwealth of Australia and a reporter for the World-Wide Press Service. I must be permitted to help my houseboy. He does not deserve this harsh treatment."

Major Terauchi does not respond. He completes his inspection of the passports. Satisfied, he tosses them on the floor.

That's enough for Ingrid. She's steamed. Jamming her fists defiantly onto her hips, she takes a step forward and stares at Major Terauchi. "Stop these atrocities. Stop at once. You have no right to treat us and Mister Drummond's servant with such untoward behavior. Release Lisan and those other Chinese passengers. Now, Major!"

Major Terauchi looks at Ingrid with disdain and does not respond. Instead, he orders Sergeant Matuso and his squad to search the coach for weapons or contraband. Two soldiers level their rifles at the group. Ingrid tries a more congenial tone. "Major, you obviously understand English."

He does not respond.

"Do I need to address you in Japanese for you to respond?"

He continues to watch her growing frustration.

Why won't he react? "You have burst into our coach and threatened us with bayonets. Taken our servant." Her eyes narrow as she stands with her arms akimbo, and in an intense voice commands, "Go away and leave us alone. We've nothing for you."

Matt realizes that Ingrid's hardheaded defiance is jeopardizing them all. He barks, "Ingrid, don't challenge him again." More softly, he continues, "Please, sit down, cool off, and remain quiet. We're in enough trouble."

Terauchi's politeness rings in a hard and cold voice. "White woman, you would be wise to not interfere with my business." He pulls a wrinkled document from his coat's top pocket. "The train's registry says that you have chartered this coach to rails-end at Chang-yeh. Why? What is your business in this remote province in China?"

Kendrick, now keenly aware of the seriousness of their situation and fearful for his daughter, adopts his best professional business mien. "Major, I apologize for my daughter's outburst. I am Randall Kendrick, a business-man from New York City. We are en route to Ho Hsien to see about rare porcelains. We have nothing to do with politics."

Terauchi with questioning eyes arches a single brow. "To Ho Hsien? Am I to understand that in these troubled times you are merely shopping for trinkets in this forsaken desert—a thousand miles from civilization?" He smiles graciously. "You take me for a fool." The major raises his right hand with palm outward when Kendrick starts to protest. "What do you know about the bandits that murdered my men and looted my supply convoy?"

Kendrick lets his very honest relief show, "Major, I assure you we know nothing about bandits. I would be stupid to associate with brigands. I don't 'cotton' to such riffraff. My business is Chinese antiquities. Nothing more."

The ruckus outside increases. Matt looks through the window. To his horror, he sees Lisan and the other Chinese being blindfolded, their hands tied behind their backs, and made to kneel with their faces down.

Wallace sees it also. He covers his eyes. He can't watch.

Matt demands, "Major! What is going on? What are your men doing to my houseboy and those other passengers?"

Major Terauchi says with nonchalance, "See for yourself, Australian."

Japanese soldiers stand behind the kneeling Lisan and the other Chinese passengers with their rifles at port arms.

A couple of hundred yards away, hidden in a thicket, the Black Viper watches the scene unfolding about the train. He takes a swig of sake from a clearly marked Japanese bottle and smiles. *The Jap is too creed-bound to search beyond the train.*

Inside the club car, Major Terauchi orders the sergeant and his men to escort everyone outside. Panic overcomes Wallace; he is unable to walk. Two soldiers drag him outside. Once on the ground, Terauchi spits orders in Japanese. His soldiers force Kendrick, Matt, Ingrid, and Wallace to stand next to the kneeling Lisan and the others. Wallace faints.

Major Terauchi barks to his soldiers. In unison, they charge the breeches of their rifles with rounds and return them to port arms. The loud metallic sounds of the bolts ramming home tells the travelers that the Japanese rifles are now loaded. Intense fear suffuses through the Occidentals.

Kendrick, resigned, does not say anything or make any untoward moves. However, to assert his position as the leader of the party, he stands upright, throws his shoulders back, and looks the major directly in his eyes.

Terauchi interprets Kendrick's actions as an affront to his authority. He slaps Kendrick hard enough to make him stumble. "Do not challenge me."

Matt tries to help Kendrick, but a bayonet keeps him in place.

Kendrick rubs the sting on his face and resumes his previous stance.

"Understand, American, I have information that the leader of the bandit gang that ambushed and looted my supply caravan is on this train. I intend to find him and administer Japanese justice. Your protestation of innocence does not convince me. You say you are travelling to Ho Hsien. The bandit I seek also travels to Ho Hsien—to arrange an arms deal with my weapons with the warlord Wu Pei-fu, I suspect." He gestures without looking. "These coolies on the ground are part of that bandit's gang."

Kendrick pleads, "Major, please understand, the man next to me is Lisan. He is my companion's houseboy. And those other Chinese men are ordinary people. They have no connection to banditry. They have been on the train with us since we left Peking."

"You are lying. They are bandits. And they shall be dealt with accordingly."

Ingrid rears back, and loudly declares, "Major, you're wrong! No one in our party was involved in any ambush. My father is correct. Lisan, the houseboy, has been with us since we started this journey five days ago. Now release him and the others, and let us be on our way."

Terauchi glares at Ingrid for her intemperate outburst. *Women do not talk to Japanese officers in such a manner—especially Western women.* He draws his pistol from its holster.

Matt sees that Terauchi is looking murderously at Ingrid. "Major, sir, please accept our condolences for the death of your soldiers and loss of your weapons. But, you have my word—"

Terauchi hisses with venom, "Your word? On your life's word? And this woman's life?"

Tension sparks. Matt and Ingrid exchange glances but neither flinches.

"Very well." Terauchi demands, "Which one is your houseboy?"

Matt points to Lisan.

Terauchi cracks orders to Sergeant Matuso. The sergeant grabs Lisan, releases his bonds, and tosses him towards the train, saving him from execution.

Matt says, "Thank you so much. Please release the other Chinese passengers."

"Chinese or Occidentals, it matters not which lives I take in retribution for my murdered soldiers. Before this morning is over, I'll take dozens more Chinese lives. Four or five or more for every man I lost." He barks out more orders in Japanese. Other soldiers grab the kneeling Chinese and drag them toward Lisan. Terauchi just stares at Matt and Ingrid, who stand mute. The major nods.

Soldiers grab both of them and force them to kneel next to Terauchi's boots. He snaps the receiver on his semi-automatic pistol to load a round and points it toward the back of Ingrid's head. "Disrespectful popinjay, you go first to meet your ancestors. The Australian will follow shortly."

Mustering the remainder of his courage, Matt takes Ingrid's hand, cracks a sideways smile, and whispers, "You're a 'fair dinkum sheila.'"

With soft tears, she squeezes his hand. "Not bad yourself, Aussie. See ya later."

In pain at seeing what is happening, Kendrick pleads, "Major Terauchi, please take me. I will replace my daughter."

In his command voice, Terauchi shouts, "No!" He pushes Ingrid's head forward and jams the barrel of his pistol's muzzle at the back of her head. The force pushes her downward and she emits a faint cry in pain.

Kendrick can't help the surge of pride he feels when he sees his daughter doesn't cry or beg.

"This woman is anathema. Her insolence toward the Empire of Japan must be revenged."

Matt tries to stand, but a rifle butt in his ribs knocks him down.

Wallace, lying on the ground, is caught between fainting or vomiting.

Lisan, realizing that Matt has taken his place, cries out in despair. The sergeant rifle-butts him, knocking him unconscious.

Kendrick is frantic, trying to figure a way out of this desperate situation. "Money! I have money! All you could want! Please!"

Ingrid shuts her eyes. Matt holds her hand tightly. On Terauchi's command, three more soldiers aim their rifles at the backs of Matt's, Wallace's, and Kendrick's heads.

Meanwhile, Lau has viewed the unfolding scene outside long enough. He digs deep under the bar and withdraws his Mauser semi-automatic pistol. He drops the magazine, sees that it is full, and with the palm of his hand, slams it home. He snaps the receiver that loads a round in the firing chamber, double-checks that the round is loaded properly, and eases off the safety.

Kendrick tries to move to take his daughter's bullet. He thrashes against the soldier who attempts to hold him—not completely successfully. Two more grab him and force him back, not allowing him to move. He sees Terauchi release the safety catch, take a deep breath, and move his finger to the trigger.

The shot rings out. A precisely aimed pistol bullet strikes Major Terauchi. He drops with a neat hole in his forehead. A second round hits Sergeant Matuso square in the center of his chest. Several more shots and several more soldiers drop. Lau inserts a new magazine and continues to fire.

A rumble of charging horses from a troop of Chinese cavalry fills the air. In a few seconds, a vicious firefight ensues and the din of battle fills the air. Kendrick, Ingrid, and Matt hit the ground flat. Matt instinctively shields Ingrid with his body. Wallace cowers behind the unconscious Lisan.

It takes only a few moments for the Chinese troops to dispatch the outnumbered Japanese. They do not take prisoners.

The melee over, the Black Viper rises unseen from behind the bushes on the hill and stands. He views the carnage. Spits. Out loud he bursts, "Idiots!" Then he sneaks back to the train and climbs aboard the baggage car.

A few minutes later, the travelers are ensconced in the coach—severely shaken, some slightly hurt, but safe from their ordeal. Wallace slouches in a lounge chair with a wet towel over his forehead. Ingrid perches on the edge of her favorite chair with her eyes closed; a forgotten cup of green tea sits untouched on the sideboard. Kendrick gulps a stiff whiskey. Lau starts to prepare lunch.

Matt sips his bourbon. He is perplexed. In the hubbub of the action, he could not identify what Chinese military group had saved them. *They cannot be from General Chiang's Nationalist army in Peking because we are too far away and they don't have the fighting skills and dogged determination this outfit demonstrated this morning.*

Outside, a corpsman tends to Lisan. He concludes that the hand is not broken but severely bruised. He applies iodine to the open wounds, wraps the hand in thick, sterile bandages, and gives him a shot of morphine. Then he inspects the wound in Lisan's head, cleans it with alcohol, closes it with several stitches, applies a bandage, and helps him to his seat in the second-class coach. With the narcotic beginning to take effect, Lisan manages only to mumble a slurred, "May your ancestors guide you."

A Chinese officer enters the coach and addresses the group. In halting English, he says, "Good morning, fellow travelers. Is everyone doing well? Not hurt too badly?"

The party manages a staggered, "Sure," "Okay," and "Swell, thanks to your soldiers."

The officer continues, "I should introduce myself. I am Captain Lin Piao of the Eighth Route Army—the fighting arm of the Chinese Communist Party." He turns and bows briefly to Lau. "Such an ordeal for our honored Occidental guests is most unwelcome." He looks about the club car and sees that the travelers are recovering. He spots Wallace, slumped in the back lounge chair. "My sincere apologies for such troubles as you have experienced."

Matt stands and exclaims, "Commies! I should have known." *Damn, during the hubbub, I didn't notice the red star on their caps.*

Kendrick rises to greet Captain Lin. "Whoever you are, Communists or whatever, Captain Piao, thanks for saving our hides. We're in your debt, big time."

Captain Lin ignores the incorrect use of his name and responds, "May I suggest that you thank Colonel Lau Jian-kang, a senior intelligence officer in the Eighth Route Army." He gestures toward the steward. "His keen marksmanship did away with the leadership of that Japanese patrol. He is your immediate savior."

Startled awe strikes the travelers. They stare incredulously at Lau, who smiles and continues preparing lunch. Matt recovers first. "Colonel Lau, you've hoodwinked us, but in the most auspicious manner I could imagine. Our sincere thanks."

Lau smiles and comments, "You must be in error. I am but a steward on this train to be of service to our honored Occidental travelers. I know nothing about military arms."

Wallace, who's been exceptionally quiet, begins to mutter something. On reflection, he remains silent and looks away, still ashamed of his overt show of cowardice.

Lau remains behind the bar, picks up the whiskey bottles, and refills Matt's and Kendrick's glasses. He goes to Ingrid, who is now more alert. "Please, Mistress Ingrid, I would suggest that you partake of this special-brand whiskey to boost your soul in this trying time."

"Thanks, Colonel." She holds up her glass. "Fill 'er up."

Kendrick comments, "Now that your cover is blown, what's your plan? Who will replace you as our steward?"

"There is no replacement, Mister Kendrick. This part of China is fraught with many dangers. I shall remain your steward. However, I must ask all of you to refrain from calling me Colonel. I am still just Lau."

Captain Lin Piao continues, "We are delighted that this contretemps has ended so successfully and you are able to continue your journey. Our leader, Chairman Mao Tse-tung, is committed to ridding China of all these evil foreigners from the black empire who rape our country." A soldier scurries in and whispers in his ear. He pauses for a second or so. "We have restored order on this train. I understand that the engineer has the steam ready. Perhaps you should be on your way."

Matt asks, "Captain Lin, how safe do you reckon it is to continue to Ho Hsien?"

Lin comments, "Your party is now under the protection of the Eighth Route Army. Proceed in pleasant harmony. Colonel Lau is your capable paladin." He salutes the Colonel and prepares to leave. "Please excuse me, I have to see to the recovery of the Japanese horses, weapons, and uniforms—always useful for a clandestine raid."

Matt makes a deep bow. "Thanks again."

Captain Lin bows, departs the train, and tends to his business on the ground.

Matt addresses Kendrick in a sincere voice. "I'm not sure what to make of Lin's comment that we are under their protection. Traditionally, Chinese Communists aren't that neighborly with Occidentals. They blame us for all of China's ills since the fall of the Qing Dynasty." He looks about the club car and rests his eyes on Lau. "As usual in the Celestial Kingdom, all frequently is not what it seems."

Matt sits next to Ingrid. "How are you doing? Okay?"

"I'm fine. Lau's nostrum is working wonderfully."

"You surprised me, young lady. That was frightfully courageous of you to stand up to the heinous Japanese officer the way you did. You've got character I did not suspect."

She slips her arm around his neck, pulls him to her, and kisses him full on the mouth. "You also, Aussie."

With her wisecracking manner boosted by Lau's special whiskey, she retorts, "Buster, you ain't seen nothing yet."

"Bloody hell!"

Kendrick, fully recovered and impatient, says, "Let's get this train moving."

18

Ala Shan Desert, Kansu Province. 13 July 1935

The full moon rides high over a clear, cool night. Its soft light highlights the parallel steel tracks that curve through the narrow canyon. The engineer carefully controls the train's speed as it creeps along the winding gorge. On the right shoulder is a deep, narrow canyon that plunges into the bottomless shadow of a long-dried riverbed below. To the left, almost abutting the twin rails, are the rugged Yin-Shan Mountains, which often black out most of the moon's bright light. The coaches sway, keeping in time with the twisting roadbed.

Sometime after midnight, Lisan carefully uses his good hand to slowly open the club car's door. His other hand hangs useless in its sling. The opening door squeaks loudly over the rhythm of the train. He winces and listens for movement in the dark coach. Nothing. He slips through the half-opened door. When the train gives a small lurch, he clutches the door frame, cursing the morphine's lingering cloud.

Satisfied that all the Occidentals and Wallace remain asleep, he cautiously pads into the lights-out club car and silently eases down the darkened hallway on soft slippers. He listens. The only sounds in the club car are the off-and-on screeching of the wheels, and snores of varying intensity and frequency. Satisfied that he is undetected, he places his left hand on the door handle to Matt's compartment and slowly tries to turn it—to no avail. The metal door is locked tight. He pauses for several seconds to confirm that he has not disturbed anyone. Then, with a sense of urgency, he raps softly on Matt's door. He waits. No response. He raps again with slightly more vigor and waits. Shortly, he hears the lock slip open and sees a faint light leak out from the door as it begins to open.

A disheveled Matt squints through the few inches of space between the door and the frame. In the dark hallway, he cannot see who is at his door. "Who's there? I can't see you."

"Mister Drummond, please to excuse me. I am Lisan," he whispers.

In a soft voice, Matt whispers, "Lisan, what the devil are you up to?" He glances at his wristwatch. "It's almost one o'clock in the morning."

"Sir, I must speak with you. There are important things happening in the forward coaches."

"Damn, we don't need another crisis. Okay, come in. But speak softly." Matt opens the door fully and Lisan slides inside. Matt quickly snaps his door closed and hits the main light switch. "What's so damned important at this hour of the morning?" He looks at his houseboy's sling and bandaged hand, and the dressing on his head. Matt gently squeezes Lisan's good shoulder and continues in a more conciliatory voice. "How are you feeling? Must be something special for you to awaken me while you are that banged up."

"My wounds do not pain me that much. That narcotic is most effective." He sways with the rocking of the train. "I am still a little woozy." He stumbles for a second. Lisan steadies himself and stands up as straight as he can. "Mister Drummond, I must thank you sincerely for saving me from the Japanese black ones. I can only repay you with my loyalty."

"Forget it." Matt grins. "I know you did not sneak into this coach and awaken me in the middle of the night to offer thanks. Out with it, Lisan. What's going on?"

Lisan speaks in a low, confidential voice. "Sir, there are some peculiar things happening in the third-class coaches and in my coach."

With impatience building, Matt demands, "What sort of things? Don't be obtuse. Tell me straight. I'm dead tired from our ordeal yesterday, and I'm not sure I am fully awake and functioning rationally."

Lisan responds in a hesitant undertone. "A strange Chinese man with a gun is drinking sake and making trouble with the other travelers." With his confidence building, Lisan says, "I am not sure, but I suspect that he is a rogue of some sort. He has a horrible face, and he has drunk a lot. And loud—he waves his pistol around, pointing it at passengers, and telling them to get down on the floor else he'll shoot them."

Somewhat frustrated at this annoyance of minor import to his mission, Matt queries, "Why doesn't the conductor stop him?"

Lisan, embarrassed for his countryman, who is supposed to be in charge of the train, says, "The conductor is afraid. That ugly fellow has immobilized him with threats and fear. The conductor sulks in a chair. May I suggest that it might be prudent if you would inspect? See if we are in danger. I heard him say that he is going to Ho Hsien."

That town name snaps Matt fully awake. "What! Ho Hsien? You are confident that this rogue said Ho Hsien?"

"Yes, sir. I heard him shout it several times. My seat is at the rear of the second-class coach. While he was in the front terrorizing the passengers, I slipped out the back door to alert you. Perhaps we should investigate."

Matt doesn't fully understand what is happening. He decides to find out who this rogue with a pistol is—jeopardizing the passengers. He starts to dress. "Lisan, you won't be much help with your wounds and fuzzy mind. In fact, you might get hurt. Stay in my compartment and listen. If the ruckus approaches this car, rouse Lau. He'll take control one way or the other." He opens the door and commands, "You understand completely?"

"Yes, sir, Mister Drummond. I will do my duty properly, you may be assured."

Matt exits the executive club car and enters the second-class car. The gun-toting rogue is not there. He sees that the passengers are recovering, returning to their seats, and retrieving their scattered belongings. They watch Matt silently as he passes, and several point forward to the third-class coaches.

He spots the conductor cowering in a chair in the front of the car. "Excuse me, sir. My houseboy tells me that there is trouble here. What is happening?"

The conductor whimpers, "It is nothing. Return to your compartment. You do not belong here."

Matt grabs him under his arms and raises him to a standing position. "Get up and rally your courage. It's your responsibility to take charge of this train. Do it. I am going to find this fellow with or without your help."

Now, standing on his own and his face flush, the conductor says, "Of course. I am feeling better now. Thank you." He stands on his own, straightens his uniform, throws his shoulders back and, projecting authority once again, reports, "That rogue with the pistol has gone forward to the third-class cars."

Matt enters a third-class car and trots down the aisle. The passengers here are surprised to see an Occidental in this humble place and they bristle at his intrusion into their domain. A few rumbles echo in the car. Unfazed, he presses forward. He searches the two third-class cars and does not find the mischief-maker.

Matt hesitates for a second as he faces the door to the baggage car. *In all probability, this is where that fellow is hiding. And I don't have a weapon. What the hell!* He kicks the door open and shouts loudly, "Hello." No answer. A solitary lantern hanging from the ceiling illuminates the car. He sees boxes, luggage, various farm animals, and hay scattered about. The stench hits Matt hard. He covers his face with a handkerchief.

Towards the front, Matt spots a man sitting on a bale of hay. Immediately, he recognizes the Black Viper from photographs in the newspapers. Matt stares at the sight of the twisted and scarred face of this dangerous bandit.

The Black Viper takes a swig of sake from a bottle labelled with Japanese characters and the radiant rising-sun logo, and draws his pistol.

He waves it at Matt and spouts, "Get out of here. I don't need company. Especially an Occidental imperialist."

Matt remains still and quiet. He tries to take the measure of the bandit and to make an educated guess at the fellow's next move. *Will he shoot, drink, or talk?* After a few moments, Matt states, "I'm a freelance reporter, and I'm here to talk with you. To find out about you."

The drunken Black Viper spits out a messy chuckle. Slurring his words, he spouts, "Occidental, you are too reckless with your words." He swigs more sake. Challenging Matt, he shouts, "So, you are a policeman and going to arrest me? Come and try."

"No. Not at all," Matt responds smoothly. "I just want to hear about your exploits and take your picture."

His drunken ego massaged, Black Viper mutters, "You are not a policeman, for true? And you will publish my picture and make me more famous?"

"Definitely. I am not a policeman, nor do I have an affiliation with law enforcement, I assure you." Matt walks slowly toward the Black Viper, holding his Leica in front like an offering. "As you can see, I am not armed." He wiggles the Leica. "This is my camera, with a flash attached."

Intrigued, the Black Viper sloshes his bottle at Matt. "Come here, reporter. I want to see you clearly."

"Very well." Matt continues to walk toward him—zigzagging his way to avoid the paraphernalia scattered about. "If we are to have a mutually agreeable interview, I would suggest that you return your pistol to its holster."

"No! I do not trust you. Come into the light."

Matt stands close to the Black Viper. He's careful to hide his shock at the bandit's disfigurement. He says, "I reckon that you are the Black Viper."

"Reporter, you speak the truth." The fellow pounds his chest several times, and with bravado says, "Indeed, I am the famous bandit Black Viper. The notorious Black Viper—and no policeman or army can stop me." He takes a deep drink from the sake bottle. "I am invincible. Do you understand?"

Matt, seeing the man's vanity, presses his advantage. "Reading your press clippings, I must say that I am impressed with your achievements. I want to take your picture and write your life story telling about your daring exploits."

"What kind of story? You take my picture? Who will see this story?"

"My photo-essay about you. Telling of your daring exploits will make an excellent feature story."

Black Viper grins widely and holsters his pistol. His ego soars with each new compliment as Matt continues to heap flattery on the blackguard. "I suspect that it was you and your gang that raided that Japanese supply train in the Yin-Shan Mountains a few days ago. Am I correct?"

The bandit laughs. "So what if the Black Viper gang did raid those damnable Japs? They have no business in China. The more I kill, the more I become a folk hero."

"In my article, I will paint you as a man of courage fighting the Japanese invaders. The story will be printed in Chinese and in English, and in the American newspapers, perhaps even in papers in Europe. And, I will make it a point to have your picture on the first page of the *Peking Times*." Matt scribbles comments in his note pad. "Why did you ambush this particular Japanese supply train? And where is the booty?"

Matt's flattery and the Japanese sake have overcome Black Viper's caution. He continues, "I have serious need for the Japs' weapons and supplies. Their equipment and supplies are now on a mule caravan on back trails in the mountains headed for Ho Hsien." He slaps his thigh and raises his bottle. "General Wu will pay a handsome price for them." The Viper points at Matt and nods. "Wu needs these arms to fight the Nationalists." Pausing, the bandit makes a show of checking to see that they are alone. "It is no secret that General Chiang is preparing for a campaign to wipe out the warlords in the northwestern provinces. And of course the Japs are getting bolder. It will not be long before they invade China in force in a full-scale war. General Wu must defend his interest."

Matt is not surprised at Black Viper's revelation. He had suspected as much when the Japanese captured the train and interrogated them so intently. Taking a new tack, Matt asks, "How did you escape from Colonel Terauchi when he searched the train?"

"You make me a hero? Yes? Good. I heard the Jap horses and saw their point rider. I suspected that the Japs were looking for me. I jumped off the train and hid in the bushes on the hill."

"That was very clever." Matt takes more notes and snaps several flash photographs with his Leica of the Black Viper, who grins broadly, distorting his ravaged face even more. Through his stupor, he snarls at the Leica's lens and avers, "I am pretty, am I not?"

19

Chang-yeh, Kansu Province. 13 July 1935

Through the night, the train had crawled through the mountains. About dawn, the train heads onto the flat plain on the edge of the Ala Shan Desert and rumbles on a straight track. It's hot and getting hotter as the sun rises. The ceiling fans rotate slowly, stirring the air softly.

Matt, perceptibly tired from his late-night encounter and interview with the Black Viper, slouches in the rear lounge chair sipping coffee. He wears a long-sleeve khaki shirt, long pants, and ankle-laced boots, and has set a wide-brimmed, light-colored hat beside him.

Ingrid enters the lounge in a flimsy sundress, ready for the desert heat. She kisses Kendrick on the cheek with bouncy good cheer. "Good morning, Dad. Sleep well?"

He sips his coffee, and looks at her. "No. It's too damn hot."

Matt waves to Ingrid and greets her with, "G'day, mate."

"And a g'day to you, Aussie."

Matt sidles over to Ingrid. "My, my, you do look fetching in that skimpy outfit, my lady."

"You know how to flatter a woman. Are you trying to seduce me, you masher?"

Matt surprises her by answering in a stern voice. "Ingrid, you'd not last four hours in that outfit in this boiling desert." He indicates his own protective clothing. "Change into something like I am wearing. This will protect you from that sizzling sun."

"Matt, I didn't bring that type of clothing. I do have boots, but nothing else like yours."

"When in dire straits, improvise. We'll make do with some of my clothes. A few safety pins ought to get them fitting you reasonably well. You won't look like the Queen of the May, but you'll have protection from that sun."

With a coy smile, Ingrid asks, "And you're going to do the fittings?"

Wallace Chung enters and greets everyone with a nod. He climbs on the bar stool and drinks coffee and nibbles on a biscuit. Ready for the hot desert, his dress resembles Matt's. Lau serves a sumptuous breakfast that he knows the Occidentals will need today: fresh-squeezed orange juice, waffles with butter and maple syrup, scrambled eggs, bacon, and biscuits with raspberry jam. He knows well to fortify his charges with wholesome food so that they might better endure the strenuous and hazardous travel they will face over the next several days.

Some hours later, amid assortments of loud clangs, squeals, and hissing steam, the train chugs to a halting stop.

Wallace Chung addresses the Occidentals. "At long last, we have arrived at Chang-yeh, a small and isolated village on the edge of the Ala Shan Desert. This is where the railroad track ends. Our executive club car will remain here until we return in a couple of weeks or so. Lau will look after it."

There is a collective groan from the Occidentals. Ingrid grits her teeth. *This trip has been hard enough in this custom coach. Now, what misery is ahead?*

Wallace continues, "Ho Hsien is slightly over one hundred miles to the northwest. I, of course, have arranged alternate transportation for us. It is not luxurious, but it is reliable and surefooted. It will take five or six days of travel to reach our destination." He pauses to assemble his thoughts. "It will be several hours before we are ready to depart. Please remain close to the station."

Matt asks pointedly, "Tell us, Wallace, what exactly is this 'alternate transportation' that you've arranged to take us to the 'back of beyond?'"

"Mister Drummond, may I answer later? I want all of you to have a pleasant surprise when you see it."

They share another groan.

"We've had enough surprises on this trip," Ingrid quips. "It won't matter much to have one more."

地暗,

Matt helps Ingrid off the executive club car. She is now more appropriately dressed for travel in the barren desert. She flashes a faint smile of satisfaction recalling the 'fitting.' She scans the hardscrabble town and the desert beyond. Shaking her head, she murmurs, "This is indeed the end of the line."

Matt responds grimly. "I fear there's worse ahead."

Lisan approaches Matt; his arm is still in the sling and bandages remain on his head. "Mister Drummond, with your permission I will hire a porter to bring our luggage to where I see Mister Chung is arranging things."

"Of course, Lisan. Look about and see what's going on."

"Yes, sir. I shall do so now."

Ingrid takes Matt's hand and starts to walk toward the town. "We're supposed to travel more than one hundred miles through that miasma of a desert?" She grips Matt's hand tightly. "Do you trust Wallace? Has he made adequate arrangements for our safety? His entire mien does not engender my confidence."

Matt responds with assurance, "He's slick, all right. But Wallace will not fail us. It's to his advantage to ensure that this Ming yellow deal is completed satisfactorily. He's too smart to jeopardize his fat fee."

Ingrid walks a few steps and comments mockingly, "So say you."
They continue walking through the town. Her oversized sleeve flaps when
she waves her arm toward the wasteland. "Look at it, Matt. Are we really
expected to traverse this desolate no man's land?"

"Knowing the stake Wallace Chung has in this adventure, I'm positive he has made appropriate arrangements. Whatever he's arranged, crude
as it may be, it'll be adequate. Frankly, I can't imagine what he's arranged."
He squeezes back with a smile. "Be prepared for a frightful surprise."

Meanwhile in Chang-yeh, caravan master Feng Ta-chao shouts orders to his drovers to move the pack mules and saddle camels into position.
Slowly the caravan begins to form for its long trek to Ho Hsien.

Wallace has arranged for drovers to have pack mules and saddle
camels ready at a staging area on the west end of town. Hired coolies un-
load luggage from the club car and supplies from the baggage car. Under
the drover's supervision, they pack this gear on the mules. Wallace rides
around the growing caravan on the back of a stout Tahki Mongolian
horse and watches keenly to ensure that the caravan is organized to his
satisfaction.

A middle-aged man in monk's robes sees the caravan assembling
and concludes that the fellow in the khaki outfit seems to be in charge. He
approaches the stationmaster and questions him in Mandarin. "Honorable
stationmaster, please tell me where that forming caravan is headed and
who is arranging it."

Seeing that the man is dressed in some sort of religious garb, he answers, "Kind sir, Mister Wallace Chung from Peking is in charge of that
caravan and it is going to Ho Hsien, I am led to believe."

"May I assume that they will travel on the main caravan trail to
Ho Hsien?"

"It is so."

"Indeed! If I may tell you my request?"

"Please do so."

"I am the leader of a group of twenty-five pilgrims returning from the shrine at Wu-chung. We have departed from that just-arrived train. I see with excellent good fortune that this caravan is going to pass through several towns along the way where my pilgrims would travel to return to their homes: Chiu-ch'uan, Yü-men, and An-shi. If it is not so, we wonder how many days it will be before the next caravan heads to the northwest."

The stationmaster pulls a notebook from his pocket and flips several pages. "I cannot say when the next caravan will form and depart for the northwest. There are none scheduled in my master book."

The pilgrim leader asks, "Mister stationmaster, would you be so kind as to approach Mister Wallace Chung to ask him if we may join his caravan?"

"I am honored to assist returning pilgrims. I too have made that pilgrimage to Wu-chung."

Wallace races about shouting nonsense orders to no one in particular. The animals are restless—camels spit at the drovers, and the mules sit, bray loudly, and refuse to obey commands.

Kendrick fusses about as the loading and packing continues. With irritation in his voice, he demands, "Is this everything, Mister Chung? You are positive? Make sure all our luggage and supplies are secured tightly on those pack animals. I don't want to lose anything."

"Of course, Mister Kendrick." Wallace scowls to himself. *If that blowhard did not have so much wealth, I would forsake him here at the edge of the civilized world. He irritates me severely. The Westerners I knew in California were much more accommodating.*

Wallace sees the stationmaster approaching. *What troubles will now plague my caravan?*

The stationmaster, a man of many years using a cane to steady himself, approaches and gives a slight bow. "Mister Chung, may I speak to you for a moment or two on a matter of some import?"

Wallace scowls, nods his head affirmatively, and dismounts. "What is so important that you interrupt me while I am supervising the loading and assembling of this caravan? We already are delayed."

"My sincere apologies, Mister Chung. I have an honest request—would you be so kind as to allow twenty-six pilgrims to accompany your caravan? If not, they will be stranded here in Chung-yeh for how many days, I do not know. There are no caravans scheduled in my book."

With incredulity that someone would ask him such an outrageous question, Wallace promptly answers, "No! Of course not. Go away, I am busy."

Kendrick overhears the stationmaster and Wallace's exchange. Though Kendrick does not understand Mandarin, the body motion of the two speaks volumes, and Wallace's negative response communicates in all languages. "Wallace, do not be so damn quick to say 'No.' Tell me what the stationmaster had to say."

With increasing frustration, Wallace says, "An addle-headed request, Mister Kendrick. He has asked me if I would agree to permit twenty-six pilgrims to tag along with our caravan." He remounts his horse. "Of course, such a request makes no sense. We are already unforgivably delayed."

But Kendrick surprises him. The old tycoon remembers his own youth bumming around the world. He knows he'd probably be dead a dozen times if not for the generosity of strangers on the road. With determination in his voice, Kendrick orders, "Mister Chung, make arrangements for these people to join us. Do you understand?"

Almost apoplectic at Kendrick's outrageous order, Wallace chokes on what he wants to say and takes a moment to compose himself. Then he mutters a stumbling, "Very well, Mister Kendrick, I shall do as you order."

Wallace tells the stationmaster that the pilgrims may join the caravan. The stationmaster bows, departs, and relays the positive decision to the pilgrims' leader.

Wallace finds the caravan master and instructs him to add the appropriate number of mules with water, victuals, tents, and other supplies to accommodate the pilgrims. Feng, surprised at this unusual request, acknowledges and discusses the additional cost. Wallace's outrage evaporates when he realizes he can turn this latest annoyance to his profit. *I will add twenty-five percent to this additional expenditure—of course, this will be in addition to my authorized twenty percent surcharge.*

"Mister Kendrick, the caravan master, Feng Ta-chao, demands one thousand pounds in advance for this additional expansion of his caravan. And there is my handling fee of two hundred fifty pounds."

Grumbling, Kendrick says, "Okay." He digs deep into his valise, withdraws a stack of British pounds, and counts out the correct amount. Suspecting chicanery, he hesitates before handing it to Wallace. "Take me to the caravan master so that I may pay him the correct amount."

Wallace skillfully hides his sharp disappointment with a half bow. Kendrick has checked his deceit. "I will bring him to you so that you may conclude the deal."

Lisan spots the pilgrims with their belongings falling in behind the caravan. Confused, he goes to find his employer, and spots him with Mistress Kendrick on the bench by the station. He approaches Matt, nods to Ingrid, and says, "Mister Drummond, your luggage is properly stored, as is Mistress Kendrick's. The loading of the pack animals appears to be proceeding properly—perhaps another hour to complete." He hesitates a few seconds to insure that what he says next is correct. "It is curious to note that a large group of people have joined in behind our caravan. I do not know who they are, or why they will go with us."

"Thanks for the report, Lisan." Matt tells Ingrid, "I'm going to see exactly what Wallace is doing. Lisan, you stay here with Mistress Kendrick." He checks his watch. "We're late already." He sees Wallace and Kendrick in an animated conversation and walks toward them. Close by, he hears Wallace giving yet another long-winded listing of the difficulties inherent in forming such a caravan properly. Kendrick suffers through it for a while. Then he excuses himself and returns to the executive coach car's bar for a dose of whiskey.

Lau has seen Kendrick's approach and has the scotch drink ready and waiting. Kendrick enters the club car, sits at the bar, and wolfs down his drink. "Thanks, Lau. I needed that. Dealing with that Wallace Chung is a serious ordeal." He smacks the empty glass down. "Fill it up."

He does. A loud clang startles them both. Lau almost spills the scotch when the club car jerks. Lau says, "Mister Kendrick, they are uncoupling our car, and there is an engine coming down the track to take it to the wye. I would suggest that you finish your drink quickly and exit this club car."

Kendrick tosses it down. "Good idea. Thanks for all your help. We'll see you, if all goes well, in ten days or so." He climbs down the steps and enters the station.

Matt, not having accomplished anything with Wallace, returns to the bench and notices that Ingrid is not there. He asks Lisan, "Do you know where Mistress Kendrick is? I thought she'd stay with you at the station."

"Mistress Kendrick needed to find a water closet. There was none in the station, and she walked into town to find one."

"Damn. She should have used the facilities on the train. What's got into her?"

Lisan responds, "It is too late to do so. Look, your club car is being towed away."

Kendrick approaches and overhears Matt and Lisan. "Don't worry, Drummond. She can take care of herself." He slaps Matt on the back. "She'll be back shortly."

Wallace comes to the station bench and comments, "It's not wise to wander off in this strange town. She should have asked for my help."

Matt says, "She is too self-confident and stubborn to ask for help."

Even Kendrick starts to worry. Concerned, he says, "Matt, see to it." Matt stomps off, looking for Ingrid.

Wallace returns to the staging area and makes a last-minute check to ensure that all's well and the caravan is ready to leave. *We've got to get the caravan moving if we are to reach our first camp before sunset. Why did Mistress Kendrick wander away?*

Kendrick waits at the station bench and wonders if he's a damn fool to have been sucked into this damnable expedition to nowhere.

Several blocks east of the station, Ingrid comes out of the public water closet looking pale and fighting the urge to gag. She looks around and sees people moving about, seemingly without a pattern or purpose, in this maze of streets and alleys. Even knowing that the caravan is due to depart shortly, her curiosity overcomes her better judgment. She begins to explore the nearby streets. She wanders deeper into their tangle while taking in the sights, sounds, and smells. Soon, she is lost.

As she rounds a corner into an alley, she comes face to face with a strange, ugly fellow. She recognizes him from the newsreels and utters a muffled scream before she catches herself.

The Black Viper is as startled as she is. He knows that she is with the Kendrick party and is headed for Ho Hsien to make some kind of a deal for the yellow porcelains.

Meanwhile, Matt looks frantically around the area near the station. There is no sign of Ingrid. He's torn—is his best strategy to stay near the station, reckoning that she is close by and will return shortly? Or should he search for her in the town? His perplexity turns into serious frustration. His fear for Ingrid clouds his mind.

Black Viper tries as best he can to ease Ingrid's fears. He steps back, demonstrating that he means her no harm. He twists his scarred face into a hideous smile. He moves to the corner of the alley and points down it, indicating that is the way she should go.

Ingrid is too stunned to move and remains frozen in fear.

The Black Viper takes Ingrid by the elbow, attempting to lead her to the main street. Instinctively, she jerks back. Black Viper backs away and points down the alley, waving his extended arm up and down in the universal body language for "Go there."

Ingrid, her fear starting to ease, is unsure of what's happening or what to do. She presses her back against the wood building next to her and points for the Black Viper to lead the way.

Finally, Matt breaks his mental lock and decides to search for Ingrid. The increased hubbub about the caravan tells him that it is ready to depart. He starts walking down the main street. Within a few seconds, he spots her turning a corner and coming toward him. He runs to get her. Spotting Matt, she turns to thank the Black Viper. He has disappeared.

Seeing that Ingrid is unharmed, Matt's worry begins to subside. But anger slips into his voice. "Ingrid! What's got into you? Why did you wander off? We've been terribly concerned about you."

Reflexively, Ingrid lashes back. "Don't raise your voice to me! I'm fine."

"You don't look fine. You look like you've just seen a phantom."

Ingrid quickly realizes that her outburst was untoward and instantly feels ashamed. "Please Matt, I'm sorry for snapping at you. I understand the anxiety you and Dad must have had. I was wrong to wander off." She goes to Matt and kisses him on the cheek. "Pals?"

"Of course. Forget it. We've got to get to the embarkation station. Let's go. The caravan is ready to shove off."

They head back to the station in silence. Ingrid is unsure whether to tell Matt about her encounter with the Black Viper.

They find Wallace pacing at the head of the caravan. Finally, he is satisfied that the caravan is ready for the long trek to Ho Hsien. He walks to Ingrid. "Mistress Kendrick, is everything all right? We were worried about you."

Embarrassed, she calms down and in a softer voice says, "Accept my apologies. I wandered into the town and shortly became utterly lost. Eventually, this strange and very ugly fellow showed me the way to the station." She pauses to clarify her story. "I must admit that when I first saw him, I was petrified. I was sure he was going to rob me or worse."

Wallace responds. "Oh, a Good Samaritan. How lucky. Is he nearby so we can reward him for his courtesy?"

Not wanting to cause more consternation among her party, she decides not to tell him that the fellow was the Black Viper. With a touch of mischief, she responds, "No. He has disappeared."

"Such a pity," Wallace remarks fatuously.

2Ø

Ala Shan Desert, Kansu Province. 13 July 1935

Finally, the caravan is ready. The mules are loaded with supplies and the party's baggage. Drovers have the mules standing. The herders wait by their saddled camels. Servants and porters fall in line to the rear. Behind them, the twenty-six pilgrims rise, gather their belongings, light joss sticks to insure good fortune on the upcoming journey, and await the signal to proceed.

Wallace guides his horse toward the Kendrick party and in his most officious voice says, "Mister Kendrick, the caravan is ready and we must leave now. Even with our delay, we can still make our first camp by night-fall. Please follow me. I will point out your mounts." Kendrick, Ingrid, and Matt follow Wallace to the caravan's staging area.

Matt demands, "What about Lisan? He is suffering from his wounds."

"I've made arrangements for him to ride on a mule."

As the Occidentals approach the assembled caravan, Ingrid gasps at the saddled camels. Herders have the pungent, grunting animals kneeling and ready for them to mount. "What are those things doing here? So this is your 'pleasant surprise?'" She's only half serious when she calls, "Wallace, you are indeed a scoundrel."

He responds, "These trustworthy Bactrian camels will take you safely through the desert to Ho Hsien, over one hundred miles of very desolate terrain."

Ingrid laughs as disdainfully as she knows how. "You're out of your mind if you think I'm going to ride one of those things."

Wallace now is frustrated at Ingrid for her hostile and ignorant display of temperament. He half-bows and smiles over clenched teeth. "Mistress Kendrick, there is no alternative. We will be traveling for several days—difficult days—over some of the most hostile terrain in all of China. I ask you to accept the inevitable." Wallace gestures toward the second camel. "Mistress Kendrick, this is your camel. Her name is Lidia. The senior herder tells me that she is gentle and will respond smoothly to your commands." He calls the chief herder over and orders him to help the Western female mount Lidia.

Kendrick strides to the camel that Wallace indicates is his. Not showing his apprehension, he climbs the beast and settles in the saddle. Impatient with his daughter's foolishness, he commands, "Ingrid, buck up and show your mettle. Get on that camel and let's get going."

Ingrid realizes that she has no choice. She accepts the herder's help and mounts the camel. To nobody in particular she asks, "Anybody going to show me how to ride this thing?" Her laughter sounds thin and forced. "Where's the steering wheel?"

Wallace smiles warmly and rests his hand on Lidia's neck. He responds, "Sway in rhythm with the animal. It is like riding a rocking chair."

Matt swings a leg over his kneeling animal and settles into the saddle.

Wallace, sitting erect on his horse, trots to the front of the caravan—now spread to a column about two hundred yards long. He takes one last look at the sprawling mass of humanity, animals, equipment, and supplies. *At long last, we are ready to proceed.* He shouts to the caravan master, Feng Ta-chao, "We go. Blow your horn."

A loud, low-frequency, howling sound permeates the area. Herders flick their tongues, making a clicking sound, and snap small switches at the camels. The dromedaries rise, spitting and growling, and take their first steps of the long, familiar journey. Drovers yank forward on the mules' halters, and the caravan slowly comes to life. It crawls in a semi-orderly fashion into the foreboding desert on what was once the great Silk Road.

Wallace, in all his life, has never had so much responsibility or ego-boosting authority.

地畳,

Late in the afternoon, the sun beats down relentlessly. The plodding caravan is in some disarray. Stragglers have stretched into a disordered line perhaps a mile or more long. All are having a difficult time maintaining the position and pace set by Feng—a muscular man of indeterminate age.

The Occidentals are managing to ride their camels with a modicum of competence. They are tired and sore; nevertheless, the prospect of the yellow porcelains keeps their spirits energized. To no one's surprise, Wallace's bravado, organizational skills, and management prowess quickly melt under the actual leadership of the complex and serious tasks of leading this caravan safely. Feng, a longtime guide of caravans in many directions in the Ala Shan Desert, assumes command by default. Wallace now rides on a camel. His horse has returned to its home in Chang-yeh. At sundown, the caravan makes camp at the desert hamlet Chiu-ch'üan. Eight pilgrims give thanks and leave the caravan.

The weary Occidentals forgo their customary banter and cocktails before dinner. They eat dinner quietly, go their tents, and retire.

地震。

Over the following three days, the Occidentals plod on, suffering searing heat, incessant pain, mind-numbing boredom, and Wallace's everlasting recitation of the history of the Silk Road. Kendrick is exasperated by the tediously long trip. *Are the yellows worth it?* He ponders once more. Then he pounds his thigh. *Damn right they are, if they're anywhere near as good as advertised.*

The travelers swelter. They are exhausted, and wonder if this dismal trek is a sample of perdition. Kendrick is just barely maintaining the set pace. He's several hundred feet behind the leader. Wallace is lost somewhere in the middle of the column. Ingrid has dropped far back, unable to keep up.

Matt is saddle sore but keeping up. He looks for Ingrid and sees that she is a straggler. Matt urges his camel to the rear. He scans the caravan's shuffling cloud of dust and spots Wallace slumped on his trudging camel, clearly in trouble. "Wallace, call a halt. This caravan is a mess. Kendrick and Ingrid are far behind and, I suspect, ready to drop. We need rest, water, and time to regroup."

Wallace, near collapse, quickly agrees. "As you can see, I am no longer in charge of this caravan. Talk to Feng Ta-chao about organizing."

Matt shakes his head and abandons Chung to his self-pity. He urges his camel forward, determined to find and convince Feng that the caravan is in trouble and that he needs to call a halt and regroup.

When Matt finally finds Feng, the caravan master concurs. "Mister Drummond, there is a small oasis just a few miles ahead. We will halt there for a time."

Matt's exhausted mind latches onto the thought of an oasis. He suggests, "It is late in the afternoon. By the time the people and the animals are refreshed and you reorganize this caravan, it probably will be too late to continue. Not so?"

Feng shrugs, considering his options. "We are behind schedule. Nonetheless, your suggestion has merit. We will camp at the oasis tonight." He tells his aide to spread the word. The welcome news quickly suffuses down the line, and invigorates the travelers to expend their remaining energy to move smartly to the oasis. The animals begin to smell water and pick up the pace. Shortly, the people and beasts move into the shade of the oasis and begin to satiate their thirst and relax. The herders tap the camels at the back of their front legs, making them kneel. Kendrick and Ingrid manage to dismount without falling. Wallace, with previous experience of camels, easily slides off his mount, then collapses on the ground.

The Occidentals and Wallace now occupy a small spot of quiet grass. The noise of the settling caravan and of people attending to the animals is confounding. Kendrick leans against a palm tree and hankers for a stiff glass of scotch to ease his pain. Ingrid lies on her side and unabashedly kneads her *derrière* where it hurts so intensely. Wallace sits with his legs crossed and stares into space. No one speaks.

Matt approaches and plops down next to Ingrid. Too exhausted to make a snappy remark, he simply says, "Cheers, mate. You look as bad as I feel."

Ingrid says, "Shut up, Aussie. I'm dying, or something close to it." She continues to massage her hurt and eyes him with a touch of envy. "Damn! You look as good as I wish I were."

Matt asks, "May I help you rub?"

She reacts with shock at Matt's outrageous comment in front of her father and Wallace. Then she realizes that Matt's forwardness under these dire circumstances does not matter. "Indeed not," she snaps in a faux formal tone. She manages to add a small, crooked smile. "Perhaps later, mate."

Feng rides to where the Occidentals are sprawled. "I see flushed faces and serious fatigue among your party and the others. I have concern that some may suffer heat prostration." Kendrick gives him a quizzical look. Feng explains. "It is a serious condition in which the body's electric system gets out of balance due to loss of electrolytes. If the symptoms are not attacked promptly, death can be the result." He orders his men to demand that all in the caravan take one salt tablet and one potassium tablet and drink at least a pint of water. "There are no exceptions. If one should refuse, force the issue." He opens the leather purse hooked to his belt, withdraws his prescribed tablets, and gives them to Matt. "Mister Drummond, I'm counting on you to ensure that the travelers in your party comply with my orders. I do not want to preside over an Occidental burial ceremony in this desert."

Matt gets the message loud and clear. "I understand, mate." He rises, walks to Kendrick, and in no-nonsense voice, orders, "Take these tablets and wash them down with water. Understand?"

Kendrick, the old hand that he is, does understand, and complies with a faint, "Thanks."

Matt distributes two tablets each to Ingrid and Wallace. "Down the gullet with these nostrums and wash them down. Shortly, you'll feel tiptop, or almost so." Without comment, the pair do as directed. Too exhausted to banter, the group lies quietly, suffering their pain, and waiting for the caravan's *chef à cuisine* to ring his large, brass gong in the call to dinner— a communal affair with no regard for one's social station.

Twilight creeps over the desert. The sky is scarlet and a cool breeze from the north engenders an almost comfortable evening. The travelers are satiated by the hearty meal of chicken and noodles, and the cool evening refreshes their minds and bodies. Wallace bangs tales of the Ming dynasty into Kendrick's ear. But Kendrick doesn't listen. His mind wanders to the yellows and to his museum in New York. He briefly worries over some details about the upcoming purchase of a newspaper chain that operates in the southwest.

Ingrid and Matt, bored with Wallace's history lesson, wander a short way from the oasis. Earlier, Feng had warned everyone not to venture too far into the desert because there are dangerous vipers about. They walk in a wide oval around the oasis. Their pace is slow and they don't say much. Being with each other is enough for now. Eventually, Ingrid squeezes Matt's hand and says, "Thanks for convincing the caravan master to call an early halt this afternoon. I'm sore all over—sore in places I didn't know I had. I'm not sure I could have made another mile."

"You're quite welcome. I was exhausted also. And when I spotted your dad slumping slightly and using all his resolve to continue, I knew I had to do something. Kendrick is a tough ol' bird. Reckon he'd keep going until he fell off his camel."

"You're absolutely right," Ingrid says. "No matter the enterprise, he taxes himself and me to the extreme." They continue their stroll holding hands. After a long silence, she asks, "So, tell me, Mister Drummond from 'down under,' what brings you to the Celestial Kingdom in these troubled times?"

Matt tenses a little at her direct question and decides to respond with a hint of evasion. "Adventure. The mysteries of the Orient. Career change. That sort of thing."

Ingrid looks at him with a crooked smile and wide eyes. "A man of your mien, sharp mind, education, and talent? I'm not convinced that's all it was, Matt." She waits, appraising, but Matt only smiles and looks out at the night. "I know you well enough to suspect that you are dissembling. There's more than that blather. Out with it, Aussie." With humor in her voice, she blurts, "No more artifice, buster."

Matt looks once more to the desert, as if for inspiration, before he turns to Ingrid. "If you must know, miss know-it-all, a 'yellow rag' reporter from the Melbourne *Herald Sun* broke the scandal regarding my indiscretions with a married, socialite woman whose husband was a prominent political leader. The story and photographs made it into the tabloids all across the British Empire, and elsewhere." He pauses to form his words carefully. "My father, a priest in the Anglican Church, rather forcefully suggested that I quit Australia for a while. So here I am. Not sure when, or if, I'll ever return. I'm using my skills to do what I enjoy. And, doing very well indeed—my photos and articles are published worldwide. Why should I return? I have a successful career, and I'm having a fine time."

Ingrid listens with increasing interest. In her smart-alecky voice she quips, and bats her lashes in the moonlight, "So, tell me, Mister Drummond, what do you do for fun in Peking?"

Matt returns her volley with a waspish quip. "I have all sorts of lascivious pastimes, Mistress Ingrid Kendrick."

Not hearing what she wants or expects, and slightly irritated, Ingrid snaps, "Really? What's the going price for those pastimes nowadays?"

Matt retorts, "No charge. They're free."

Again she's caught off guard by the Aussie's response. "Excuse me? I don't understand 'free.'"

"It's simple. I am the dart-throwing champion of the Bloody Mary Pub on Ling Po Road and of all the other pubs within the International Settlement. Loser buys the round. I haven't bought a whiskey in months." Matt winks at Ingrid. "Then, there are the ladies in the International Settlement."

Before Ingrid can respond, and as the pair complete the circuit around the oasis, she hears Kendrick calling them back to camp.

They head that way, but not before Ingrid fires a final shot. "You *roué*, I'm not letting you off without more details." She squeezes his hand tightly.

21

Yü-men-shih, in the Foothills of the Ch'i Lien Shan Mountains.
18 July 1935

It's shortly after noon. The sun is at its zenith and has no mercy on those who dare challenge it. The ragtag caravan ambles along the twisting high-desert trail in the foothills of the mountains. None of the Occidentals has mastered the technique of riding the camels. However, each day their camel-riding skills improve slightly. With some success, they all ride together, and they halfheartedly banter among themselves to try and boost each other's morale as they share the purgatory of this caravan. Resigned to their fate of continuing pain, blistering heat, and mind-numbing boredom, they persevere with dogged determination in the now sprawling caravan. They have difficulty maintaining Feng Ta-chao's relentless pace—set to maintain some nonexistent schedule. It's the treasure of a lifetime that lies ahead—the Ming yellow porcelains—so they press on. Kendrick seems to hear the yellow porcelains calling,

Earlier this morning, nine pilgrims left the caravan to return to their homes in Lao-chün-miao, a burg a few miles south of the Silk Road. An old man of obvious and determined stamina approached Ingrid and offered her a dozen joss sticks. In a dialect that Matt could only partially understand, the fellow asked Ingrid to accept his joss sticks and to please light one every few hours of her travel. He assured her that they would keep away the evil spirits that he knew haunted this road. She accepted the gift and nodded her head in thanks. The fellow bowed deeply to the white woman with flaming-red hair and hustled after his fellow pilgrims, now several yards away.

Pleased, yet perplexed by the offering, Ingrid asks Matt, "What should I do with these? That was very kind of that old pilgrim. I did not know how to thank him properly. I wonder what sort of evil spirits hang around this trail," she says, with a hint of humorous skepticism.

Matt, more familiar with Chinese customs, doesn't laugh with her. He responds, "I reckon you ought to light them along the way. The world here is full of secrets. In this ancient civilization, one cannot know them all." Teasingly, he continues, "Though I've never seen an evil spirit or a ghost of any kind, some of my pals in the Bloody Mary Pub claim that they've had narrow escapes from them. A lighted joss stick was the key to shooing them away."

"Damn you, Matt Drummond, you 'bloody rotter.' You tax my soul with your nonsense. How am I to know when you're teasing me? When I should I believe you?"

Before Matt can form an appropriate quip, Wallace arrives. "Ahead is an ancient lamasery, long since abandoned, a few miles east of the hamlet of Yü-men. Feng plans to call an extended halt there and get this caravan reformed. It has stretched out for almost two miles. He is concerned that some of the laggards will get lost or have other troubles that he could not attend to."

The Occidentals, almost in unison, cry, "Thank God!" "About time!" and "None too soon."

Wallace continues. "It is believed that this lamasery functioned for many years during the Tang Dynasty, sometime from about 600 through 900 *Anno Domini.* It was an integral stopover on the Silk Road. In those days, there was abundant crystal-clear water from several springs in this valley." He continues with his recitation of ancient Chinese history, but he has lost his audience. The Occidentals round a bend in the trail and spot the structure just a hundred yards ahead. Their energy surging, they urge their mounts to move faster.

Shortly, they and the first elements of the two-mile caravan approach the abandoned site. Kendrick yelps, "Finally, the ruins! Perhaps Feng will let us camp here this evening." He whips his camel and starts toward the monastery at a gallop. "Let's see the accommodations."

Wallace whips his camel to follow. He shouts, "No! No. It is not for us. Mister Kendrick! Please come back. That place is not safe."

Kendrick snaps back, "Nonsense, Chung. This place is abandoned. Let's explore it. Who knows what we'll find. I'm a ghost-towner from way back."

Wallace shouts, "Stop! Stop! Do not enter. This place is cursed with devils—savage demons that attack without provocation or mercy."

Kendrick is several yards ahead and he presses on. He refuses to pay attention to Wallace's pleas. His stubborn curiosity has overwhelmed his good sense.

Matt uses his cane to whip his camel into a canter. *Kendrick's recklessness is going to get him killed one of these days.*

Ingrid maintains pace with Matt. Although she knows Wallace would not be so forceful and demanding if the ruined lamasery were not dangerous, with false bravado, she tells Matt, "Over the years, Dad has done great. He has bested more rogues than we could imagine."

Kendrick reaches the ruin and dismounts, eager to explore. He sees that it is in very poor condition. Most of the roof has collapsed and many walls have fallen, their stone blocks lying in a mosaic of complex patterns. The place is overrun with weeds and junk from the centuries. His arrival startles an ibex eating the thin ground cover. It bolts. In an instant, it vanishes into the hills. Clenching his jaws at his enduring saddle-soreness and deep pain in his leg joints, he strides apace up the steps like a younger man and enters the opening that once was the door.

Within a few seconds, Ingrid, Matt, and Wallace reach the entrance steps in time to hear Kendrick's piercing cry for help. "Ingrid! Matt! I need help NOW!"

Matt reckons that bandits have captured Kendrick. He immediately looks for and finds the lead herder, who is just a few yards away. Ingrid, with an instantaneous adrenaline boost, runs helter-skelter up the steps and into the ruin. She spots Kendrick frozen in place. At his feet is a cobra with its neck flared in the strike pose. Ingrid screams, "Father!"

"Be still. Be quiet," Kendrick urges Ingrid. The cobra sways back and forth in the ruckus with its eyes fixed on him. With his eyes, Kendrick indicates Ingrid should scan the entire room. She sees that her father stands in the middle of a cobras' nest. Some have been aroused by the commotion and are moving around.

Matt hears her scream, scrambles up the steps, enters, and immediately grasps the entire, dangerous scene. "Dear God!" he exclaims.

Though only a few steps inside, Ingrid is frozen in place as several of the irritated cobras slither near her. Kendrick carefully puts one index finger to his lips to signal continued quiet, and says, "No more talking or moving about." She grips her hands into tight fists and uses all her willpower to remain still and quiet.

Wallace, not sure what the ruckus is about, chooses to remain outside. *Fools! They challenge the demons.*

Matt slowly draws his hunting knife. He sights quickly and, with a quick flick of his wrist, his knife sails true and slices off the head of the cobra threatening Kendrick.

Kendrick, with beads of perspiration dripping from his face, remains motionless and says softly, "Be still and quiet." In a minute or two, the no-longer-irritated reptiles gather at the back of the ruins. He slowly backs out of this 'cursed' place. He takes Ingrid by her arm and guides her to the steps. She grabs her father and hugs him. "Thank God you're safe."

"Thank Matt. He's the fellow that saved me with his expert knife-throwing skills."

Matt slowly eases out of the lamasery. "You folks doing okay?"

Ingrid grabs Matt in a bear hug and kisses him full on the mouth. "Thanks, my 'down under' hero."

Kendrick takes Matt's hand and shakes it vigorously. "Thanks, Drummond. You're a good man. I'll not forget."

Wallace asks, "What has happened? I heard the shouting and wondered if the evil spirits had captured you or something worse."

Kendrick says, "No evil spirits. I walked into a nest of cobras, and Matt saved me with his knife-throwing prowess."

Wallace, with alarm, spouts, "This place is indeed cursed."

The last stragglers enter the area. Feng orders his drovers to work quickly to reform the caravan. "We must get to the lamasery in Yü-men before nightfall."

Kendrick and Matt both groan at his words.

Ingrid lights three joss sticks, places them in front of the abandoned lamasery's steps, and in a half jest, murmurs, "Demons, be gone!"

22

Yü-men, Nan Shan Mountains, Kansu Province. 18 July 1935

An hour later, Feng and his drovers have reorganized the caravan. He orders all to mount and on his signal the caravan begins its crawl over the rocky trail that winds through the Nan Shan Mountains. Their destination is the lamasery at Yü-men, several miles ahead.

Matt sways in his saddle, enduring the aches. He'd thought his top-notch physical condition was enough for him to withstand most any hardship. Now, he's struggling to endure. He is the first to spot the cloud of dust in the distance. He moves up to Feng. "What do you make of it?"

"Horsemen, no doubt—a squad of soldiers galloping to intercept us."

"Coming to attack this unarmed caravan?"

"Not sure, but I doubt it." He shades his eyes from the fading sun and looks intently. "Probably from Ho Hsien."

Kendrick, farther back, sees the cavalry ahead closing rapidly and snaps, "Dear God! More Japs! Another assault?"

Ingrid asks, "Who are they? Is it a military raid?"

Wallace would like to enjoy their fear a little longer, but he interrupts to ease their anxiety. In his most assuring voice, he comments, "Please do not be concerned. Those soldiers are coming here to guide us to Ho Hsien. General Wu has sent them, I'm sure."

Matt, not convinced, demands, "If that is so, why are they coming so fast?"

"They are no doubt anxious to greet us."

Feng rides ahead to meet the soldiers. Despite Chung's continued efforts, everyone tenses, and the silence grows heavy.

In a few minutes, Feng returns to the caravan. "All is well. These soldiers represent General Wu. They will escort us to Yü-men this evening and to Ho Hsien tomorrow."

The soldiers arrive at the caravan, and their leader, Captain Tze Pie-fu, dismounts. Projecting a professional military mien, he gives a snappy salute to the group and says a few words of greeting in Mandarin to Wallace.

Matt notices Ingrid's interest in the ruggedly handsome, black-eyed young man.

Wallace looks to the Occidentals and says, "May I present Captain Tze Pie-fu? He is an old acquaintance of mine."

Captain Tze bows deeply, and in stilted English addresses them. "Good afternoon to all of you. My father, General Wu, sends his sincere greetings and welcomes you to his home at Ho Hsien. I am here to escort you and see to your safety."

Matt leans and whispers in Kendrick's ear, "Good God! These are warlord troops. I don't trust them. They are more bandits than soldiers. Their modus operandi is terror, thievery, rapine, and pillage."

Kendrick brushes Matt off his shoulder and remarks, "A little paranoia is healthy, but don't let it overwhelm you."

Matt responds with wariness, "Perhaps. But I'm leery. We've had enough trouble on this damn trip."

"Enough, Matt." Kendrick addresses Captain Tze. "You scared the living dickens out of us, charging in that way. I thought your horsemen were the Apocalypse descending on us."

"My apologies if I alarmed you. That was not my intention. It is merely that the hour is late. We must reach the lamasery at Yü-men before dark." He cracks a small smile, bows, and snaps a salute. He mounts his horse and orders his troops to encircle the caravan.

Wallace nods at Kendrick. "I am sure that Captain Tze does not understand your biblical reference. Do not be concerned; he is a fine soldier indeed. With his leadership and protection, we will surely reach the lamasery at Yü-men before dark."

Feng inspects the caravan and sees that it is ready to travel. He nods to Captain Tze. Tze makes a last check and sees that his father's guests are mounted and prepared. He orders Feng, "Blow your horn and get this caravan moving."

地門,

At twilight's end, the lumbering caravan arrives at the lamasery. Expecting the caravan, the head abbot greets the travelers. He's standing just outside the huge oak doors. A cruelly wide, pink scar runs from his eye to his chin—a fresh memento of General Wu's raid to steal the Ming yellows. Others linger in the courtyard at the rare sight of an Occidental female with red hair. When they see Wu's soldiers, they scurry inside. Many still nurse wounds from the raid some weeks ago.

Wallace dismounts and approaches the abbot. "Greetings, Honorable abbot. May we ask for your hospitality for the evening? We are weary, having traveled far these past six days."

The abbot looks askance at the large group and scowls as he sees General Wu's soldiers. He remembers all too well their raid.

Wallace Chung, keenly attuned to assessing the body motion of his clients, sees the abbot's concern. "Please do not fear these soldiers. They mean you no harm. They are to escort us to Ho Hsien. Will you accommodate us?"

The abbot clasps his hands to stop them from shaking before he answers, with some apprehension, "You are welcome. Perhaps you and your Occidentals will accept our hospitality and join us for supper after you have refreshed." The old man raises his chin and glares at Tze and his troop. Captain Tze bows and salutes the abbot to show respect and to alleviate his fears.

Intimidated by General Wu's soldiers, the abbot offers to Feng, "The soldiers may tend their animals in that barnyard and sleep in the shed. The others can wash and eat in that structure over there." He nods over his shoulder towards a rundown shack that once was a horse stable. Feng responds, "Our thanks, Honorable Abbott. Your offer of hospitality is most welcome."

Wallace tells the Occidentals, "The head abbot has agreed to let you be his guests this evening. Please dismount and follow the abbot inside. I'll have Lisan bring your belongings."

Matt snaps, "Lisan?"

"Do not be concerned, Matt. Lisan shed his sling and the bandage on his head two days ago. He is quite fit—his ol' self, so to speak."

The senior fellow of the remaining nine pilgrims tells Wallace, "We will continue our journey to our homes at Tun-huang, only a few miles to the southwest." They thank him profusely and each offers him several joss sticks.

Captain Tze bows to the abbot from his horse. His voice is smooth as he says cordially, "We are grateful for your hospitality. We will be no trouble—be assured."

The head abbot instructs one of the novices to show the soldiers to their bivouac.

Exhausted from the long journey, Kendrick is unusually quiet and hopes Drummond will answer for the group. But the Aussie won't lift his head enough to look out from under that ridiculous hat. So the tycoon rallies. "Wallace, tell this priest thanks, and let's get moving. I'm tuckered out, as are the rest."

Wallace counters, "He is a monk. Not priest. Please be more respectful."

"Whatever. It doesn't matter. What matters are a hot bath, a fine meal, and a soft bed."

Wallace interprets the abbot's greeting to the Occidentals. "Sirs, it is my honor to offer the hospitality of this humble lamasery. Permit me to show you your quarters. Supper will be served shortly."

Ingrid needs no translation. She's done a respectable job of hiding the fact that she is exhausted, with intense pain tearing through her every joint. She is energized at the thought of a hot bath. She has six days of desert-travel filth encased on her body. Matt, in about the same condition, puts his left arm around her shoulders. They lean on each other to remain upright.

The Occidentals and Wallace follow the head abbot. Wallace launches into a history of this famous lamasery on the Silk Road. Kendrick listens but does not hear. His thoughts have locked onto the proffered meal, hot shower, and a clean bed. He is not disappointed.

他陪，

After sunset, the heat dissipates quickly in this high desert. Tonight, it is cool enough that it's prudent to wear a light jacket.

Matt, freshly washed and satiated, strolls across the moonlit court-yard for a relaxing walk to iron out some of the pain in his joints. He spots Lisan tending to the luggage and goes to him. "Lisan, I see that you have recovered from your wounds. Feeling fine?"

"Yes, Mister Drummond. I am whole now."

"Excellent. I have a task for you."

"Yes, sir. How may I be of service this evening, Mister Drummond?"

Matt, with his voice muffled, "I want you to keep a watch on Wallace Chung. I have serious misgivings about him. I understood some of the Mandarin dialect that Captain Tze and he were speaking. Something is askew. I cannot pinpoint it, but all is not what it seems. See where Mister Chung goes. Who he talks to. What he does."

A faint smile creeps over Lisan's face. "As you say, Mister Drummond."

"Be cautious. Don't let him spot you, and keep me informed."

With a hint of bravado, Lisan puffs out his chest. "I understand. I will be most careful." He bows and moves into the dark courtyard.

Matt continues his stroll until he spots Ingrid standing in her doorway. She waves to him. He wonders what their relationship is or ought to be. *I've loved many women in my day, but I've never been seriously in love. This woman is special, very special.* He approaches and gives a snappy bow. "Good evening, Mistress Ingrid Kendrick. All's well?" He cracks a large smile. "Ingrid, you could pose for a soap bar advertisement, all freshly scrubbed and hair combed."

She retorts, "I'm not sure that's a compliment," then smiles. "But I'll take it for one." She loops her arm around his. "You look spiffy yourself." She kisses him lightly on the cheek.

They banter for a few minutes, talking about their adventures. Suddenly, Matt holds up his hand for silence. They're being watched. He points at some of the younger monks on the balcony, barely in their teens, who are giggling and nattering. A senior monk shoos them away.

Ingrid asks, "What are those fellows doing?"

"Best I can tell, they are wondering if you are my wife or concubine."

Ingrid frowns at Matt as if she is offended. He looks bewildered and stammers a few unintelligible sounds. She laughs heartily.

他陰.

Her room is clean and Spartan, lit by a lone candle. Matt lies on the simple steel bed's thin mattress. Ingrid fidgets with her belongings at the wood dresser. She turns and smiles. "Get up. It's been a long day and I'm going to sleep."

"So am I." He spreads his arms wide. "Come here."

Before she can react, there is a cautious knock on her door. Ingrid asks, "Yes. Who is there?"

"I am Lisan. Please excuse me, Mistress Kendrick. I must speak with Mister Drummond."

Ingrid is awkwardly embarrassed that Lisan knows that Matt is in her room this late in the evening. She quickly slips into her robe and fluffs her hair. "You may come in, Lisan."

He enters and bows to Ingrid and Matt. He looks shyly at Ingrid, deciding what approach would be appropriate. After a few seconds of awkward silence, he says, "Good evening, Mistress Kendrick. May I speak with Mister Drummond in private? I have urgent information."

Matt, impatient to hear his news, says, "It's all right, Lisan. You may speak freely. What have you found?"

"Mister Chung is not in his room."

"Well, where is he? Is he with Captain Tze? Out with it."

"No. Captain Tze is with his soldiers. Mister Chung is at the entrance of the lamasery with ... Mister Drummond, you should see for yourself. I fear that trouble is brewing."

Ingrid looks at Matt questioningly.

"What's that Wallace Chung bastard scheming now?" Matt dresses and charges Lisan, "You stay here with Mistress Kendrick until I return."

Ingrid responds, "That's not necessary. I'll be all right." She takes Matt's arm. "Be careful. Since we started on this caravan, I've had an uneasy feeling about Wallace. I've no concrete evidence, but there's something about his ways that puzzles me."

Matt takes her right hand, squeezes tightly, and says, "Will do." Moving silently, he reaches the inside of the lamasery's entrance and kneels quietly behind a roaring-lion statue that's guarding the entrance. He sees Wallace talking with the Black Viper in quiet, conspiratorial tones. He can just pick up the drift of their conversation in Mandarin. Trying to move closer to hear more clearly, he stumbles on a loose rock.

The noise alerts Wallace and the Black Viper, and they spot him.

"Is that you, Matt? Why are you skulking around in the dark?"

Discovered, Matt rises and tries to act nonchalant as he approaches the pair. "Trying to find out what you're up to, ol' chap. Some sort of skullduggery, no doubt, with this bandit, the Black Viper."

"Not so, ol' chap. Just passing the time with this interesting fellow. He has the most fascinating tales to tell. I must say I'm surprised that you know the Black Viper. How is it so?"

With his anger rising at Wallace's clear obfuscation, he snaps, "Frankly, Wallace, it's none of your concern how I know this bandit." Matt is not willing to reveal that he's interviewed the Black Viper and is working on a feature-photo story about him.

The Black Viper is pleased that Matt recognizes him. He bows and asks, "Photographer man, when will my picture be in the newspapers? Send me copies to the post office in Chung-wei. Yes?"

Matt responds, "Of course." He points to Black Viper's belt buckle. It has the rising-sun symbol engraved on it. Though he already knows the answer, Matt wants to continue the charade, so he asks, "Where did you find that belt buckle? It's Japanese."

Black Viper proudly shows off the belt buckle. With a surge of pride, he answers, "I retrieved it from a dead Japanese soldier I found in the mountains. Some of his comrades were about, but they were lifeless also. Those soldiers must have stumbled into some sort of serious trouble." Then he bows to the two men and says with a distorted grin, "Goodbye, Australian man. Make a good story about me."

When the Black Viper is out of sight, Wallace whispers to Matt, "We are very fortunate. The Viper's scouts are reconnoitering throughout this area. His intelligence will be invaluable in getting us safely to Ho Hsien. Already they have spotted Japanese patrols south of here. And there are some other soldiers to the northwest, perhaps rogue Nationalists."

Wallace does not bamboozle Matt. He knows Wallace too well to be snookered. Clearly, Wallace and the Viper are in cahoots about some knavery. To disconcert Wallace, he asks, "Shouldn't Captain Tze have been in this meeting? He's responsible for getting us to Ho Hsien safely."

Wallace responds with faux sincerity, "Captain Tze is strictly a by-the-book officer. Actually, in many ways he is a dolt. He does not have the subtlety to analyze intelligence and use it effectively. It would only have confused our strategy to have Tze here."

"What strategy, Wallace? You and the Black Viper? That's insane."
With his ire rising, Matt has heard enough of Chung's pat answers and
demands, "And how, may I ask, do you know so much about Captain Tze?"

Wallace, unruffled, responds, "Recall, old chap, my family has lived
in this province for many generations. Not much happens here without
our notice."

Matt is not convinced.

23

Ho Hsien, Kansu Province. 19 July 1935

Early the next morning, the caravan plods along a straight, desolate, and narrow road. Feng and his crew work assiduously to keep the smaller caravan orderly. It's an easier task now that the pilgrims and a number of miscellaneous followers have left the caravan.

Kendrick moves next to Wallace. "Are we lost? Last night you said that Ho Hsien was nearby. We've traveled all morning and into midafternoon and all I see is more of this damn desert. Where the hell is this city?"

"We are not lost, Mister Kendrick. I assure you that we are on the correct road. The town is only a few miles ahead."

Ingrid overhears her father. "Well, Dad, we might as well be lost. At the rate we're going, I'm about ready to give up and go back. Can anything on this planet be worth the cruel wretchedness we've endured these past seven days?" Answering her own question, she continues, "This close, we'll press on. Those yellow porcelains had best be the treasure of all time."

Matt moves his camel until his leg brushes close to Ingrid's. "If those porcelains prove to be fakes, whom will you liquidate first? Or do you have something more sinister in mind?"

Ingrid arches a brow and waves her camel rod like a scepter. "Mister Matthew Drummond, stick with me and find out."

The caravan tops a small hill. In the distance, looking almost like a mirage, is the citadel of Ho Hsien.

"Mister Kendrick!" Wallace exclaims. "There is Ho Hsien. We are almost there. Just a few minutes more." He smiles disdainfully and swats his mount for speed. "You see, we were not lost."

The caravan arrives at the citadel's ponderous wooden gates. On a signal from Captain Tze, the sentries work to open it. The two massive doors slowly widen outwardly amid sundry creaks, squeals, and groans. The travelers give a faint cheer and then laugh at themselves. At long last, their ordeal is almost over.

Matt is impressed with the gate, the ancient walls that surround the town, and the fortified towers. He uses his Leica to snap several photographs of the scene and then focuses on Kendrick, Ingrid, and Wallace. Next, he points his camera at the soldiers and the remains of the caravan. He makes a point of snapping a close-up of Captain Tze on his horse.

The captain leads the caravan as it slowly winds its way through the maze of narrow, filthy streets. The residents cower in fear as it passes. A few who have never seen a white woman find the courage to stare at Ingrid and her red hair.

Matt moves to Wallace's side. They pass rundown barracks and grim-faced soldiers lounging about in dowdy, ill-fitting uniforms. The soldiers carry a mélange of primitive weapons—General Wu's army.

Matt whispers, "What I've seen so far is a piddling excuse for an army. This is not the image one gets of General Wu from the newsreels. With the Nationalists on the offensive, and the Japanese nearby, I see why he's offering the yellows for sale. He needs the money to build these vagabond pikers into a fighting army."

Wallace pouts a little at the indirect slight. "Of course, your assessment is correct, I must say." Wallace sits straighter in his saddle. "I understand that General Wu is well aware of what his army lacks. In fact, I am told, an agent of his is negotiating with several soldiers of fortune who are looking for a commission. These fellows are from Germany, Russia, and Great Britain. I believe Wu offers a handsome salary, an apartment in his personal compound, and a concubine or two." Wallace chuckles. "Art for guns, one might say."

"Indeed, one might," Matt retorts.

"Do not be deceived. General Wu is a crafty and intelligent soldier. He will counter the upcoming Nationalist offensive head-on. Wu is on his ground. General Chiang Kai-shek does not know this land, and his supply is a line that stretches long and far from his base." Wallace smacks his camel and scoots ahead.

By late afternoon, the travelers are standing in front of the gate to General Wu's compound. A stout hardwood fence topped with barbed wire surrounds the compound. Sentries spot the travelers, and the corporal-of-the-guard indicates that they are to enter. Servants from inside slowly open the massive door outward and escort the guests into a lavishly decorated courtyard. A magnificent manor rises before them—in stark contrast to the squalor in town.

Bright flowers outline the walkways, and ancient shade trees scatter the sunlight. Lisan trails three coolies toting the Occidentals' luggage.

Captain Tze approaches. "General Wu welcomes you to Ho Hsien and his humble home. The guest quarters are there, to the right. He is confident that they will be satisfactory." He indicates a cadre of servants standing by. "Our servants will escort you to your quarters. We have tried to stock your rooms with the amenities you might need. Bundle your laundry and your servant will process it and have it ready before the twilight ends."

Ingrid, somewhat awed at the splendor inside the compound and anxious to relax in comfortable quarters, comments, "Thank you, Captain Tze. That's most thoughtful."

Tze addresses Kendrick. "Mister Kendrick, General Wu requests the honor of your company at dinner this evening. Please bring Mister Drummond. Mister Chung already has his invitation."

Kendrick, somewhat puzzled, comments, "Captain, you did not mention my daughter's name, Mistress Ingrid Kendrick. She is also invited, I would assume."

Captain Tze has his orders. But they did not include this confrontation. He knows that the female is not invited and he does not know how to respond. An awkward silence prevails.

Wallace intervenes. "Mister Kendrick, sir, it would be inappropriate for Mistress Kendrick to attend dinner with us this evening. I'm sure that other arrangements have been made for her."

Kendrick bellows, "What the hell! Why is she not invited?"

Wallace tries to appease Kendrick. "Please be calm, Mister Kendrick, and understand. Culturally, it is unimaginable for a female to dine with us when we discuss business of great import."

Kendrick, with his ire rising, jams his index finger at Wallace. "Well, he can start imagining, Mister Chung! Either she attends or I do not! Is that unequivocally clear? Mistress Kendrick manages my business affairs. She will sit with us or else I'm heading for Peking. Understand?"

The silence stretches. Wallace looks back and forth between the motionless Tze and Kendrick. Neither flinches as the tension rises. Ingrid remains silent, but her eyes narrow and her lips press tight.

Matt says, "Wallace, listen up. You've got to be the tie-breaker here."

Wallace takes several deep breaths. He's determined not to let the deal of his lifetime crumble. He pulls a handkerchief from his pocket and pats his sweaty brow. "Mister Kendrick, I'm sure I can make a satisfactory arrangement." He looks at the manor as if he were seeking instructions. With pain on his face, Wallace continues, "By all means, please bring Mistress Kendrick with you."

Tze charges, "It is your decision, Chung." He addresses the guests. "We've made arrangements to bring you to dinner."

An hour later, the sun dips below the horizon. The refreshed Occidentals wait in front of their guest quarters for their escort to take them to General Wu's manor.

Kendrick is fashionably dressed in his 1920s tuxedo and his black bow tie is tied expertly. He has a half smile on his face as, unheard by others, the jazz tune "The Charleston" plays jauntily in his head.

Ingrid wears a brilliant emerald-green cocktail dress with long sleeves and a high bodice. For the first time in many days, she has applied some cosmetics—just enough to enhance her natural beauty. A whiff of Tabu perfume suffuses about her.

Matt wears a four-pocket, custom-tailored bush jacket, a white shirt, black tie, jodhpurs, and polished riding boots. He takes a few steps to stand next to Ingrid. "My, my, you do look positively spiffy this evening, *Mademoiselle.* If your dance card is not complete, may I escort you this evening?"

Ingrid smiles broadly and bats her green eyes, adopting a coquettish mien. "Shades of the Empire. Matt, you look as if you just stepped off the steamship from Indjiaah." She takes his arm and kisses him on the cheek. "Indeed, you're a hail-fellow-well-met, Mister 'down under.'"

Wallace Chung steps out of his room and says, "Good evening. Our transport to the house will be here shortly." He has managed somehow to have his white suit cleaned and pressed. He's as dapper as if he were hustling the marks in Peking.

General Wu's servants, dressed in fine silks, arrive with three ornate sedans.

Kendrick complains, "Three rickshaws! Where's the fourth?"

"They are sedans, Mister Kendrick," Wallace corrects.

"Whatever they are, we need one more. Or, are you going to walk, Chung?"

Matt intervenes. "No need. I'll squeeze in next to Ingrid."

Impatient, Kendrick says, "It matters not. Let's get going. Tell these fellows to giddyup."

The sedans arrive at General Wu's manor. It's surrounded by beautiful, tended gardens. Servants dash to help the dinner guests from the sedans and to escort them to the large front door, which is decorated with red, white, and blue bunting. Two sentries in smart uniforms and with fixed bayonets snap to attention. The clank of their rifle butts on the concrete entryway reverberates throughout the courtyard.

Kendrick nudges Drummond and comments, "Now, isn't this something? Finally, a little civilization and some military élan."

The door opens with a flourish, revealing General Wu standing with arms akimbo and legs apart. He is a tall, powerful-looking man with piercing black eyes and a "Fu Manchu" mustache partially hiding his moody mouth. He is dressed in full military regalia festooned with an array of medals and honors, some from the Qing Dynasty, some from nearby countries—all largely unearned—and some of his own design. He looks as if he were a character from a Gilbert and Sullivan comic opera.

He rushes forward to greet his guests.

Wallace bows respectfully. Wu lifts him up, grabs him in a bear hug, and speaks in passable English, with a rough edge to his voice.

"Welcome home, my number *one* son!"

The Occidentals gape at each other and are flabbergasted at this startling revelation.

Matt's surprise quickly turns to anger at Wallace's deception by omission. He blurts, "That scheming scoundrel! That stinking 'rotter'! I should have been more suspicious. This whole shebang of a trip for rare treasures now makes some sense. That 'bushranger' Chung has hoodwinked us. And God knows what else."

Kendrick, an old hand at chicanery, feels slightly amused at being duped by the young Chinaman. He says with admiration, "Damn, Wallace Chung. I take my hat off to you. You're a clever sonofabitch."

Ingrid is ready for a pleasant evening with interesting companions. She nudges Matt, "Calm down! I don't care who Wallace is—he's all those things and perhaps lots more. It's done. Let's eat and drink tonight and then get the yellows and get out of here tomorrow."

General Wu approaches Kendrick to shake his hand. He freezes when he spots Ingrid.

Wallace, ever ready to keep control, uses Mandarin to whisper in General Wu's ear. "Father, honorable sir, the American millionaire insisted that his daughter must join us. I tried to explain."

Wu mutters under his breath at first but, as his anger rises, so does his voice's volume. "There will be no female at my dinner table. It is intolerable!"

Wallace pleads, "Father, please be calm and lower your voice. Our Occidental guests will not understand. Think clearly. We need our army refreshed more than we need to uphold old traditions."

General Wu pauses and listens to the validity of Wallace's reasoning. His number one son makes sense. His anger subsides and he grabs Kendrick's hand with a vigorous handshake. "Everyone inside. Time to eat."

Wu hooks one arm around Kendrick's, and the other around Wallace's, as if he's escorting two potentates to dinner. Kendrick hides his discomfort at being so close to Wu, but accedes.

Ignored, Matt and Ingrid follow. She asks, "Any idea what's on the agenda?"

"No idea. Let's follow and find out. Game, ol' girl?"

24

General Wu's Compound, Ho Hsien, Kansu Province. 19 July 1935

The coterie enters a large, oval entryway opulently decorated with tap-estries depicting classic Chinese landscapes. A *maitre d'hôtel* dressed in white tie greets the party with a deep bow and shows them through the main hall and into the formal dining room. Big-band jazz tunes greet the diners from a wind-up gramophone. Male servants in stiffly starched, formal dinner attire bow even more deeply to honor the Occidentals. They escort each guest to brilliantly colored, silk-covered chairs surrounding a solid teak table trimmed in ebony and rosewood. One servant waits behind each diner's chair. The table is set with a pale-green silk tablecloth woven with threads of gold. Gold-rimmed dinnerware, pellucid crystal glasses, tall crystal flutes etched with animal scenes, and highly polished, antique sterling silverware complement the table setting. Flickering candles light the scene.

Kendrick emits a slow whistling sound. "Can you believe this lavish theatre in the middle of this miserable desert?"

Matt wonders how many lives are invested in the riches of this milieu. The ambiance and setting would do the Peninsula Hotel in Hong Kong proud.

Ingrid shakes her head back and forth in disbelief at the opulence of the table and instinctively begins to estimate the cost in United States dollars.

Matt nudges her gently and, with his eyes, he indicates the guest across the table in dark shadow. She is stunned to see that it's Black Viper. He is dressed in a rich, gold silk robe. He rises and manages a faint smile of recognition. The pair, though intently curious about his presence at Wu's dinner table, do not acknowledge him. Instead, Ingrid whispers in Matt's ear, "Any idea of why that bandit is here?"

"Not definitively. But, I suspect that there's skullduggery afoot. Last evening, I stumbled upon Wallace and him in a hushed conversation that positively rang with conspiratorial overtones."

General Wu, standing at the head of the table, sees that his guests are placed properly and are impressed with his extravagantly formal table setting—precisely correct according to proper British etiquette. "You are most welcome to my home, Mister Kendrick. And your family. We have a fine time tonight." Nodding towards the Black Viper, he introduces him with, "There is Chin Mao-shu, a longtime business associate."

Kendrick knows the Black Viper's reputation and just nods his head slightly to acknowledge the notorious bandit. He returns his look to General Wu, waiting for him to introduce Ingrid and Matt.

Instead, Wu sits down—a signal for the others to do so also. Wu claps his hands and, almost instantly, the servants pour champagne, chilled to forty-five degrees, into the crystal flutes. Other servants set several appetizer dishes filled with pan-fried dumplings, peanut zongzi, fried pork belly, and other offerings, on the table.

Wu raises his flute. "A toast to my new Occidental friends." He empties the flute in one gulp. The guests raise their flutes in a toast and sip the wine.

Matt tastes the wine generously. His eyes flicker with tacit approval. As the servant attempts to refill his flute, Matt takes his hand, turns the bottle, and examines the label: *"Krug, Brut, Grande Cuvèe, 1918."* He releases the servant's hand and widens his eyes in exclamation.

Ingrid cocks her head questioningly.

Matt, in a low voice, says, "I'm not a sommelier, but I know enough to understand that this champagne is extremely rare and outrageously expensive."

Wallace has watched Matt's inspection and overhears his comments. He interrupts with just a hint of sanctimony, "Not as barbarian as you thought, ol' chap."

Matt cracks, "My congratulations to your father for his fine wine cellar stocked with such a rare vintage." He pointedly turns away from Wallace and engages Ingrid in badinage regarding the wine, the extravagant scene, and its ambiance. Black Viper and other matters are of no import. They snack and listen to the music of the Paul Whiteman and Shep Field bands. Ingrid hums along with Field's arrangement of the Cole Porter tune *You'd be so Easy to Love,* and wonders if it's true.

The bandit sips his wine and remains mostly silent, keeping his own company. Nonetheless, he sagaciously observes the unfolding play.

Wu monopolizes Kendrick and recounts the intricate details of his fierce campaign in Meng-Chiang Province shortly after the revolution that overthrew the Qing Dynasty in 1912. Discussing the battle has conjured a troubling incident; he rubs his left shoulder vigorously.

Kendrick asks, "Arthritis?"

Wu's eyes glaze for an instant and he vaingloriously retorts, "No. A bullet from a Nationalist soldier—now with his ancestors." He empties his flute and immediately a servant refills it. "I was young and strong once. Able to kill a man with one hand. Only if he deserved it, of course." He smiles more to himself than to his guest. Reflexively he murmurs, "Too many battles. Too much chaos. Try my champagne."

Kendrick sips the wine, savors its excellent taste, and smiles generously. "General, this is excellent champagne. From France, I presume." Kendrick raises his right eyebrow, making his statement a question.

"Yes. From France." Wu drains his flute and continues, oblivious to the servant struggling behind his chair to refill his moving flute. "Last autumn, the train to Chang-yeh had an unfortunate accident. A few freight cars derailed several miles south of the town. Fortunately, I was nearby and salvaged several dozen cases marked for the French Legation." The look that creeps over his face speaks volumes. "It is curious because there is no French Legation in this province or any province west of Peking. Perhaps some scalawag was playing a scheme on the importer." He smiles and says, "Too bad." His smile enlarges singularly.

Sampling a different appetizer, Matt makes eye contact with the Black Viper but does not comment.

Seeing an opening, the Black Viper nods toward Ingrid and speaks in Mandarin.

"This woman is yours?"

Matt responds with an unequivocal, "Yes!" He dissembles because if he had not replied in the strong positive, Ingrid would surely be Black Viper's prize. Matt maintains steady eye contact with the Viper until the bandit grins and shrugs. Matt nods, confident now that since the bandit knows the female is "his," he will probably leave Ingrid alone.

A parade of servants laden with an array of bowls of exotic food arrives and places them around the table. General Wu speaks in a loud voice. "Eat. Do not be hungry. Enjoy my table."

Ingrid comments, "Dear Lord! We've just had the appetizers? This orgiastic feast just keeps coming."

Proudly, Wallace raises his glass and says, "As a matter of pride, my father is lavish with his guests."

The conversation fades, and the diners fill their plates with dishes Oriental and unknown. Guilt creeps over Ingrid as she feasts on this obscene bounty of delicacies. She recalls the gaunt look of the citizenry of Ho Hsien she had passed as she rode to this manor. Their expressions of despair matched Dorothea Lange's haunting photographs of Americans in the Dust Bowl in this Great Depression. Nonetheless, Ingrid continues to eat—fearful that if she does not, she'll offend their host.

Some minutes later, as the diners slowly continue to satiate their appetites, General Wu speaks. "Do not be hungry. Eat. Indulge. There is more coming."

Kendrick pushes his almost empty plate away. "Thank you, General. That's enough for me."

General Wu stares at Kendrick with questioning eyes. "You are not satisfied with my food?" He gestures at the other diners, who continue to eat. "What would you want? I'll have it prepared instantly for you."

"General, many thanks for your superb dinner. I've tasted all your plates and they are delicious. But, I've had my fill." He glances at Ingrid and Matt, and sees that they too are completing their meals. "We are much obliged for your generous hospitality."

"No more food, eh? Too bad. I have more prepared in the kitchen." Somewhat mystified by the Occidental's meager appetite, he concludes, "Very well. Now, drink. I have more bottles of this champagne chilled and waiting for you."

Kendrick smiles, pats his own stomach conspiratorially and, in his best political voice, says, "General Wu, may I decline your kind invitation? I have enjoyed this fine meal perhaps too much."

Wu draws back. His servants pull away their bottles.

Matt intercedes, and whispers in Kendrick's ear, "Do not offend our host. Accept his offer of champagne. Sip slowly if you must, but accept."

Kendrick quickly nods. Understanding the protocol, he says, "On second thought, yes, indeed, I'll have more of your delicious champagne. General Wu, your hospitality is superb. I've never had such a fine meal. My compliments."

Wu cracks a large smile. The servants push forward with their bottles. He has won the first round. "It is my pleasure to serve you. Now drink."

Kendrick complies and then leans in slightly. "May we talk business about the Ming yellow porcelains? I would like to see them, if that's convenient."

Matt overhears and interjects, "Kendrick, you ought not to talk business while we are dining. It's not seemly. Later, please."

Frustrated, Kendrick says, "Damn. Too many customs in this country for my liking."

General Wu, half-tipsy, guffaws. "How true, my American friend."

Wallace turns to Ingrid. "It appears that our fathers are getting along famously. Their business should be harmonious."

Ingrid surveys the scene. Her father's body language tells her that he is uneasy parlaying with General Wu. *He's fidgety and not drinking much— not his style.* Across the table, she sees Captain Tze in his military uniform standing next to the wall. *Why is he not joining us? I'm perplexed by this* opéra bouffe, *and I do not understand the subtle interplay.*

Suddenly, Wu bellows a command. A servant changes the record on the gramophone to Tchaikovsky's *Swan Lake.* Seven beautiful courtesans, dressed in skintight cheongsams, gracefully enter the room. Three of them give a startled gasp when they see Ingrid. Wu claps, spurring them to start their sinuous dance.

Startled at their erotic movements, Ingrid grabs a champagne bottle, fills her flute, and swigs it down. She nudges Matt in the ribs, and coquettishly charges, "Don't you dare lust after them." She offers the bottle to Wallace, but he places his hand over his glass.

General Wu notices that his son has refused a drink from a female, and leans towards Kendrick and says, "I fear your daughter is more of a man than my son will ever be."

Kendrick accepts the general's comment as a compliment. He smiles broadly, but suspects that there is a subtext in Wu's message that he cannot savvy.

Following through, Wu presses his shoulder into Kendrick's. "How many sons have you?"

"Ingrid is my only child. Her mother died in childbirth."

General Wu responds, "Most unfortunate, I extend my sympathies."

"It was a long time ago. My wounds have healed. I've been both father and mother to Ingrid and she has become a loving and compassionate daughter. My pride and joy."

Now crassly curious, the General asks, "And how many wives?"

Kendrick, surprised at Wu's question, responds, "Only one. Just Ingrid's mother."

Wu is taken aback. "My heart breaks for you. No number one son and no wives."

"It's all right. My number one daughter is the love of my life. Ingrid is smart and tough and manages my business with professional competence—better than any man could. And one of these days, not too soon I hope, she will own it."

"With no wives, do your concubines substitute suitably?"

"General Wu, I have no concubines. It is not the custom of Westerners to own females."

General Wu does not know how to respond to this alien concept. He takes another deep draft of champagne. "I was not tough enough with my number one son. I have doubts that he can take my place and keep Kansu under our family's control. He has had too much education and not enough fighting."

Kendrick, trying to appease the General, says, "So far, he's done okay. Perhaps there is more character in your son than is apparent."

Suddenly, the servant serving Wallace draws a Beretta 32-millimeter subcompact pistol and aims it at General Wu.

Unobtrusively, Captain Tze has been standing behind this servant with his saber drawn and tucked by his side. Seeing the fellow draw his pistol, Captain Tze impales the man with his weapon, sending the assassin's shot awry.

Ingrid immediately looks to her father, startled by the loud report. "Dad! Dad, are you all right?"

Matt grabs her about the shoulders and he forces her to the floor, where he covers her body with his.

The courtesans and servers scurry away.

Wu stands to see what is causing the ruckus. With reflexive action, the indomitable Kendrick tackles Wu and they hit the floor hard.

The potential assassin falls to the floor next to where Wallace crouches. Captain Tze kneels over the dying fellow.

The mortally wounded assassin, with his final burst of energy, stares at Wallace with lifeless eyes and with his dying breath mumbles, "Wu dead?"

Captain Tze glares at Wallace and then wipes his saber across Wallace's napkin. He flicks his saber toward his older brother. "Wallace, this is your doing! With a nod from father, I'll run you through."

Wallace turns away from his brother, tears dripping down his cheeks. In a whimper, he appeals to his father. "I am innocent, father. I do not know this assassin."

Wu stands now with his arms akimbo. He did not need to hear what the assassin said to understand what almost happened.

Matt, Ingrid, and Kendrick huddle in a tight group. They are horrified at the bloody action and unsure what to do. Ingrid murmurs nervously, "We can't continue this dinner. Let's get out of here. This yellow porcelain deal is finished."

Kendrick puts a steadying hand on her arm and snaps, "Easy, Ingrid. Don't make a rash move. Let's see how the rest of this kerfuffle plays. We've come too far and endured too many arduous days on this journey. The yellows are here and in our reach. Now is not the time to quash the deal."

Matt interjects, "Instinctively, I agree with Ingrid. We are on a dubious mission fraught with bugaboo and danger." He shrugs. "But we've got too much invested to quit this near to closing the deal. Besides, how do we know that General Wu would even release us? Much less provide a caravan and escort back to Chang-yeh. We are totally in his power. He could kidnap us, or worse."

Ingrid, now calmer, says, "Very well. We'll stick together and complete this adventure to its end, one way or the other. Deal?"

Taking control of the room, General Wu waves his hand and shouts commands. Two bodyguards rush in and drag the assassin's body away.

Wu returns to his chair, empties his flute, and commands, "Sit. Eat! Everyone eat. Have more wine. Sorry for the interruption." Servants quickly refill his flute and the flutes of the others.

Matt winks at Ingrid and comments, "This is insane. Will nothing stop this dinner?"

Wu raises his glass and looks at his guests. "A toast to our friendship, my Occidental friends."

Kendrick quickly finds his glass and returns the gesture. He gives Ingrid and Matt a look imploring them to join the toast.

All empty their flutes, and the Occidentals sigh with partial relief now that calm has returned to the dining room. Nonetheless, a leaden pall imbues the atmosphere throughout the room.

Wallace, engulfed in fear, is near catatonic. He stares at his plate. Captain Tze goes to General Wu and speaks to him in a low voice.

General Wu glares at his number one son.

Wallace cannot face his father.

Finally, General Wu reaches across the table and slaps Wallace in the face as hard as he can, knocking him reeling. Then he calmly addresses the Occidentals. "My number one son schemed to have me assassinated this evening! He could not wait for nature, or for a Nationalist or Japanese bullet." He makes a toast. "My heartfelt thanks to my number two son, Captain Tze, who dispatched the assassin before he could complete his foul deed."

Kendrick asks Wu, with an incredulous look at the taciturn captain, "Captain Tze is your son? What's next?"

Ingrid and Matt are as surprised as he. Matt says, "I should have expected this surprise in this Byzantine maze we've entered." With finality he asks, "Where is Lewis Carroll's rabbit hole?"

Tze speaks. "Father, I recognized this assassin posing as our servant. We were students at Whampoa Military Academy in Canton. He was in the class two years ahead of me. Fortunately, he did not recognize me because seniors did not socialize with underclassmen. Clearly, he is a spy in the pay of Colonel Peng's Nationalist Intelligence Agency. I did not act until I knew what his play was." Captain Tze glares at Wallace, who now is slumped in his chair with his head on the table. Tze places the point of his saber against the nape of Wallace's neck. "You, my brother, were going to deliver Ho Hsien and all of Kansu province to the Nationalists. Is that not so, my father's number one son? How much gold has Colonel Peng promised you?"

A shaking Wallace points a trembling hand to Captain Tze. "Father, can you not see what your number two son is doing? He is attempting to steal my birthright."

General Wu glares at Wallace a moment longer, heartbroken, in stark disbelief that his number one son would engineer an assassination attempt. Recovered, he points to Wallace, and he orders his bodyguards, "Take the traitor out of my sight."

Two bodyguards grab Wallace's arms. He thrashes about wildly and pleads with his father. "No, Father, I did not do it. It was Tze. Father, don't do this. I have not betrayed you."

Without compassion, Wu commands, "Put that running dog in the corner cell."

Wallace screams and flails about more furiously as the bodyguards drag him away. He screams at his brother. "Tze, I will kill you! You'll see. I will kill you."

An uneasy silence grips the room. The Occidentals empty their flutes nervously. Matt can't help but wonder how the next scene in this morbid melodrama will unfold. He leans over and whispers to Ingrid, "I hope the general doesn't have any more sons."

The Black Viper had sat unmoving throughout the botched assassination, seemingly unfazed. He continues silently picking at his meal with deliberate precision. Nonetheless, he astutely assesses the brouhaha and devises a plan to best turn it to his advantage.

General Wu, still standing, issues a final command—causing Ingrid and Matt to flinch. "Enough of this theatre. Dinner is over. Time to see my Ming yellows. Follow me." He rises and quits the dining room. The guests hustle to follow him.

25

General Wu's Compound, Ho Hsien, Kansu Province. 19 July 1935

General Wu leads his guests to the rear of the manor. As they pass through a conservatory, Ingrid sees that this room has a large skylight. Wu pauses in front of a locked steel door and Tze hands him a key. Wu opens the door, then cautions the Occidentals, "Proceed carefully. We will descend a dozen steel steps into an underground room. The steps are lit only with two oil lamps."

A few minutes later, the group is standing in front of an inner chamber secured by a heavy steel door. Wu digs deep in his robe's pocket, withdraws a large key, and inserts it in the ancient lock. He swings the massive slab open on squeaky hinges. The room is pitch black. Servants scurry in with lit lanterns. A large teak table in the center of the chamber stands as an altar to a Ming patrician. It's covered with a black silk cloth. On it, the twenty Ming yellow porcelains seem to float in a harmonious tableau.

The flickering lanterns' light generates a dramatic chiaroscuro. Matt nods, his photographer's eye impressed by the general's grandiose display. He studies the shifting shadows on Wu's face and now understands Wallace's charlatan nature—it's an inheritance of immense wealth.

Kendrick gasps, awestruck by the majesty of the milieu. He moves to the table and stares at the treasures—the *raison d'être* for this accursed trip to the ends of the earth. *Damn. It was worth it.* He's tempted to reach for the yellows and caress them but understands that it would be inappropriate. With keen appreciation, he finally whispers, "Most impressive, General. Most impressive."

Wu smiles broadly with pride at his yellow porcelains and tries to anticipate the exceptional bounty his ill-gotten treasure will fetch. He offers, "Please, Mister Kendrick, you may examine my porcelains."

Kendrick gravitates to the most spectacular piece, the large vase. As he is about to touch it, Ingrid whispers in his ear. Kendrick nods in agreement and steps away from the table.

"General Wu, we are privileged to see this magnificent art. Unfortunately, because the light is flickering and dim, I cannot view these yellows clearly enough to evaluate them." He pauses to form his next response with professional respect. "May I suggest that you have these yellows moved to your conservatory?" His hands grip emptily and he forces himself to look away. "Tomorrow morning, when we return, the sunlight will highlight their beauty."

General Wu considers Kendrick's suggestion. "Of course. You make an excellent point. I am embarrassed that I did not plan to display the yellows there. Tomorrow that table and the yellows will be in the conservatory." He cracks a crooked smile. "Now I have a special treat for my special guests."

Led by General Wu, the Occidentals exit his manor and enter the courtyard. About midway, they spot the courtesans arrayed in a line. Ingrid nudges Matt, "What's happening now? Why are these women waiting here?"

"Don't know. Wu is a devious fellow, for sure, and there's no point in second-guessing his schemes."

General Wu grabs Kendrick by the shoulder and points to the courtesans. "Honored guest, you choose. Which one would please you the most? Two, perhaps?"

Ingrid is mortified that Wu would devise such an unseemly proposal. Wu's act is a direct insult to her. She grabs Kendrick's arm, and with intensity demands, "Dad, let's get out of here. I'm incensed that General Wu would proffer these whores to you. We'll have no part of this charade."

Wu sees that Ingrid is markedly agitated, and smiles at her discomfort. *Western females are too prudish and do not understand the nature of our ancient customs.*

Kendrick, with his most professional mien, grips his daughter's hand hard and looks her in the eye until he's confident she'll calm and remain silent. Then he smiles at Wu. "Thanks for your generous hospitality, General, but I must respectfully decline your kind invitation. I've had a long and hard day and I need to rest."

General Wu's wide smile withers on his face. He makes a show of inspecting the girls before grumbling at Kendrick's refusal of his generosity. "Do they not please you? I will order more to appear."

Kendrick flushes with embarrassment at this scene in front of his daughter.

Matt, sensing how bad the scene could become and with insight into Chinese customs, enjoins, "Kendrick, please. At least approach one of these women and pretend to give her a once-over. If not, your refusal would show great disrespect to the General and most likely will hinder your purchase of the yellows."

"Damn it, Matt, these bizarre Chinese customs confound me. How can I explain my embarrassment to Ingrid and assuage her obvious distress?"

"Tomorrow morning we'll tackle that problem. Now, we'd best at least pretend to accept General Wu's gracious hospitality. He's waiting for you at the end of the concubines' line."

Captain Tze, who has followed the Occidentals, notices Ingrid's discomfort. He goes to her and chivalrously puts his arm out for her to take.

She tries to smile in appreciation, but cannot. Her distress overwhelms her. She manages a quiet, "Thank you, Captain Tze," and takes his arm. They begin walking to her quarters. She turns around for a moment and sees one of the courtesans flirting with Matt. Ingrid quickly turns away and, with a quickened pace, breaks away from Tze and flees to her room with tears in her eyes.

26

General Wu's Compound, Ho Hsien, Kansu Province. 19 July 1935

Two guards with fixed bayonets stand guard over Wallace's prison cell. The new moon has slipped behind a tall cumulus cloud—Wallace's cell disappears in the inky night shadows.

Wallace sits on the cot in his dungeon-like cell, unhinged that his plot has failed. *In all probability, my father will have me killed tomorrow, most likely by crucifixion.* He wonders if the rest of his scheme is still viable.

The Black Viper and two of his gang sneak up behind the guards. Without a sound, they slit the guards' throats. The Black Viper tears the key ring off the belt of one of the fallen guards and opens the squeaking cell door.

Wallace, in wonderment, eases toward the door, unsure how his ally views him now. "I am surprised that you are here, Chin. After the assassination failure, I imagined that you would abandon me to my father's justice."

Shaking his fist at Wallace, the Black Viper demands, "Be quiet, you dolt!" But, he softens when Chung cringes back into his cell. In a quieter tone he continues, "There's still much to do, my craven ally. Perhaps in the next phase you will be more adroit." The bandit and his men grab Wallace and they escape into the night before the weak moon emerges from the clouds.

27

General Wu's Compound, Ho Hsien, Kansu Province. 20 July 1935

The rising sun has just peeked over the horizon and faint sunlight bathes the compound. It's filled with Wu's soldiers in full battle dress standing at attention next to their horses. Captain Tze forms them into six-man squads and issues search instructions to the corporals. On his command, they mount and canter out of the compound to search for Wallace Chung and the Black Viper gang.

The ruckus wakens Matt. He rises and watches the soldiers ride away. *What the dickens is going on? Maneuvers? And why are those soldiers standing guard around this area? Odd, but so what. I have more pressing concerns. Ingrid!*

Matt approaches the door to her room. He almost turns away, hesitates, and then knocks lightly. There is no answer. He knocks again—this time with more energy. Again, there is no response. With his frustration building, he asks, "Ingrid, are you awake?"

Ingrid responds in a raspy voice, "Yes. Go away. Leave me alone."

Matt puts his hand on the doorknob. There are no locks on the doors of the guest quarters. He slowly opens the squeaky door and peeks inside the dark room. Ingrid sits up and stares at him. Her eyes are puffy and red.

He waits just inside the doorway, and his expression is that of a mischievous child caught in a forbidden pursuit.

"What are you doing here?" She demands.

He says softly, "I'm checking to make sure you are safe, after all that happened last evening."

Ingrid says, with more energy, "I'm fine, and I've nothing to say to you." She begins to sob. "Get out! You whoremonger."

"You're jealous because of the—"

"Go back to your slut!"

"Those women are not whores. They are courtesans."

"Spare me the lesson in Chinese culture."

"Jealous? Come on, Ingrid, jealousy is not your style."

She snarls through her tears, "Don't be ridiculous!"

"I'm here to explain."

"Get out!" She throws the pillow at him. It misses.

He ducks, nevertheless. "Very well." Matt retrieves her projectile and tosses it back to her. "I know you care for me."

Ingrid throws everything she can reach at him. She is enraged because his comment is true, and she is wounded deeply that Matt would consort with such a female, almost in her presence. *He has no shame.* "Such conceit, Mister Matthew Drummond." When she runs out of projectiles, she takes a moment and pushes her hair back off her face. "I'll have you know that I find the Black Viper more attractive than you."

Her remark stings Matt, and he realizes that it's time to be forthright. "Please listen, Mistress Ingrid Kendrick. Nothing happened last evening. It was all pretend. Your father and I went through with the charade to keep General Wu pleased. I would imagine that the nattering in his seraglio this morning is quite bountiful."

Ingrid realizes that her improvident jealousy was unfounded and has hurt the man she deeply cares for. Wiping away her tears she says, "Damn you, Matt. Come here."

俾咆,

As the sun rises higher over Wu's compound and the desert warms, Matt hears a quiet knock on Ingrid's door.

"Who is there?"

"It is Lisan, Mister Drummond, with important news."

Not wanting to further embarrass Ingrid, Matt says, "Stand by. I'm coming outside."

After the dim, curtained twilight of Ingrid's room, the sun hits his wide-open eyes hard. Squinting deeply, he asks, "What is this news, Lisan?"

"Sir, I do not mean to disturb you. But you should know that the soldiers guarding Wallace Chung are dead. Their throats are slashed! And Mister Chung and the Black Viper have disappeared." He looks about. "General Wu's soldiers are after them."

"Zounds!" Matt exclaims. "What's next? Thank you, Lisan. Be watchful and report any unusual activity."

"Yes, sir."

Matt retreats inside Ingrid's room and briefs her on the developing scenario.

"Damn, Matt, what conspiracies have we plunged into?"

"Don't know. However, I'm leery. We can be sure that those two scoundrels are up to deviltry of some sort."

Kendrick comes out of his room also roused by the military activity. He sees soldiers standing guard about the compound. Alarmed, he knocks on Ingrid's room. "Ingrid, it's your father. Armed soldiers are guarding the compound."

"I've heard. I'll be out shortly. I'm dressing."

"Where's Drummond? Is he still asleep?"

"Kendrick, I'm here." Matt adjusts his shirt. "I'm coming out."

Kendrick comments, "I suspect that this martial activity has something to do with last evening's family reunion."

Matt affirms Kendrick's supposition, "You are correct. Earlier this morning, Lisan told me, Wallace escaped. The Black Viper killed the two guards, released Wallace, and they rode away."

Kendrick, puzzled, asks, "You reckon—"

Ingrid continues Kendrick's thought, "That the General thinks that we had anything to do with the assassination attempt?"

Matt interjects, "Not hardly. Wu is a 'smart cookie'. He'd realize that there is no gain for us to pull such an untoward stunt."

Captain Tze approaches Ingrid's open doorway. Two soldiers nearby snap to attention and salute. He does not return the salutes, rather he addresses the Occidentals. "Good morning. I trust you slept well."

Kendrick answers with a touch of pique. "Considering the contretemps of last evening, I'd say we're surprisingly okay. We have a general notion of what happened last evening. Please recount the details."

Tze says, "Regretfully, I am sorry to say that there was murder in our compound last night. It appears that the Black Viper killed two of my men and released my brother. Both have escaped into the desert. Wallace is now a fugitive and in company with the Black Viper and his marauders. He will be gravely dangerous. I am sending patrols to search for their tracks."

Kendrick asks, "Will these events hinder our purchase of the yellows?"

"Not at all." He backs out of the doorway and says, "Now, if you will follow me, General Wu is waiting to offer you a meal to break your fast and to continue your business regarding the yellow porcelains."

The victuals consist of coffee, cakes with honey, and figs—enough to satiate the Occidentals' hunger. Kendrick is fidgety—anxious to conclude the sale.

Wu enters the dining room. "Good morning." He sees their empty dishes. "Finished, I see. Excellent." He jams his fists on his hips and thrusts out his chest. "Forget last night's unpleasantness with those scoundrels. Not to worry, we have everything under control." He winks at Kendrick and grins. He commands, "Now we go see the yellows."

Captain Tze leads the guests to the conservatory. Two servants open the door and bow deeply to welcome the Occidentals. Kendrick immediately spots the dazzling Ming yellows. Each piece shines in the clear morning light and highlights bounce off the porcelains in a kaleidoscope of yellow and dark reflections. Kendrick emits an involuntary whisper in amazement at the tableau.

Ingrid and Matt stare at the yellows' sparkling beauty. She takes Matt's hand and squeezes it hard. The infinitely deep yellow glaze electrifies their senses. "My God! Have you ever seen anything so radiantly beautiful? They're amazing. I could not have imagined that these yellows were so spectacular." She pulls Matt a little closer. "Perhaps our trip was worth the torture."

Matt whispers, "I'm astonished. Their elegant artistry truly is *nonpareil.*" He focuses on the large vase—the prize of the collection. Some seconds later he whispers, "I'm benumbed by the yellows' depth and intensity. It's unnatural. It's a phantom." He returns Ingrid's squeezes. "Perhaps there are spirits in the Celestial Kingdom." He straightens up and nods with a smile. "You're correct. This trip is well worth the adversity we've endured."

Wu, anxious to get the business started, suggests, "Mister Kendrick, approach the table and inspect my Ming yellow porcelains. Please to see the depth of the yellow. Does it not dance before your eyes?" With his paw-like hand, he gestures toward the collection. "Please check the inscriptions to confirm that they are authentic."

Kendrick and Matt carefully examine the yellows piece by piece, checking the designs and symmetry, and looking to see that they are free from cracks and chips and have consistent depth of color. Matt uses his ten-power loupe to study the orthography on their bases and checks them against the photographs. Some of the glyphs are faint, others are bright and clear. Finally, Matt comments, "Kendrick, you know that I'm not an expert on Ming porcelains. The inscriptions seem to be authentic. Accordingly, I would conclude that these yellows probably are genuine—'dinkum,' as we'd say 'down under.'"

General Wu says, "You see that my yellows are authentic? Yes? It's time for business."

Kendrick avers, "Let's."

General Wu says, "Please to understand that all bids will be in British pounds sterling."

Ingrid is caught off guard by the word "bids." "What?" She cries. But in the excitement of the moment, her exclamation falls on deaf ears. Soon she dismisses her concern. *Probably Wu misspoke because of his poor English skills.* She wonders, though, why Wu wants payment in British currency and not in U.S. dollars or in gold troy ounces. All eyes watch her, waiting. She knows that hunger in her father's eyes and realizes that all she can do is try to keep him from spending his entire fortune. Ingrid understands clearly that she does not have any leverage against Wu. She says, "Agreed."

Kendrick, anxious to conclude the deal, blurts, "I offer 50,000 pounds for these yellows." Confident that General Wu will accept his offer, he cracks a big smile and approaches the table to pick up a bowl.

A loud voice booms from a dark corner in the conservatory, "75,000 pounds."

"What the hell," spouts Kendrick. He spins around and sees Wuhan Wei-ku walking out of the shadows and toward the yellows.

"Wuhan?" Matt sputters.

Wuhan responds, "Indeed, I am he." With a sly smile and to announce that he is a player, he continues, "I am Wuhan Wei-ku, the proprietor of the Antiks shop in Peking. I am most pleased to visit with you again."

Kendrick, alarmed and seeing his cheap buy fade, shouts into the antique dealer's face. "Hells bells! What are you doing here, Wuhan? How did you get here? What's your game, Chinaman?"

Wuhan pretends to ignore the affront and responds with calm, "Mister Kendrick, I am here to bid on the Ming yellows. More details later, perhaps. Let's proceed with the business at hand."

But Kendrick now angrily demands, "Whom do you represent? Yourself? Someone else? Answer me!"

Wuhan, stoic as usual, replies, "I am not at liberty to say. May we continue with the bidding?"

General Wu watches their exchange with a large smile, relishing his little joke on the Occidentals.

Kendrick, frustrated beyond reason, insists, "Tell me, or I'll choke it out of you. You devious Chink."

Disregarding the threat from the raving barbarian, Wuhan calmly responds, "I must respect my client's confidentiality. Suffice to say, I represent an honorable collector from the great city of New York."

Kendrick backs off and tries to regain his composure. "Damnation! It's Wickham. Gaspar Wickham. That bastard. I'll beat him. He'll not get these yellows."

Ingrid lets all of her frustration explode at their host's double-cross. "General Wu, we risked our necks to come here and to negotiate in good faith for these yellows. Now you hoodwink us? You tricked us. It's not professional! Or honorable."

General Wu's smile hardens. Women do not address him so. He regains his composure—not wanting to compromise this bidding war he's so carefully orchestrated. "Mistress Kendrick, neither my son nor I have guaranteed you anything except an opportunity to purchase the yellows. You are a businesswoman and know that competition gets the best price."

She says to her father, "The general has duped us grandly." She pauses to regroup. "We've no choice. Might as well continue."

Neither Ingrid nor Kendrick is sure what their next action should be.

Matt pulls the pair into a huddle and whispers, "There is a bright side to this episode. If Wuhan is bidding this kind of money on these yellows, we can be assured that they are authentic."

General Wu says, "It is time to continue. Mister Wuhan bids 75,000 pounds. Mister Kendrick, your bid."

Ingrid stammers, "Father, …"

Kendrick squeezes Matt's shoulder and nods. He's decided Wuhan acting as Gaspar Wickham's cat's paw doesn't matter. All that he cares about is getting those yellows. With his resolve fixed firmly, he spouts, "100,000 pounds."

Wuhan replies, "150,000 pounds."

"200,000 pounds," affirms Kendrick in a too loud voice.

Matt silently exclaims, *That's one million U.S. dollars. This is insane.*

Wuhan counters, "300,000 pounds."

Ingrid, now seriously alarmed, shouts to no one in particular, "Dear God! That is a million and a half United States dollars." Only Matt listens. She sighs deeply. "We're in a deep economic depression."

Ingrid and Kendrick look at each other. She pleads with her father, "Dad, that's enough. Quit. Let's get out of here and go home."

Ignoring her entreaty and with firm resolution, Kendrick bellows, "400,000 pounds." Wuhan does not respond immediately. The American smiles briefly because he sees Wuhan falter.

Wuhan recovers. "450,000 pounds."

Kendrick pauses and looks at Ingrid. He knows now that he can win.

Understanding that Kendrick has his mind locked, she comments with a smile in defeat, "You've come this far. What's the difference now, another 100,000 pounds or so? This is not the time to resign. Think of what we've been through to get here."

Emboldened by his daughter's words, Kendrick takes a deep breath and with resolution, he bids in a loud and clear voice, "500,000. One half million British pounds sterling. Genuine coin of the realm, as it were."

Wuhan is stoic. He mentally evaluates his instructions from Wickham once more. Already he is over the New York man's limit. Wuhan looks at General Wu and shakes his head negatively. "I cannot continue." He goes to Kendrick and shakes his hand vigorously. "Congratulations, Mister Kendrick. You are a worthy opponent. Please consider me as your agent for your next purchase."

"Thanks, Wuhan. You did Wickham well. You're a cagey and perceptive opponent."

Kendrick and Ingrid hug. An ecstatic Kendrick slaps Matt on the back. "Wahoo! We did it. A pretty price for such little things. Wickham is going to have an apoplectic fit." Kendrick beams at his new treasure. "Wow!"

General Wu shakes Kendrick's hand to seal the deal. "I commend you for your excellent play on the bidding for the yellows. Only you could conclude this business with such purpose." The General is ecstatic. The price he realized for the yellows is far more than he had hoped. *Indeed, competition brings the best return.*

Matt uses his Leica camera to thoroughly document each yellow piece and to capture images of the participants as well as the ambiance of the scene.

Ingrid seizes the moment. "Thank you, General. We must make arrangements for shipping the yellows."

The general interjects, "First, we'll discuss payment." He smiles. "You will make the deposit to Captain Tze's account in Barclays Bank in Peking."

Ingrid responds, "That arrangement is acceptable—with a caveat. I will make the deposit to your son's account only when I have confirmed that the yellows have arrived, are without damage, and are safely stored in the Pacific and Orient's Customs House at Tsingtao. And not before."

General Wu scowls. *This white witch needs to be taught manners. A good flogging, perhaps?* Realizing that she has set the terms without compromise, and he has no choice, he nods in agreement. "And what deposit will you make? Twenty percent would be acceptable."

She counters forcefully, "There is no deposit, General Wu. We are not stupid enough to bring that sort of cash with us. You know very well who my father is. His word is his bond. No guarantees are necessary."

General Wu has no leverage, and he knows it. He desperately needs the money to rebuild his army for the upcoming conflicts with the Nationalists and the Japanese. He addresses Kendrick. "You do indeed have a number one daughter. She will run your business admirably. I envy you with such good fortune."

Kendrick smiles. "Thank you, General. My daughter is a far better businessman than I." He takes her hand and squeezes. "I'm very proud of her."

General Wu continues. "To ensure the safety of your party and the yellows, I have ordered Captain Tze to go with a squad of his best-trained soldiers to escort you to the railhead at Chang-yeh."

Ingrid interrupts, "Chang-yeh! Not good enough, General. We and the yellows need protection all the way to Peking and then to the port at Tsingtao." She pauses for emphasis. Then she speaks in her determined voice, "I demand it!"

Captain Tze looks to his father with a question in his eyes.

Wu frowns deeply. *That female!* Reluctantly, he nods positively.

Tze enters the conversation. "Mistress Kendrick, I will provide protection for you and the yellows all the way to the Custom House."

Wuhan interjects, "Mister Kendrick, may I have the pleasure of your company to the railroad station at Chang-yeh?"

Kendrick responds, "Of course, Wuhan. We have lots to discuss. I can always use a man of your skills."

2日

Lamasery, Yü-men, Kansu Province. 20 July 1935

aptain Tze leads the small caravan along the ancient camel trail en route to the lamasery at Yü-men. This afternoon, the blistering sun bathes the caravan in intense heat. The nonmilitary part of the caravan consists of five camels: three bearing the Occidentals, one for Wuhan, and one for Lisan. The herders ride stout Mongolian horses. In the center of the caravan are the herders with the five pack mules laden with their precious Ming yellow cargo. Before they began their journey, Tze had cautioned the herders to be especially diligent. "Take no chances."

Scattered about the caravan are twelve of General Wu's best-trained soldiers. Scouts ride far in front and outriders are on both sides.

Preparing the yellow porcelains for the long and rough trip to the railhead at Chang-yeh took far longer than Tze anticipated. Porters wrapped the yellows in several layers of straw, covered them with tarpaulins, and secured all with stout ropes. Accordingly, the caravan departed Ho Hsien several hours later than Tze had planned. He urges the column to move at a hard pace, determined to reach the lamasery before the monks close the massive oak doors at sunset. *I do not want my charges to spend the night in the desert. Black Viper and the renegade Wallace Chung probably are in the area.*

Kendrick is beaming. He congratulates himself on closing the deal. *The Ming yellows are mine! I've trumped that scoundrel Gaspar Wickham.* He looks once more at the five pack mules. *Let's see him top this coup. So what if I paid significantly more that I should have? It matters not. I've got them—that's what counts.* The mountains burn in the lowering sun. *These yellows will be the highlight of my collection.*

Matt and Ingrid ride side by side and review the morning's proceedings. Though pleased for her father, Ingrid worries that she'll have to sell assets to raise the 2.5 million dollars to pay for these trinkets. After a while, she reckons that the most likely candidates to sell are the gold mines in Portuguese Mozambique, British Southwest Africa, and the Italian Somaliland. She's been thinking about liquidating them anyway. Two years ago, President Roosevelt had signed an Executive Order that forbad ownership of gold in any form by individuals or any type of organization. *Yes, that's what I'll do.*

She discusses her decision with Matt, primarily to hear if the deal makes sense when described aloud.

Matt, not skilled in the intricacies of high finance, cannot comment with cogency. "I reckon it's okay. Gold still is viable in the British Commonwealth."

She arches her brow and decides she doesn't expect Matt to be proficient at everything. Then she moves the topic to the damned heat, then to nothing in particular.

Kendrick spots Wuhan riding slightly behind him. He makes a hand signal to Wuhan to ride in close beside him. Kendrick smiles at the crafty old man. "Tell me, Wuhan, were you in Ho Hsien before me? When we spoke in Peking, Mister Drummond and I thought that you were unaware of this yellow sale. Fill me in."

"Actually, I arrived at the same time as you. Wallace Chung had contacted me several weeks ago—knowing that I had worldwide clients interested in Oriental art. He told me about a patron of his who had these Ming yellows for sale. He gave me the yellows' inventory and showed me that saucer. I verified its authenticity by the inscriptions. I based my conclusion in large measure on Mister Drummond's excellent close-up photography. Mister Chung suggested that I remain incognito—reckoning that you'd have a singular obsession with purchasing these porcelains. I contacted several of my clients about the yellows. Alas, only Mister Wickham expressed interest at the estimated price I thought might be the successful bid. After intense negotiations, he and I made the deal. Mister Chung contacted his patron, and he agreed to participate in our charade."

Kendrick exclaims, "Damnation! That duplicitous Chung is a clever scallywag. I give him credit for that. Tell me, how did you get to Ho Hsien?"

"It was quite simple. I was on the same train as you. However, to cloak my identity, I rode in the third-class railroad car with the servants. At Chang-yeh, I melded with the pilgrims in the caravan. I saw the members of your party several times." With a twist of a smile, he continues, "All we Chinamen look the same to the Occidentals. Not so?"

"Well, I'll be...." Kendrick cracks a big smile. "You fellows surely did hoodwink me. Congratulations on a most successful ploy." He pauses to formulate the final twist. "But I got the yellow porcelains."

"So you have." Wuhan gracefully falls behind as Matt, who has overheard the conversation, sidles next to Kendrick. "Hoodwinked, indeed. Wallace, Wuhan, and General Wu played a skillful hand and duped all of us—the worldly Occidentals. The Chinese are clever businessmen. Yet we continue to underestimate them and seldom do we best them. Wuhan said it correctly. Such is the price we pay for not respecting them as equals and individuals."

"Very perceptive, Aussie." But Kendrick is not amused. "Life's little lessons." He turns to watch his treasure for a while. "Go keep Ingrid company. I'm in no mood for your 'down under' wit."

The sun is low on the horizon and long shadows on the desert stretch until they seem to march in time with Tze's pace. The caravan slowly winds its way to Yü-men. Captain Tze nods at the discipline of his handpicked soldiers.

Ingrid and Matt are again riding side by side. With her cotton hand-kerchief, she wipes the perspiration from her brow. "Damn this heat. I as-sure you this is the last desert trip I'll ever take."

Ingrid squints, looking ahead, hoping to spot the lamasery. Instead, she sees that the caravan is several hundred yards ahead. It seems that no one has missed them. She whips her camel and shouts at Matt, "We're lag-ging. Get the lead out, Aussie."

"Yes, Your Highness."

They close on the caravan and move past the mules. Ingrid looks behind to ensure that they are in their assigned places. She spots a rising cloud of dust. She points; the words for some reason stick in her throat. A horseman is riding hard toward the caravan. She finally forces herself to cry out, "My God! Matt, look behind our caravan. There! Here comes trouble." But she's already calming down, assessing. *A bandit? I think not— not as a solo rider.*

"What say you, Matt? Another crisis?"

"No clue, m'lady. He's coming fast so he must have important infor-mation. Let's see."

The outriders fall in with the approaching horseman. They gallop to the front of the caravan. The rider is an *aide-de-camp* from General Wu. He salutes Captain Tze and speaks to him in Mandarin. With a look of con-cern, Captain Tze nods and shouts orders to his men. Ten of his soldiers immediately turn around and gallop hard towards Ho Hsien.

Kendrick demands, "What's going on, Captain? Why are your sol-diers leaving? We are without protection."

"Bad news, I am afraid, Mister Kendrick. One of General Wu's scouts reported that yesterday a Japanese patrol raided Tun-huang, a village a few miles south of Ho Hsien. I understand that they have massacred most of the citizens, looted what little there was, and burned everything."

Ingrid screams, "My God! That's where those pilgrims went to their homes yesterday. What a horrid place, this forbidding desert." Distraught, she goes to Matt. Tears are in her eyes. "We've got to leave this place. As soon as we can. I've had all the savagery I can stand."

Captain Tze continues, "The General expects that this raid is just a precursor to a powerful Japanese attack on Ho Hsien. To bolster his defenses, he has ordered most of my men to return to the citadel."

Frustrated and a little frightened for his valuable treasure, now more vulnerable to thievery, Kendrick says, "We're in peril out here alone with this treasure. What about you, Captain?"

"My orders are to ensure that you and the yellow porcelains arrive safely in Tsingtao. Two of my men and I will remain with the caravan."

Matt and Ingrid ride to the head of the caravan and listen with growing concern.

Kendrick continues, "Captain Tze, we're stripped of meaningful protection and the yellows on those mules are an enticing temptation to those brigands. We're in peril. What's your plan?"

Ingrid interrupts, "If any of us are hurt, or if any of those yellow porcelains don't arrive safely or get stored completely undamaged in the Pacific and Orient's Customs House in Tsingtao, there'll be no payment of five-hundred thousand pounds. Understand?"

Captain Tze realizes that the caravan is in grave peril, and there is no point in minimizing the risks. *My father has forced me to throw in his lot with the Occidentals. The Black Viper gang and Wallace must be in the area and are probably tracking us. Surely, they have seen my soldiers leave.* He looks at the Occidentals. "The prize in this caravan is too large for them to resist." With his most reassuring voice he says, "Mister Kendrick, I understand your concern. Our immediate goal is to get to the lamasery before sundown."

Deep concern suffuses through the Occidentals. They understand the peril and are not satisfied with Tze's immediate goal of reaching the lamasery before sunset. Matt speculates. *What happens tomorrow and the day after? And the day after that? How many days to Chang-yeh and the railroad?*

Captain Tze understands his charges' concern. He simply doesn't have the resources to change the scenario. He says, "Move out. There is less than an hour before sunset."

他畸,

The head abbot has told the visitors that the evening meal will be served in about an hour. After washing their grimy bodies, Matt and Ingrid lounge in her room discussing the day's journey and the potential danger that they'll face tomorrow. They scold themselves for not asking General Wu for weapons. Matt says, "With all the chaos of the last two days and your father's victory with the yellows, our minds were preoccupied." He continues with chagrin, "Nonetheless, I should have recognized our situation and asked Wu or Tze for rifles. Damn!"

To alleviate Matt's distress, Ingrid says teasingly, "Aussie, we all failed." She pats the bed next to her. "Come here and kiss me to make it well."

Matt responds, "We don't have time. Dinner will be called shortly."

"Very well, you cad." She looks away from Matt for several seconds. Eventually, she comments, "Matt, never would I have expected to be a participant in this harrowing trek to the end of civilization. And I certainly never expected to meet such a sterling man as you." She turns to face the Aussie. "Oh, Matt, it's such a joy to see Dad get what he wanted—the reward that he has earned. You'll have a great story to write."

"True. And lots of negatives to develop and print into big, glossy photographs."

Ingrid teases, "A Pulitzer Prize, perhaps?"

He frowns. "Not likely. The cognoscenti on the committee could care less about an ultra-rich guy spending several fortunes on some yellow porcelains to hoard in a private collection. My story will not have the cachet to match their unwritten criteria that focus on sophisticated stories that expound the human condition. It matters not that Kendrick faced life-threatening dangers, incredible hardships, duplicity, and murder. No, my story is more a type of gruel for the proletariat."

Somewhat surprised by his flippant answer, Ingrid continues, "What's your plan when we return to Peking?" She rises, winds her arms around his waist, and asks, "Maintain your course or aspire to roguish challenges?"

"Don't know. Honestly. I've not thought about it. I'm not sure what my future is. Maybe I'll go home. See my father. Work on a newspaper. Or perhaps, with the stake your father's paying me, I'll start my own wire service, or a newspaper."

With the stage set, she offers an idea she's been nursing for some time. "If you're not sure, consider coming with me to New York." She pauses for effect. "I need an Executive Editor for my World-Wide Press."

Blindsided by her unexpected offer, Matt is silent for a moment. He stumbles in his response. "Your offer comes from out of nowhere." He rises and walks about her room as his mind whirls with possibilities. "It's tempting." He continues to pace. "How do you fit into this equation?"

"Actually, I want you to run the Service. You've got the smarts and verve to kick the Press in the rear end to modernize it and make it the leader in this business. I've got to attend to other divisions of Dad's organization. I need someone I can trust. I'd want you to mold the Press into a multimedia conglomerate—mold it into the forerunner of the upcoming technical communication modernization." She takes a deep breath. "Give my offer some thought, Matt. I'd love to have you on my team."

Finally, Matt says, "It's a tempting offer. Regretfully, I reckon that I must decline."

She drops onto the bed and a deep frown creeps across her face in disappointment. Recovering, she offers, "There's a generous salary. Liberal expense account. And off-the-book perks."

Matt takes a minute, not wanting to misstep, trying to form a respectful response. "Your offer is enticing. That's not it. I just feel that it would be inappropriate for me to accept."

Puzzled, she decides not to pursue the issue now. "Very well, Matt. But, I do ask you to keep an open mind. Deal?"

"Deal, my fair damsel." He grabs her and kisses her full on the mouth.

29

Lamasery, Yü-men, Kansu Province. 20 July 1935

Many years ago, when the lamasery was thriving, the large, high-ceilinged room was an assembly hall. Now, travelers relax here and discuss the events of the day. Over the remains of a tasty dinner of fried pork, rice, peas, and green tea, Matt rises and says, "Please excuse me. I'm going to make sure that Lisan is okay."

A loud explosion coming from the courtyard rocks Matt back into his chair. He shouts, "The gate! They've blown the gate." Matt jumps up and heads for the window. Seeing Black Viper's gang pour through the gaping hole, he exclaims, "It's the bandits. Damn! Black Viper's gang is invading this lamasery."

Kendrick snaps, "The yellows. They're after my yellows."

Captain Tze rises, draws his pistol, and announces, "That's serious trouble; I am going outside." Before Tze can exit, the Black Viper, Wallace Chung, and several members of the Viper's gang burst into the dining room with their weapons drawn.

Wallace only has eyes for Tze. He demands, "My brother, drop your pistol, else I will fulfill my promise I made to you last evening." Two gang members drag Matt away from the window and push him back into his chair. Others surround the diners.

Tze commands, "Get out! Get these brigands out of this lamasery and leave us alone."

Wallace continues. "Brother, no need for alarm; we come in peace."

Tze retorts, "Wallace, your perfidy is obvious. We are not fools. If indeed you come in peace, then holster your weapons and go away in peace."

Wallace counters, "That's a clever retort for the dolt you are."

Kendrick demands, "Come on fellows, we've had enough of these shenanigans. Why don't you two go outside and settle your dispute Old-West style? Leave the rest of us alone."

Black Viper snickers at Kendrick's naïveté and rumbles a few words in Mandarin.

Ingrid, terrified, chides her father. "Be quiet, Dad. Do not provoke these fellows."

Wuhan, with no stake in the play at hand, remains stoic and watches the goings-on with calculating eyes. *Surely there is profit for me somewhere in this matter.*

Matt asks angrily, "Wallace, what the bloody hell are you doing here with the Black Viper and his gang? If you're so damned peaceful, why did you have to blow up the gate to enter this lamasery? That's a terrorist's act."

Wallace, with false bravado and a straight face, shrugs. "Perhaps it was." He grins at the Viper, who waits with bright eyes. Wallace continues, "We saw those ten soldiers depart your caravan. Black Viper and I are here to provide additional protection for the Ming yellow porcelains." Wallace snickers. "We will be your guards until you reach the railroad station at Chang-yeh." He stares at Captain Tze. "I am acting in good faith to prove to my father that it was Tze who framed me."

Tze, angry, puffs up, and steps toward Wallace. A soldier bars his way. "Brother, you and everyone else know that you are the traitor. You are a hunted man. When our father captures you, your crucifixion will be in the town square at Ho Hsien—you will hang for two, perhaps three, days in agony, begging death to visit you quickly. Leave now while you still have the opportunity to escape and you have not provoked more harm."

Wallace smirks and responds, "Do you believe that we are as stupid as you? General Wu will never find me. Shortly, within two days at most, General Wu will have the fight of his life. A brigade from the Japanese Kwantung Army will head for the citadel. They want Ho Hsien as their base for deeper forays into central China. They have artillery and heavy machine guns. Our father, that oaf of a faux general, will not be alive to hunt for me."

Black Viper follows the interplay between the siblings with keen interest.

"Wallace Chung, you have betrayed our family." Tze's eyes narrow in unbridled hatred. "I will hunt you down."

Kendrick is impatient with the contretemps. "Calm down, fellows. Keep your family feud away from us. I've had enough of both of you."

He begins to rise. Ingrid shouts, "Father, sit down!"

The Black Viper, whose understanding of English is limited, mistakes Kendrick's move for an act of aggression. Reacting reflexively, he pistol-whips him across the face, knocking him unconscious. He stands over the fallen Occidental, points his pistol at his head, and utters imprecations in Mandarin.

Wallace shouts, "Not yet!"

Ingrid shrieks, rushes to her father, kneels beside him, and cradles his head in her lap. She sobs mournfully.

Matt tries to lunge at the Black Viper, but he's pinned tightly between two bandits.

"Heads up, Ingrid," Matt calls out. "Tend to him. Say nothing."

In a futile attempt, Ingrid tries to use the tail of her shirt to wipe the oozing blood off her father's face.

The Black Viper grabs Ingrid's right arm, yanks her upright, and twists it behind her back. She screams in searing pain. The bandit cracks a sardonic smile. "Mine now, you woman with the flaming hair."

She yells, "Stop! Let me go! Matt, help!"

Matt struggles desperately to free himself. A bandit nicks his chest with the tip of his bayonet. A trickle of blood stains Matt's shirt. He is helpless to respond.

A loud crash of porcelain disintegrating stops the theatre.

Wuhan exclaims, "The yellows!"

Matt cries, "Those idiotic bandits have smashed the yellows?"

The head abbot pauses at the entrance to the dining room. He shakes with fear at the scene and stands amid the shards of dinner plates.

Alarmed by the noise, the Black Viper reacts defensively. Using his free hand, he fires several rounds at the abbot—hitting him in his upper left arm and his stomach. He falls to the floor among the porcelain fragments and murmurs in pain.

The Viper shouts orders in Mandarin to his gang and several hustle outside to prepare the mules with the yellows for the gang's escape.

Now, only one bandit guards Matt. As the bandit tries to see the red-headed woman, his pistol points loosely.

Black Viper sadistically increases the pressure on Ingrid's arm. He wants to hear her scream again, to tame her.

Stubborn and with sterling mettle, she'll not give the blackguard satisfaction. She grits her teeth, flares her nostrils, and takes deep breaths as her green eyes glare with venom. Black Viper continues to apply pressure. Eventually, when her arm is near breaking, she can no longer endure the agonizing pain. Her screams assault Matt's ears.

Matt yells at Black Viper, "You're dead!"

The Viper glances at Matt and laughs under his breath. He increases the pressure.

The pain is unbearable, and she no longer can endure it. She faints.

Matt, in desperation, commands, "Wallace, tell that ugly bastard to release Ingrid!" He yells, "Now!"

"Not my concern, ol' chap."

Infuriated, Matt knocks his guard's pistol to the floor and lunges for the Black Viper. Before he can get to the bandit, two gang members grab him and hold him at bay.

Wallace dangles his pistol, strolls over to Matt, and cavalierly says, "You do not give me orders, ol' chap. I am in control." He pats Matt on the cheek. "Now the Chinaman has power over the foreign devil." His pat turns into a single, final slap and he levels his gun. "I no longer need kowtow to the white man."

Black Viper releases Ingrid and signals to a couple of his gang. They bind her with ropes. She awakes and resists as best she can, but to no avail. One of them jams a dirty cotton rag in her mouth and binds it with a large gag.

Wallace presses his pistol into Matt's chest. "Shall you buy me a gin and tonic, Aussie, His Majesty's subject?"

The Black Viper eyes Matt's Leica. He knows it's a camera, but has no idea of how to operate it, its worth, or its critical importance to Matt. He draws his knife and cuts the strap holding the camera around Matt's neck. Not sure what to do with the Leica, he looks into the lens and sees nothing. *What good is this black thing?*

Matt says, "Give my camera back. It's of no use to you."

Black Viper, not fully understanding Matt's words, believes them to be an imprecation calling a curse of some sort on him. He swings the Leica and it smashes into Matt's face, sending him to the floor, next to the dying abbot. Blood drips from Matt's nose and from deep cuts on his cheek and forehead.

Lisan, roused by the hubbub, creeps into the courtyard unnoticed. He sees the Viper's gang working with the treasure-laden mules, preparing them to leave. The banditry is occurring, as he knew it might. He crawls, below the building's eaves, and peeks into the window. He immediately understands the unfolding scenario within. Helpless, he reckons that his best strategy is to remain hidden and silent and wait for an opportunity to help Mister Drummond. He does have an emergency option, however.

Captain Tze stares at Wallace and nods his head toward the Black Viper. "These are the animals you have allied yourself with. You inane fool!"

"You, my younger brother, are the fool—the General's trained pet. You do not understand that the time of the warlord is over. The Nationalists will wipe out all of them, bringing our country under one national central government. China must be united to fight the Japanese, who continue to rape our land—even now they are on our soil."

Tze evaluates his options. He has none. He remains silent and wait for an opening or for the inevitable.

Matt is dazed, and blood oozes from his mouth. *I'm going to kill those bastards.*

Wallace smirks and focuses on the wounded Matt. He nudges the Australian and kicks the unconscious Kendrick. "When that arrogant bone-head awakes, tell him we'll be in touch to negotiate an appropriate ransom for his beloved daughter. We shall take excellent care of her to make sure that she is returned unharmed." He laughs uproariously and slaps Ingrid's *derrière*. "Though she might be slightly soiled, as the song says."

Matt, keenly alarmed at Wallace's forewarning, spouts with sprays of blood, "You stupid guttersnipe. Kendrick will have every intelligence agency in the world after you. Interpol will have your photograph in every police station on the planet. Save yourself now. Release Mistress Kendrick and be on your way. You've got the yellows. That ought to be enough."

The Black Viper catches bits of this conversation. The Occidental's pleadings amuse him. He looks at Ingrid, standing in the iron grip of one of his gang. Her right arm hangs loose. He nods to one of his gang. The bandit flicks his saber, ripping Ingrid's shirt open and exposing her upper torso. The fellow takes a moment to enjoy her nakedness.

She squirms uselessly. She finally accepts and closes her eyes. Soft tears drip onto her cheeks.

The miscreants have a hearty laugh at the female Occidental's embarrassment.

Wuhan pays no attention to Ingrid's plight. Ever the opportunist, he concludes that the bandits are committed to stealing the Ming yellows and calculates how he can turn a profit from their thievery. He speaks in Mandarin to Wallace. "Mister Chung, please be extra careful with those priceless yellows. By now, I assume you've heard of Mister Kendrick's exorbitantly successful bid—500,000 British pounds sterling, if I am correct. Roughly, in United States dollars, that is 2.5 million dollars. When I return to Peking, I may be of assistance to you in disposing of those yellows. I have clients worldwide who would not look too closely at their provenance." With assured finality, he continues. "Contact me from your sanctuary. We can negotiate a mutually profitable deal, I am confident."

Wallace stares at Wuhan, unsure if he will shoot him or embrace him as his 'swagman' for the yellows.

Black Viper has been staring at Wuhan and then at Wallace. *Imbeciles.*

Matt, lying by the wounded abbot, realizes that the tapping in his side is from the dying man. The abbot is trying to communicate with him. The abbot subtly looks at his right hand, hidden inside his robe. Matt slowly parts the abbot's robe and spots a stiletto hidden in its folds. Matt checks, and sees that Wallace and the gang are looking at Ingrid and making inappropriate comments. He carefully reaches into the abbot's robe and palms the stiletto.

Captain Tze notices Matt's play and tries to distract Wallace and the gang away from Matt. He avers, "Word of your theft of the Ming yellow porcelains will spread like wildfire throughout China and all of the Far East—even to the Americas and Europe. You will be infamous. Brother, you are already as dead now as you will ever be. If not by our father's hand, then by the Nationalist Army, some other intrepid warlords, or the international police."

Wallace and the Black Viper stare at Tze. Wallace says, "So you wish, brother?"

To continue the distraction, Tze continues. "They will hunt you to the ground. The secret police of the Soviet Union, Italy, and Germany will follow your trail to the end. Do not forget the intelligence agents of Mao

Tse-tung's Communists. You may be assured that they will have a keen interest in these yellows and will track you down with relentless vigor. There is no place on this planet where you can hide."

An enraged Wallace screams in Tze's face, "Don't call me brother!" He's heard Tze's screed and his words ring true. To bolster his courage, he shouts, "You speak nonsense. I will now fulfill my pledge to you in the compound. You die." He cocks his revolver and presses it to Captain Tze's forehead.

Wallace, focusing his attention on Captain Tze, does not see Matt. Just as Wallace is about to pull the trigger, Matt flicks the stiletto. It slams deeply into Wallace's heart. He is dead before he hits the floor.

The Black Viper lets out a hearty guffaw. He turns to Matt and points to the dead Wallace. "Englishman! I thank you for the favor—saved me the trouble of killing this mongrel myself." He continues laughing at his little joke.

The Black Viper tosses the Leica back to Matt. Matt catches it, then lets it drop to the ground. His concern is with Ingrid.

Matt struggles to rise and addresses the Viper. "I don't care about the camera. Release the woman and save yourself. Kendrick will see that the Nationalists hunt you down. You and your gang will end on the cross praying for death."

The Black Viper draws the trigger back on his revolver with a loud click and points it at Matt's chest, debating whether he should kill him, Kendrick, Tze, and Wuhan. *Best to be rid of witnesses.*

3Ø

Lamasery, Yü-men, Kansu Province. 20 July 1935

Kendrick regained consciousness several minutes ago. From his early days in the West, he knows that sometimes it's best to 'play possum' and wait for an opportunity. He lies still and quiet, with his eyes closed—listening to all the banter. He recognizes the click of Black Viper's revolver and slowly he opens his left eye. The Viper stands close, with his back to him, facing Matt Drummond. Ingrid is not in his field of view. He almost smiles when his eye lands on Captain Tze's Mauser pistol lying close to his right hand. He grabs it, releases the safety, and fires a round into the back of the Viper's knee. The Black Viper screams, and falls to the floor in intense pain. The gunshot report reverberates throughout the dining room. Viper's two bodyguards rush to his aid. Kendrick doesn't hesitate. He tosses the Mauser to its owner. Tze catches it, and with two shots drops the bandits.

Before the bandits outside can react, Captain Lin Piao and his mounted company of soldiers from the Communist Eighth Route Army rush through the blown-away gate. They surround the lamasery and within minutes disarm the remaining bandits. Lin and some of his men enter the dining room with weapons drawn. He quickly assesses the scene. Pointing his pistol at Captain Tze, he commands, "Your weapon."

Tze, without comment, turns the handle to Lin and hands him his weapon.

Lin walks to the prostrate Black Viper. "Finally, Chin Mao-shu, you've tasted a bullet. You are my prisoner."

The Viper, now only somewhat under control, asks, "Who are you? Nationalists? Bandits? Mercenaries working for the Japanese? Not the Soviets?" His face strained, he displays his broken teeth, and cringes. "You would not shoot an unarmed man? Would you?"

Lin responds with military precision. "We are members of the Communist Eighth Route Army. Our first priority is to make China safe for the proletariat and rid our country of riffraff such as you."

Black Viper gasps. His false simpering quickly turns real because he knows that the omens are not looking favorable for him.

With a hand signal from Lin, two soldiers drag the screaming Black Viper away. Others remove the two dead bandits, Wallace Chung, and the abbot. Lin orders a pair of soldiers to release Mistress Kendrick.

Matt rushes to Ingrid and grabs her in a big hug. He removes his jacket and helps her slip into it. Ingrid sobs and buries her head on Matt's shoulder.

Tze helps Kendrick rise and escorts him to a chair.

Now that the room has returned somewhat to normal, Lin bows and says, "My apologies for being late. We saw Lisan's red rocket flare. En route, we stumbled upon a Japanese patrol and the firefight took longer than it should have. Only three of my men were wounded and none too severely. The Japanese won't need medical assistance."

Ingrid goes to the wounded Kendrick, carefully cradles his head, and whispers encouragement. "It's over. Dad, it's over. Thank God. We are all, more or less, okay." With a catch in her voice, she says, "Let's go home."

Kendrick wipes his bloody head with his handkerchief, smiles, and says, "You've got a deal, darling daughter." He hugs her deeply. "That's a deal."

Lisan enters and goes to Matt. Chagrined that he could not help his employer directly, he says, "Mister Drummond, I am so delighted that you have survived this tragedy and your associates also. I saw this scene un-folding from the window, but was helpless to interfere. All that I was able to do was signal with a rocket—given by an acolyte. You understand?"

"Yes, Lisan. I understand. Thanks for your help. Prepare our things for tomorrow morning's early departure."

"Yes, sir, Mister Drummond."

Wuhan had remained silent and unmoved throughout the gunplay scene. By outward appearances, he seems to be unfazed by the unfolding events. He addresses Kendrick. "Mister Kendrick, if it is possible, may I have the privilege of accompanying you on the caravan to Chang-yeh?"

"Sure. Do whatever you like," snaps Kendrick.

Captain Lin orders Sergeant Pai Chung-hsi, "Search the bandits, confiscate their weapons and supplies, and bind them securely. They are due for Chinese justice." He bows to the Occidentals. "Our corpsman will be here shortly to attend to your wounds. We will meet in the morning."

The Occidentals, their emotions running high, jabber noisily about the evening's events. Ingrid remarks, "This evening's tragedy resembles a Greek play: the *deus ex machina* arrived just in time to save us. And in this play, they've also saved our treasure." Their excited prattle continues. Shortly, they are interrupted by an incessant, noisy chatter of machine guns that emanates from the courtyard.

Matt comments, "Communist justice is swift."

31

Lamasery, Yü-men, Kansu Province. 21 July 1935

The air is crisp this morning. High cirrus clouds combine like a patchwork in a red-and purple-tinted sky. The assembled caravan is ready for the travelers to mount. Lisan stands with the camel that Matt will ride.

Kendrick, Ingrid, and Matt come out from the monastery—looking as if they have just been treated in an emergency room. Kendrick's head is bandaged. Ingrid's right arm is in a sling. Matt has a swollen lip, a bruised cheek, and a bandage around his head. Last evening, the Occidentals were keenly appreciative of Lin's medical corpsman's professionalism.

Wuhan follows shortly and nods toward Kendrick. He remains silent as he goes to his camel and a drover helps him mount. He's concerned that his offer to help Wallace Chung the evening before may have damaged his ability to work with Kendrick in the future.

Captain Tze approaches Kendrick. "I am returning to Ho Hsien to help my father. Deposit the British pounds in my account in Barclay's Bank in Peking." He hands Kendrick a folded paper. "Here is my banking information." He mounts his horse, salutes the travelers, and rides away. No more words need to be spoken.

Kendrick is amazed at Tze's trust in him. *It's that simple with these fellows.* He now realizes that there is no protection for the caravan. He's seriously concerned. *Who is going to protect us on the road to the railroad at Chang-yeh?*

Captain Lin Piao's men are assembled by their horses ready to leave. Lin addresses Kendrick. "Mister Kendrick, are you well enough to travel— and the others? It is over a hundred miles to Chang-yeh and that desert is going to be hot this afternoon."

Kendrick responds, "I'm okay, I reckon." He rubs his jaw. "Haven't been cold-cocked like that since my prospecting days in Montana."

Lin continues, "Perhaps you should stay a few days in the lamasery and recover more fully. Yes, that would be prudent. Not so?"

"'Not so' is correct, Captain. I'm anxious to get those yellows to the Custom House in Tsingtao." He extends his hand to shake Lin's. Lin does not accept Kendrick's offer. Instead, he bows, and in a half-mocking voice says, "In the Celestial Kingdom, the bow is appropriate."

Caught off guard, Kendrick mutters to himself, *I knew that.* "Captain, I must say, we're in your debt for saving our skins last night, but I have to ask, what in the hell are you doing here?"

"We have been tracking you since you left Wu Chung in the Yin Shan Mountains. You might say, to look after you and your party, and to ensure success with the yellow porcelains. You have done a great service for China. We thank you sincerely."

"I didn't catch the Black Viper. You did."

Captain Lin Piao remarks, "I am not referring to the Viper. I am referring to—"

The noise and shouts of several soldiers urging forward the mules with the Ming yellows interrupt Lin. The soldiers lead the beasts to the lamasery's entryway.

Kendrick shouts, "Hey! What are you guys doing with my yellows?"

Ingrid puts a restraining hand on her father's arm. "Father, don't strain yourself. I'm sure that Captain Lin will explain."

Matt doesn't share her faith in Lin's motives. Worried, he asks, "Indeed! Why are your men taking away the Ming yellows? Are you coming to the train station with us? Explain!"

Captain Lin responds professionally, "I am not going with you to Chang-yeh. My duty requires that I get these yellows to safekeeping in the

Socialist-controlled area, many miles south of here. Sergeant Pai Chung-hsi and six of my soldiers will escort you to Chang-yeh. The Chinese people thank you for recovering our priceless national treasures. Your dedication will be remembered."

Kendrick is crestfallen as he watches Lin's soldiers lead the yellows-laden mules out of the courtyard and turn south towards the Nan Shan Mountains. He is numb, unable to move at the realization that this entire enterprise was for naught. He murmurs aloud, "Five hundred thousand British pounds sterling worth of priceless trinkets." He slaps his knee, stomps his foot, and spouts, "It is I, Randall Kendrick, multimillionaire from New York City, who got hoaxed by a Commie. Damn! What an adventure."

Lin proudly announces, "These Ming yellow porcelains will be displayed in the Great Hall of the People in Peking after we defeat the Japanese, halt the Soviets' advance into our country, and overthrow the corrupt Kuomintang Nationalist Government. There will be a bronze plaque with your name inscribed as the donor of these yellows."

Kendrick responds, "That's something. I reckon what we've endured these past weeks is worth a bronze plaque."

Ingrid says, "Just think, Dad, you'll be famous all over Communist China." With mockery in her voice she continues, "Isn't that wonderful?"

Kendrick ignores her jibe and addresses Captain Lin. "I thought both Wuhan and Wallace trumped me, but you made them look like a couple of tomfools. I reckon that you knew why I was headed to Ho Hsien when you saved our hides from the Japs!"

With a deadpan face, Lin responds, "We have friends in Peking, Mister Kendrick."

"I see," snaps Kendrick. "Your spy conveyed our plans to your intelligence people and they concocted this scheme to have me do your dirty work—buy the Ming yellows so you could relieve me of them. And damned if that's not exactly what happened." He smiles. *It's not often I get bested, and this time, once more by a Chinaman.* "Clever! Very clever, Captain Lin Piao."

Captain Lin says, "My soldiers will ensure that you have a safe trip to Chang-yeh. I am returning to our base in Yunnan province, where the yellows will be secure until we can display them. If you will excuse me." Captain Lin salutes. He and his soldiers ride away, leaving the Occidentals stunned at the tragedy of last evening and the loss of the yellows.

Ingrid, with regret, laughs. "Some adventure. We won the yellows and we lost the yellows. We were nearly killed twice. You, Dad, almost three times, when you angered that cobra." She laughs again when they all just stare at her. "Instead of crying over spilt yellows, let's be grateful that the Communists saved our hides." She pulls Matt's jacket a little tighter and says, "Let's get going."

Matt snaps a few more photographs to make sure his Leica still works before he shoves it in a jacket pocket.

Kendrick, in an attempt to save face, remarks, "We lost the yellows, but damn, we didn't pay for them. We're ahead, I reckon."

Ingrid says, "It's easy to be philosophical when no money changes hands."

地震。

A couple of weeks later, the travelers are gathered in the Executive Club Coach lounge enjoying a relaxed evening. Lau checks his watch and announces, "In a few hours, we will arrive in Peking. Our coach will be deadheaded onto a siding and you can take your time gathering your things and departing."

Kendrick asks, "And you, Lau, what about you?"

"I shall depart unobtrusively later tonight and rejoin my cadre."

"You've done a fine job taking care of us. Thanks. You've got a second career waiting."

"Actually, Mister Kendrick, before I joined the Communist party, I was the head waiter at the Oriental Hotel in Peking."

"I should have guessed."

"Sergeant Pai has briefed me on the success of our mission. It is I who thank you, Mister Kendrick, for your splendid cooperation in our plan."

Kendrick has a flash of insight. "Damnation! It was you who concocted this scheme. Wasn't it?"

"Who is to know?" Lau bows. "Now, please excuse me."

Matt and Ingrid have ignored the others since boarding the train and tonight is no different. They sip whiskey at the bar and review their adventures one more time. At a break in their conversation, Matt figures it propitious to change the subject. "We did not finish our conversation the other day as we were leaving Ho Hsien."

Ingrid looks deeply into his eyes. "I apologize if I made you uncomfortable, Matt. My offer for the Executive Editor job is genuine."

"It's not that. It's the way I feel about you. I just don't know if I ought to work for you." Now that the truth is out, he is embarrassed and looks away. "I don't even know your full name."

Ingrid caresses Matt's face. "It's Ingridandra Theodora Kendrick."

"As beautiful as you."

She leans towards him and kisses him full on the mouth. "You're a sweet-talking rascal."

When Ingrid and Matt return to the lounge area, they find Kendrick and Wuhan discussing Chinese antiques. Ingrid interrupts, "Father, what's on your mind now that our trip is almost over?"

"Lesson learned, my dear. My obsession wasn't worth risking our necks. Especially yours. I'm sorry, Ingrid, for endangering you."

"No need for an apology. I had the adventure of my life." She takes Matt's hand and coyly adds, "And I had a little fun in between."

Kendrick turns to Wuhan. "So, Mister Wuhan, what are you going to tell Wickham about our adventures with the yellows?"

"Simple. He was outbid by a half million pounds sterling. The Communists saved your life and then stole the yellows. It is very simple."

The Occidentals are surprised at Wuhan's candor. That's not his style.

Wuhan, seeing an opportunity, speaks in his most sincere voice. "Mister Kendrick, in my business I have the ear of many collectors. Some tell me the most astounding stories. And, I myself have seen fabulous treasures—waiting to be had."

Silence pervades the room. Everyone looks at Wuhan in anticipation that he will continue, but he stalls to create more interest.

Kendrick's curiosity is aroused, along with his impatience. He demands, "Out with it, man. Don't play games. What treasures?"

"Please, sir. A few months ago, a White Russian *émigré* sold me a spectacular emerald broach. On my question, he assured me it once belonged to the Grand Duchess Anastasia Romanov." He withdraws a loupe from his coat pocket, puts it close to his eye, and says, "I verified the inscription on the lock myself. The Cyrillic letters spelled 'Victoria Regina.'" He returns the loupe. "We know that this broach was Queen Victoria's wedding present to her niece, Empress Alexandra—Anastasia's mother."

Kendrick comments, "That does not make sense. We were led to believe that all the royal treasures disappeared when the Bolsheviks overthrew the Romanov Dynasty and assassinated the Czar and his royal family."

Wuhan responds in a quiet, conspiratorial voice, "Later that evening, this *émigré* told my niece, Yen Hei-Lan, that most of the Romanovs' jewelry is hidden in an abandoned Buddhist temple in western Sinkiang province. You understand that, quite by accident, he let this key information slip from his mind."

Kendrick sits up brightly. "Can you imagine the look on Wickham's face if I were to return to New York with that treasure?"

Ingrid and Matt look at each other in disbelief. Kendrick can't be serious. Or can he?

EPILOGUE

Shortly after the travelers returned to Peking, Matt and Ingrid realized that there could be no long-term commitment between them. There was too much distance between their stations and temperaments. They parted as great friends and promised to write. We have no record of their correspondence.

Kendrick died of a massive heart attack a few months after his return to New York. Ingrid donated his Oriental collection to the Antiquities Department in Nanking. The Japanese Army looted the collection during the "Rape of Nanking" in December 1937. The Ming yellows disappeared during the War. To this day, they remain missing.

General Wu and his army were wiped out by the Japanese in July 1935.

Lin Piao died in a mysterious airplane crash while flying over Mongolia in September 1971. The Communist Party condemned him as the leader of a counter-revolutionary clique plotting a coup to oust Mao Tse-tung as Chairman of the party.

Lisan joined the Communist Eighth Route Army, fought valiantly against the Japanese Kwantung Army, survived the war, and advanced in the party hierarchy to become head of China's intelligence agency, the Ministry for State Security. During Mao Tse-tung's Cultural Revolution in December 1976, the Red Guards purged him for having Western thoughts.

Great Britain declared war in September 1939 on the Axis powers: Germany, Japan, and Italy. Matt volunteered for the Australian army and was assigned to the 8th Division in Singapore as a photographer. When the Japanese captured the city in February 1942, he was taken prisoner and condemned to help build the infamous railroad bridge over the Mae Klong River in Burma. He did not return from the War.

Ingrid took total control of the Kendrick empire, and held it together during the War. Afterward, she built it into a massive conglomerate with divisions worldwide. She never married. Throughout the years, she groomed her son, Matt, to become the Chief Executive Officer.

Dear reader, please see my novel titled *St. Catherine's Crown* to follow these treasure hunters after the Romanov jewelry.

About the Author

Captain Shelton is retired from active and reserve U.S. Navy service. He attended the Naval School of Photography and documented Navy and Marine Corps activities in Korea, French Indochina, and other areas in the Western Pacific. Commissioned as a Photographic Officer, he then served in Vietnam and other Pacific regions.

Shelton earned his Master of Arts Degree (Cinema) at the University of Southern California. For thirty years, he produced a host of information and documentary motion-media shows, winning over forty awards in national and international film competitions and festivals. His peers elected him a Fellow of both the Information Film Producers of America and the Society for Technical Communication. He served as the President of the Information Film Producers of America.

Shelton has published extensively in trade magazines, peer-reviewed journals, and commercial publications. His professional book, *Communicating Ideas with Film, Video, and Multimedia,* garnered the Best of Show award in the Society for Technical Communication's Spotlight Publication Competition.

Currently, he is writing historical novels whose *mise en scène* is the Far East and Africa. His action-adventure novel *St. Catherine's Crown,* published in

2013, garnered wide acclaim from reviewers. The narrative is set during the Russian Revolution. Following the regicide of the royal family, the harrowing post-Revolution adventures of Grand Duchess Anastasia and her cousin Lieutenant Kirik Pirogoff begin, as they travel the Trans-Siberian Railroad to refuge in northwestern China.

Details regarding his literary work are posted on his web site, sheltoncomm.com.